Montana Promise

Other Books by Caroline Fyffe

Montana Promise

A McCutcheon Family Novel

Book Ten

Caroline Fyffe

Dedicated to my dear sister-in-law, Lauren Roe Nesbit, with love.

Chapter One

The woman stared at the body splayed across the floor of her tiny cabin. The man's empty eyes gazed unseeing at the wooden beams above. Blood trickled from the gash on the side of his head, creating a dark crimson halo on the pine floorboards. Rings of sweat marred his plaid work shirt, and dust covered his boots. Until a moment ago, Benson had been her husband of one year.

Heat scorched her face. A burning chunk of coal had replaced her heart. Benson never returned before noon! At least, not until today. She fisted her hands, and her nails bit into her palms. The man beside her still clutched the fire iron. "Look what you've done!"

"I had no choice," the man gritted through a clenched jaw. "He saw us. Through the window. You couldn't explain your way out of this. I did the only thing I could." He gestured to the gun in Benson's holster. "He would've killed me. Maybe you too."

Blanche clutched the base of her throat. That was fact. As kind and patient as Benson had been, he had a temper too. She'd seen signs when their marriage had begun to sour. He'd warned her enough times what would happen if she ever looked elsewhere. Benson wasn't a saint.

Her gaze darted to the window, and her throat tightened. Morning shadows from the mountains covered the aspens and pines nestled near the cabin. Still, the day would be here within minutes.

With a shaky hand, she fingered her hair and tried to swallow with her dust-dry throat. She hadn't believed a marriage to a freighter would be so horribly boring. Living out here on the outskirts of town, away from everyone, had been suffocating to say the least. She glanced sideways at her cohort, thinking she should be thankful he'd had the guts to actually take action when he did. She couldn't have. Blanche slowly returned to the middle of the room.

"What should we do with the body?" she asked softly, as if an animal skulked about that might hear her words and scamper to town to alert the people. "And what will I say when folks start asking questions? You know his sister can't go two days without her dear darling brother coming for a visit."

The man nudged Benson's shoulder with the toe of his boot, not minding the blood. "I'll put him in the river. He'll wash away fast enough."

"And if he doesn't? This time of year the river is low. Too many rocks and branches. We can't take that chance." She gripped the folds of her skirt. "We'll have to think of something else."

"I'll dig a grave where no one will find him. That's our best choice."

That decision was risky. Keeping the body anywhere might be a mistake. The newness of *this* relationship had already worn off. Their affair was over. After what they'd done, she couldn't stomach another encounter. But what if he wouldn't go away quietly? Would he blackmail her? Turn her in? Say *she* was the one who killed Benson? She discreetly eyed Mr. Romantic, thinking he'd do just that to spite her. She needed to be extremely careful.

He was looking at her. Waiting for a response.

She pulled back her shoulders. "You're right. I'll say Benson never returned from his last job. After a while, people will come to believe something must have happened on his way home. We'll roll him up in a blanket, and then tonight you can take the body south, maybe all the way into Wyoming."

He smirked. "You have this all figured out, don't you? Won't people wonder when I don't show up for work?"

His sarcastic tone set off alarm bells. She swallowed. Placing a hand on his arm, she tried to smile. "Thank you for taking action. I think you saved our lives." His color was still high. She'd never noticed before how his lips twitched when he was nervous. She'd need to be shrewd. Her word against his. She gasped and whirled to the window.

"What?"

"His pack animals! If Benson is here, that means his animals must be outside in the corral." She paced to the wall, her breath coming fast. "It's already morning. We can't get rid of three mules, a horse, all his gear, and Benson's body without leaving evidence behind. Someone will see us."

Shaking overtook her hands, and then her arms. Surely they'd both hang for what they'd done. "If this is a nightmare," she moaned through a tight mouth, "please, *please* wake me up." Another look at Benson made her stomach squeeze painfully. "I think I'm going to be sick."

Her companion reached to pull her into an embrace.

She stepped away. They had too much to think through. No time existed for his one-track mind.

"We have to do *something*. Before any more time is wasted, I'll dump his body in the river. That's our only chance."

He was so stupid! She tried not to watch as he wiped an unsteady hand across his mouth. The face she'd thought so handsome before sharpened. What had inspired her to start carrying on with him in the first place?

"You can't. His mules are here. And his horse. No one will believe he came home and then just disappeared."

"Then you say he got kicked in the head and fell down the bank. Before you could help, he'd slipped into the water."

She flung her hand toward the corral. "By those mules? They're as docile as lambs. Besides, he was an expert. And the river is a quarter mile away. No, no, that won't work." Her eyes kept straying back to Benson's surprised face, his expression mocking. He would exact his revenge on her cheating even in his death.

Outside, the whinny of a horse brought her around. Fear ricocheted through her body. Was that one of Benson's animals or someone else? She ran to the window. "Someone's coming!"

"Do I have time to hide the body?"

"No. He's already dismounted by the leaning pine and will be at the door in a moment."

"Who is it?" he whispered.

"Don't know. He's tall, whiskered. Looks untidy. I don't recognize him or his horse."

"A drifter?"

"Yes. I believe so." *Did she dare?* She placed her hand on his chest. "Do you think you should get rid of him too?"

He roughly gripped Blanche's shoulder. "I'm not killing anyone else! You'll have to yourself if that's what you want."

The scowl on his face sent a chill up her spine.

A small smirk replaced his glower. "He's probably looking for something to eat or directions. Out this far, can't be any other reason. We'll pin this whole mess on him."

The pressure on her shoulder increased threateningly.

"You hear that, Blanche?" His brows bunched in a frown. "No matter what, he doesn't come in. Then, when he's gone, you'll have the perfect alibi. There'll be tracks and all. I'll have to rough you up a bit, but that can't be helped."

"What?" Her mouth fell open as a strong knock sounded. After one last glance at Benson, she cracked open the door and slipped out.

Chapter Two

Priest's Crossing, Montana Territory, July 1887

"**M**cCutcheon!" The cheerful greeting rang above the din of thirty or so people crowded into the warm, medium-sized schoolhouse where Luke and his adopted son, Colton, stood with their backs to the wall, hair combed, wearing their Sunday best. Each held a cup of punch. The building, which also doubled as the church on Sundays, was decorated with streamers, paper hearts, and vases filled with wildflowers. The pine floor had a newly polished shine, and the four glass-paned windows were open to let in the breeze.

Happiness surged through Luke as he put up his hand and waved. Joe Brunn, his father's good friend from way back, weaved his way through the guests, his new wife's hand clutched in his own. The wide smile on Joe's face and his high color were good indications he was having the time of his life. The bride looked to be close to Joe's age. She wore a soft blue dress and matching hat.

Been a while since I was in Priest's Crossing. A lot had happened in four years. This was where Ward Brown had carted Faith off to all those years ago, as well as her stepson, Colton, and newborn, Dawn, and forced her to marry him. Luke cut a quick look out the open windows to the undertaker's building down the street, where she'd been roughed up by Ward amid Dawn's cries of distress. The fact no one had stepped in to help Faith still rankled. Colton had filled Luke in on every moment of that horrible day. Of course, the marriage had been invalid, but that didn't stop a blackness from descending over Luke. He reached forward and grasped Colton's sturdy shoulder, the hold erasing away the bad memories.

"Luke, you son of a gun, you came!" Joe glanced around. "Where's Flood and Claire? And your brothers?" After a second, his brow creased into a frown. "They're not here?"

"Everyone's real sorry. With all that's happened over the brutal winter, Flood's off to Cheyenne with my mother, Mark, Matt, Brandon, and Charity to the Stockgrowers Association annual meeting. As you know, ranchers were hit viciously hard this past year. The loss of cattle has wiped out countless breeders. Any other time, they would have skipped the meeting, Joe. They're disappointed not to be here for you but send their sincere congratulations." He smiled at Joe's wife.

Joe sighed. Flood and Joe had traveled together to Montana Territory when they were strapping young men. They had a long history. "I understand. We were affected here as well. But I wonder why Brandon went? Being sheriff, I'd think he'd stick around town."

Luke nodded. "You're right. He and Charity are taking that long-postponed honeymoon. They're sightseeing while the others are at the meeting."

"Makes sense."

Luke hoped his good friend understood. After the winter they'd just lived through, everyone needed a break. "Won't you introduce us to your beautiful wife?"

Joe slipped his arm around the woman's waist, bringing a smile to her lips. "I'm sorry. In all the excitement, my manners have flown right out the window." He gently pulled the medium-height, delicately built woman closer as he gazed into her eyes. "Dear, this is Luke and Colton McCutcheon. Son and grandson of my good friend, Flood. They hail from Y Knot. Luke and Colton, this is Pearl Van Gleek, now Pearl Brunn."

"It's a pleasure to meet you, Mrs. Brunn. You've lassoed yourself a good man," Luke responded and then waited a moment to give Colton a chance to speak up. As much as his son had come out of his shell, the lad still got tongue-tied around the opposite sex, even with someone old enough to be his grandma.

"Ma'am," Colton said softly. "I'm pleased to meet you." With everyone's gaze on him, Colton's cheeks darkened to a ruddy bronze.

Luke smiled to himself, proud of Colton's manners. The boy didn't spend a lot of time around the womenfolk and was normally a little shy, even for twelve. Boys his age were usually awkward at a gathering of strangers. Luke needn't have worried about him. He was doing fine. With everyone else off to Cheyenne, the journey to Priest's Crossing had turned into the father-son excursion he'd wanted for some time. They'd had quite a few enlightening conversations along the way as Luke taught him about camping, ranching, and life. They'd talked about Luke's true heritage, the fact that he was half Indian, and that Flood wasn't Luke's real pa. Luke's darker hair and skin. Things a boy his age might wonder about but lack the courage to bring up. Each night, as they stared into the campfire, Luke waited for his son to voice any questions he might have about women or queries along a more personal line, but none came. Perhaps the boy got some answers from Billy, Luke's nephew, who was a year older than Colton. They had brought along Colton's new rifle Luke bought last Christmas at Stan Lock's in Waterloo. And this was War Bonnet's, Colton's horse, first time off the ranch. His son had a lot on his mind.

Pearl fluttered a small fan in front of her face. "Thank you, Luke, Colton. The pleasure's all mine."

Luke thought her voice suited someone not yet twenty. The soft, high-pitched tone almost made him blink.

Colton's lips twitched several times as he looked up at Luke. The silent communication telegraphed his humor.

"Joe has shared many stories about your family and ranch," she went on. "He thinks the world of all the McCutcheons. Please, call me Pearl."

Joe's proud smile was heartwarming.

"Now I understand why we haven't seen him around Y Knot for some time." Luke chuckled and thumped Joe affectionately on the shoulder while being careful not to jar Mrs. Brunn. "You've been courting. Your letter inviting us to your wedding surprised us all."

"Sure did, Mr. Brunn." Colton smiled at Joe. "Everyone was excited."

Luke puffed out his chest. His son was growing into a well-spoken young man.

"Even the ranch hands," Colton continued. "They've been taking bets on what your bride would look like."

Pearl softly gasped and looked indignantly at Joe, whose mouth promptly fell open.

Colton, with eyes as wide as harvest moons, hung his head, wishing, Luke was sure, that the ground would open under his feet. His gaze jerked up to Luke's for help.

Desperate to fix things, Luke blurted out, "I didn't know that! If they are, I'm sure those crusty cowboys are all just jealous. I'll be happy to report back Mrs. Brunn is as pretty as springtime in the high plains and sounds like an angel." Luke searched his mind on how to change the subject. He'd be sure to remind Colton that what was said in the bunkhouse was not to be repeated. Anywhere! No exceptions. "The service was real nice. I wasn't aware Reverend Crittlestick was making the trip. Looks like he's enjoying the festivities as much as everyone else."

Luke gestured to the front of the room where Y Knot's circuit preacher was surrounded by a handful of chattering women.

"That he is," Joe said after giving a hearty laugh. "That's Widow Kane who has his ear. Mildred doesn't act like an eighty-year-old." He grasped Luke's hand. "Thanks for making the trip."

Luke lifted a shoulder. "We've enjoyed the time away. Colton has a new horse he's wanted to put to the test in new surroundings. We've taken our time and done some hunting."

"How long will you stay?" Joe asked.

"We'll take a day or two to see the town, then head back. We don't have any solid plans. I left a gift for you and Pearl over on the table. From all of us."

A sentimental expression crossed Joe's features. "You didn't need to do that. Just having you here is a present enough."

"Just a little something." Luke waggled his eyebrows.

Joe scrubbed a hand over his face. "I wish we had more time. Pearl and I are leaving tonight, going north for a few days."

"That just means you two will have to plan a trip to Y Knot. Lots of folks there will want to meet her."

Pearl nudged her husband. "Joe, have you seen Blanche?" she asked softly. "I haven't and I'm worried." She smiled at

Luke and Colton "I'm sorry to change the subject, but my brother had to be away on business, and I'm watching over his little wife while he's away."

Joe patted her hand. "She's here somewhere, darling. Blanche, being Blanche, can do for herself just fine. I'm the only one you should be thinking about today!"

Luke chuckled. "Go, get socializing. We've taken too much of your time already."

Joe and Pearl turned and were instantly corralled by several twittering ladies.

"Don't know why women put so much stock into weddings," Colton said quietly at Luke's side.

"You'll understand someday, Colton. But until then, you best not lose any sleep over the matter. Until you're the one saying the vows, marriage never makes a lick of sense." He recalled his vows with Faith, getting a light, squishy feeling in his heart. "There's just something about that tie that binds. You hungry?" He glanced at the buffet table.

"Sure am."

"Let's go see what they're serving. I'm hungry too."

Women's heads turned as they made their way through the crowd to the long table covered with a white cloth and an array of foodstuffs. Luke reached for the top dish when a low, sexy voice brought him up short.

"If it isn't Luke McCutcheon, in the flesh. I thought I'd fallen asleep and was dreaming."

His eyes shot wide open, making the young woman laugh. "Tilly?"

Before he could think better of the reaction, Luke looked her up and down, not with desire but surprise. The young saloon girl who used to work at the Hitching Post looked very respectable in a blue calico dress that covered everything up to her chin. He'd never have recognized her in a month of Sundays if she hadn't spoken up. A white lace shawl covered her shoulders, and a feminine ribbon wound through her hair. At one time, she'd set out to marry a McCutcheon, any McCutcheon, and Luke, being the last single brother in town, had garnered all her attention. Tilly then ventured to Priest's Crossing to take the job Faith had been after in Christine Meek's mercantile.

"The one and the same, handsome." She smiled sweetly at Colton. "This can't be the same little boy who came to town with your wife? He's all grown up." She held out her hand waist high and winked at Colton, making his face flame red. "He was only this tall when I saw him last."

Luke cleared his throat. "It's him, all right. Getting close to being all grown up but not quite." Tilly, being Tilly, laughed heartily. Seeing her again was good, but so strange in this setting. He was used to fending off the woman's advances over a shot of whiskey. "Tilly, you look wonderful." And she did. "I can see the change in scenery was just what you needed."

Luke had had a friendly, teasing relationship with her for several years, as did his brothers, and so falling back into the old routine was easy. Before he knew what she was about, she wrapped her arms around him for an affectionate hug. Only then did he notice the bulge in her midsection he knew all too well, still too early to be easily seen. He stepped away.

"That's correct, Cowboy. I can see you noticed." She quickly gazed around the room until she spotted whoever she was looking for. She waved her arm. "Someone is here I'd like you to meet."

A bookish-looking man made his way over and stopped at her side. He was average height, clean-cut, and well dressed.

"Luke, this is Neil Huntsman, my husband. And the light of my life."

Happiness for his friend lifted Luke's chest. He thrust out his hand to grasp that of the fellow who had given an ex-saloon girl a chance on a new life. "Pleased to meet you, Mr. Huntsman. I'm an old friend from Y Knot."

"Not that old," Tilly practically purred.

Her familiar tone almost made him chuckle.

"At one time or another, I had a different McCutcheon in my sight—and you the longest, but to no avail. And now I'm glad. You know what they say about unanswered prayers."

"A pleasure, Mr. McCutcheon." For a moment, Neil gazed lovingly at his wife and then ran a hand down her arm.

He seemed in no way threatened by Tilly's flirtatious nature. Luke felt certain Mr. Huntsman knew his wife's history and didn't care a lick. "Call me Luke," he responded. "And this is Colton, my son."

Neil shook Colton's hand.

"Nice to meet you, Mr. Huntsman."

Tilly's brows arched. "Such nice manners. Takes after his pa."

She always was a tease. "I think congratulations are in order."

"Neil is the bookkeeper at the bank next to the mercantile where I work. I spotted him as soon as I arrived." She leaned into his shoulder. "It was love at first sight."

At that proclamation, the man's eyes warmed.

Whatever they were doing, they were doing it right.

"Three weeks passed before I dredged up the nerve to speak with him. I opened an account at the bank with a whole four dollars. Say, where're you staying? At the hotel or with Joe?"

Luke shifted his weight. "At the hotel. I wouldn't intrude on a man's wedding night."

"Mr. Kasterlee at the hotel is a charmer. Good thing you didn't bring Faith along—not that *you'd* have to worry, Luke. Still, he tries so hard to act shy, but in reality—"

Luke wrestled the smile from his face. "And how exactly do you know all this?"

"I stayed there my first few days in town. We're good friends—but just friends. I only have eyes for my husband."

Neil calmly stood there and kept the smile on his face.

Luke was glad he didn't seem threatened in the least by his ex-saloon-girl wife. She deserved all the happiness she could find. He lifted his glass, intending to take a drink, but Tilly stopped his arm, looking at his knuckles where the skin was torn away.

"What happened?"

"Nothin' much. Skinned 'em last night wrestling some stubborn firewood. Not deep but stung pretty good."

"You cowboys should take better care of yourselves." She lifted one of Neil's hands admiringly. "Women notice these things."

Chapter Three

Luke and Colton meandered down the street, having left the reception after the festivities concluded. On the main road, down from the hotel, a row of rectangular buildings housed the post office, a newspaper, and a general store. The clang of metal on metal announced the presence of a blacksmith's shop. Still, beyond the scattered houses, swaths of emerald grass cut through the mountains, and the hilltops were crowned with colorful flowers. Warm air brushed at Luke's shoulders, whisking away a portion of last winter's heartbreak. Much more time would have to pass before the heaviness of loss would lift from his soul.

"Look at that, Pa," Colton said in the midafternoon light. He pointed through the window at a newfangled icebox. "That sure is fancy. I've never seen anything quite like that."

"Me either." Luke couldn't imagine much need for the likes of that contraption in a small town like Priest's Crossing, but one never knew.

Colton stepped away and looked up and down the street. "I'm sure glad that wedding is over. Think we might get in some hunting?"

"Not until we head back to the ranch."

Colton groaned. "But I want to get a deer with my new rifle."

"You had your chance several times." He gave his son a pointed stare. "For the next couple of days, we're relaxing. Enjoy being somewhere different. The town is small, but we don't get away often. Who knows? We may discover something interesting. Or have an adventure."

Colton jerked his face up to Luke's, his eyes wide. "In Priest's Crossing? This town makes Y Knot feel like a city."

"How would you know what a city feels like?" he said on a laugh. "By the way, things you hear in the bunkhouse aren't to be shared with the world. Especially any topic about women. That situation could have gotten messy today. I'm thankful she didn't want an apology."

By his expression, Colton was chewing on his statement.

"The ranch hands get colorful sometimes, I know. Not everybody needs to hear that kind of talk. Do I make myself clear?"

"Yes, sir."

"Good. I thought poor Mrs. Brunn was going to faint." He chuckled and riffled Colton's hair, as he'd done so many times before.

This time, Colton pulled away.

"You got something stuck in your craw?"

"Just I'm not a kid anymore, Pa. You're treating me like a baby."

"Guess I am. It's not intentional."

Colton's mouth flattened.

He was growing up, Luke supposed. Maybe Colton had a point. "Sorry if I do. I'll work on that. I just sometimes…"

"This place don't even have a boardwalk," Colton complained.

"*Doesn't even* have a boardwalk. Your mother wouldn't be happy to hear you using incorrect English."

Colton shrugged off the comment.

A handful of riders passed by, looking the strangers over. Luke chuckled.

"I don't think they liked us," Colton whispered when they were far enough away not to be overheard. "What'd we ever do to them?"

"They're just being cautious, like we would be with strangers in Y Knot."

Colton suddenly pointed. "Look!"

"Well, I'll be." They started across the street a few buildings away. "I wonder what Trent Herrick's doing up here. I didn't see him at the wedding. Trent," Luke called when they were within hearing distance.

Trent was climbing down from the high seat of his buckboard in front of the hardware and leather shop.

"What're you doing in Priest's Crossing? I didn't hear any talk of you heading up this way."

The man's face lit up when he saw their approach. "Luke. Colton. This is a surprise." He grasped Luke's hand first with a hearty shake and then Colton's.

Luke nodded to himself. *That may help the boy from feeling like a child.*

Trent hitched a thumb over his shoulder. "Me and Pa are buying out the shop. All the tack and leather goods."

The shop he was referring to was rundown and in need of repairs. The gray, grimy window needed a wash. No shingle, sign, or other marking indicated what kind of business resided within the four walls.

Trent beamed and lifted his chest. "Been haggling the details of the sale for about three or four months. The old man's tough and been holding out for the best deal he could get, and I don't blame him. I'll load up everything tomorrow, lock, stock, and barrel, and head back to Y Knot. Should increase our leather and tack inventory by a good twenty-five percent."

Luke nodded and smiled. "Congratulations. That sounds like good business. Y Knot is growing. I'm sure you'll do well."

"I hope so."

An older man stepped from the shop, his hands tinted brown from some kind of dark stain. "You gonna stand out there all day, Trent, or are we gonna finish our business? I may die of old age before we get this transaction done."

Trent nodded. "I better get moving," he said quietly. "Don't want him to be crankier than he already is. Pa and I have been after him for some time to retire and let us buy him out. We were surprised when he finally agreed." He rubbed a hand across his forehead and glanced at the hotel. "Will I see you two before tomorrow morning? I figure that's when I'll be heading back to Y Knot."

"Most certainly. We're just enjoying ourselves before we leave on Monday."

Fifteen minutes later, Colton and his pa entered the hotel lobby, the establishment a fourth of the size of Cattlemen's Hotel back home. The room's musty smell stuck in Colton's nose. He headed for the stairway, drawing from his pocket one of the two keys his pa had entrusted to him for safekeeping.

His pa went to the counter, picked up a newspaper and then glanced at him halfway up the stairs. "You go on, Colton. I'll find out the best place for supper tonight." He nodded to the three vacant tables in the corner of the room that constituted the hotel's own restaurant. "I don't think we'll eat here."

Colton nodded and turned to go.

"That's him, Sheriff," a female voice said softly. "I'd know that face anywhere."

Colton swung around to see two women in the hotel doorway standing behind Jack Jones, the former deputy sheriff of Y Knot who'd been fired last fall. His tall, rangy stature was familiar. At times Jack's face could be warm and teasing, but at the moment his eyes twitched with what looked like indecision and a bit of fear. His mouth hung wide like a barn door, as if totally surprised. In the same instant, he snapped his lips closed and his face hardened, his gaze granite-edged.

Jack pulled his gun from his holster. "You sure?"

An unsure waver filled his voice.

A pretty girl clutched the arm of the accuser, who had purple bruising around her right eye and face. Her swollen lip looked painful. She hunched in one direction, holding her side.

Luke straightened and turned toward the door. "What's this?"

Colton's gaze cut to his pa's face and then back to Jack Jones.

"Yes. I'm positively sure, Sheriff. Who could forget those eyes? They'll haunt my sleep until the day I die." She burst into tears.

The younger female turned the battered woman and helped her out the door.

"I'm taking you in, McCutcheon! You're under arrest."

Pride shot through Colton when an easygoing grin spread across his pa's face. He wasn't scared of nothing.

"Is that right, Jack?" Luke drawled. "You and what army? If I remember back, you're pretty much afraid of your own shadow."

The barrel of Jack's gun pointed at his pa's chest.

"Just keep talking, big fella. You're digging your grave deeper with each second that passes, I can promise you that."

Luke slowly relaxed his elbow back on the hotel counter and, with unhurried, precise movements, inched up his hat with a fingertip. "Okay, Jack, just calm down. I can see you're serious. This is some kind of misunderstanding, is all. Why don't you put away your gun and explain what's going on? I'll help you figure out things—like Brandon used to in the old days. No need to get testy."

His pa's voice was calm and cool even though Jack's gun hand quivered in front of him. Colton held his breath. He wished he possessed one quarter of his pa's courage.

"We arrived into town late this morning," Luke went on evenly, darting a quick look to him to make sure he was out of harm's way. "For Joe's wedding. We barely had time to stable our horses, get a room and clean up, let alone get mixed up in a crime you think I'm guilty of. Take a deep breath until your heart rate settles, and then we'll solve this puzzle together."

Suddenly, before Colton realized what was happening, a man came through the back hall, swiftly stepped forward, and smacked the back of Luke's head with the butt of his gun. His pa crumpled to the hard floor with a thump.

Chapter Four

Luke's hand flopped on the stone floor, the cold bringing him fully awake. What happened? When he tried to sit up, a wave of queasiness sharply twisted his gut, causing a low moan to slip out of his lips.

"Pa! You awake?"

Luke forced open his eyes and then assumed a sitting position even though the floor tilted sharply and unsettled his stomach. He was in a cell, and Colton stood at the bars, wide-eyed and frightened. "Colton, what happened?" Fragments of the past few minutes were jumbled in a head wracked with pain.

"A deputy came in the back door. Knocked you out."

The wavering panic in his son's voice made him hurt more than the knot on the back of his head. He looked around the area, empty except for the two of them. Two other cells and a bench against the wall. "Don't be frightened, Colton. This misunderstanding will be worked out. Did Jones say why he was locking me up? What crime does he think I committed?"

Colton shook his head, his hands still fisted around the bars.

Luke went to stand but thought better of the action and stayed seated on the cot. "Like I said before, this is all some sort of mix-up. We'll get everything straightened out in time for a hot steak supper tonight. Go now and see if you can find him, but be careful."

Colton nodded and hurried out the door.

With a grip on the cold iron bar, Luke pulled himself to his feet, causing pain to ricochet across his eyes. A window about seven feet high was on the back wall of his middle cell. To see out he'd have to climb onto the cot, and he didn't feel steady enough for that. He paced to the cell door and gave it a good shake, his anger mounting. That good-for-nothing Jack Jones was back to haunt him. Brandon hadn't heard a thing from the man since he'd left Y Knot. Wasn't difficult to figure out he'd have a vendetta against Brandon, and him and his brothers as well, for his own stupidity and shortcomings. Always blaming his ineptness on everyone else. And now—Jack had the power to exact pain from him. Feeling helpless, he pounded a fist against his thigh.

Colton was back, skidding to a stop in front of the cell door. "I can't find him or the deputy."

Leaning against the bars, Luke glanced at the window, thinking the sun had already gone down. Soon a summer night would fall. The small room was hot. Little air could be felt from the window. "That's okay. He'll be back soon enough. Did you happen to see a telegraph office around?" *I didn't even look when we rode in.*

Colton let out a shaky breath. "No."

"Well, we won't need that, anyway. I'll explain to Jack we haven't been anywhere except on the trail." Why was Jones hiding out? Probably scared now that he'd actually locked him up. Joe Brunn was a respected person in this town. Best to search him out before he had a chance to leave on his honeymoon. "Go back to the church and see if Mr. and Mrs. Brunn are still there. You remember where the church is?" *Not that I want to flop this mess in their lap on their wedding day, but that can't be helped now.*

"Sure. Just down the street."

"If you can find Joe, bring him back here. If not, see if Trent Herrick is still at that leather shop, or Reverend Crittlestick. We need to find someone to tell us where Jack Jones is"—*hiding out. No, I can't say that*—"and then we'll be in business."

Colton turned to go.

"Don't dally, son. Do what you set out to do and get right back. If not, I'll worry."

Colton's brows scrunched together. "I'll find someone, Pa. I can take care of myself."

To fortify Colton, Luke forced a smile. The boy must have bad memories of this town already because of Ward Brown, his infamous uncle. If those memories made Luke uneasy, how much worse were they for Colton, having witnessed the calamity and unable to help? He'd only been eight at the time—but such a trouper. "I know you can. And I'm proud of you. And plenty relieved you're here to help."

Colton took a step back. "I best get going before it's dark."

"You're right. Go on and get back. See what you can find out." A thought gripped him so tight he almost gasped. "But if you see Jack, best to keep your distance. Only approach him if someone else is with you. That man may have a few loose boards upstairs." He tapped his temple.

Colton's nostrils flared. "Be back soon."

With that, Luke was once again alone in the stuffy five-by-eight enclosure, itching to get his hands on Jack Jones. What that man was up to could be anything.

Chapter Five

A knock on the front door brought Ashley Adair out of their guestroom bedside chair, and she hurried to the front room.

Ashley's mother, distraught with grief over the happenings in their sleepy little town, looked from the kitchen alcove with red, puffy eyes.

Ashley pulled open the door. "Sheriff Jones. Deputy Clark. Please, come in." She stepped aside.

Both men removed their hats, wiped their boots, and entered.

Because of her mother's cooking, the air in the room was thick and uncomfortably warm despite the wide-open windows. What Ashley wouldn't give for a blessed, cool breeze.

"Blanche still here?" Sheriff Jones asked.

"Yes. And she'll remain here until she's ready to go home," Mrs. Angelia Adair said, coming into the room. "She finally fell asleep. Poor thing is beside herself over Benson. She loved him very much."

Ashley couldn't stop her gaze from straying to the hall that led to the bedrooms. What had happened to poor Benson was atrocious. He'd been such a nice fellow, always saying hello to everyone. Careful with his words so as not to speak crudely, not like some of the other freighters that now and then came through Priest's Crossing. He was a true gentleman through and through. And now Blanche was a widow at twenty-nine years old. Amazingly, she'd lived through the vicious attack by that horrible man locked up in the jail. *The half-breed,* her mind whispered. *Like the man who killed my father.* She'd collapsed onto their guestroom bed in a storm of tears and had finally fallen asleep from exhaustion. Her face was badly beaten. What she'd gone through shouldn't happen to anyone, let alone a woman like Blanche. Her friend would need much care to get over this heartbreak. "Has he confessed?" Ashley asked, clasping her fingers tightly together. What made a man snap like that?

"No," Jones replied flatly. "He was still out cold when I left. But with Blanche being an eyewitness, he'll have a hard time making anyone believe any different."

Deputy Clark scowled.

With his bloodshot eyes and wrinkled shirt, he looked as if he hadn't slept a wink last night. She thought she detected a slight scent of whiskey.

"What will you do now?" Ashley's mother asked. "Since you have the perpetrator already locked up? Seems like a closed-book case."

Feeling like a swarm of bees battled in her stomach, Ashley stepped to the window and looked out on the sleepy street that ran into town. The school, where she had taken over as teacher for Blanche when she married Benson, could barely be seen a quarter mile away at the end of Main Street. The gigantic oak stood guard over the building as if this evening was the same as any other in the year. "It's horrible," she whispered, still gazing out. "Murder in our own little Priest's Crossing. And in cold blood." She turned back. "No one should die because of money."

Sheriff Jones rubbed his chin. "That's the part I don't get. Luke McCutcheon is one of the richest ranchers in the territory. He could buy and sell this whole town ten times over with his petty cash."

Ashley's mother straightened. "Are you saying Blanche isn't telling the truth?"

The sheriff jerked as if he'd been slapped across the face, reminding Ashley of when he'd first come to town. During the Christmas social, he'd pestered her nonstop and even tried to kiss her. She hadn't slapped him, but she'd wanted to and told him so in no uncertain terms. Since then, he'd been a gentleman. After he became sheriff, he seemed like a whole different person.

"Of course we believe Blanche," Hoss Clark, the powerfully built deputy, said before Jack could open his mouth. "She's lived here all her life."

Ashley cocked her head. "No, actually, she hasn't. Not her whole life. Just since becoming the teacher nine years ago. She's from Chicago."

A vision of Miss Lowrich, her name until marrying Benson, standing at the blackboard on the day her mama brought Ashley to school for the first time hadn't faded over those years. Blanche was twenty and the most beautiful woman Ashley ever saw: independent, strong, with a tiny waist and thick, midnight-colored hair. She had stories about the exciting people and goings-on in the world outside Priest's Crossing. Sometimes this little town seemed much too small to contain her. When the teacher took a shine to the skittish nine-year-old, perhaps because both were new arrivals to town, Ashley had felt special. Still healing from the violent death of her father, Ashley had soaked up Miss Lowrich's attention and praise like a thirsty rose.

The deputy lifted a shoulder. "That's plenty long enough to be one of us. But that don't make any difference. She's a trusted member of the community, and McCutcheon is an outsider."

Thinking of Blanche's battered face, Ashley blinked against the burn of tears behind her eyes.

Her mother came to her side and put a comforting arm around her waist.

"She's my dear friend," Ashley said. "She believed in me. Gave me a chance. Helped me take my teaching test right here in town and then hired me. In my book, no one is as unblemished in kindness or character."

Both lawmen nodded like twins. *Good.* She was thankful they were in agreement. Blanche had already been through a nightmare of unfathomable proportions, losing her beloved husband and then suffering at the hands of his murderer. Ashley wouldn't let any more sadness befall her in the days to come.

Chapter Six

Darkness had long since fallen. Luke, the dizziness having faded away, climbed on his cot and stared out back, not a soul in sight. Where was Colton? What was taking him so long? Not being able to protect his son was the worst part of this charade.

A hot wind puffed inside, and his anger was replaced with a mustard seed of alarm, a feeling he was unaccustomed to. What would happen? Did Jack really believe he could get away with something so dishonest? Or did the thick-skulled man really think Luke'd committed a crime? He still didn't know what he was accused of. The look of the battered woman pointing at him was burned into his mind like a red-hot brand.

Scuffling sounded. The door between the cells and the office opened. Still standing on the cot, Luke looked over his shoulder at the sight of his dejected boy approaching the cold steel bars. He stepped down and went to his son.

"Colton." He tried to infuse calm into his voice. "What did you find out?"

"Nothin', Pa," Colton responded. "Couldn't find the sheriff or the deputy. I did find out the telegraph operator skedaddled out of town last month, taking most the equipment."

Okay, there are other ways. "Did you find Trent Herrick?"

"He's nowhere, Pa. I went to that shop and banged on the door until someone else came from next door and told me to stop making a ruckus and go away. I tried to ask him about Jack Jones or the deputy, but he just shooed me off."

Luke sucked in a deep breath. *Let's not panic.* "And the church?"

"Everyone's gone. Even the reverend. I went to the livery to see if Mr. Herrick's team was still there, and it is. As well as his buckboard."

Still a chance to get word home. "That was good thinking, Colton. At least we know Trent hasn't left town."

"I'm sorry I let you down." Colton's shoulders slumped, and he didn't even try to shake away the hair that had fallen into his eyes. Smudges of dirt marked his shirt that hadn't been there before he'd left.

"Come here." In the dark jail, Luke reached through the bars and took hold of Colton's hand giving it a shake. "Don't worry. They can't hold me for something I didn't do. Tomorrow, this situation will get straightened out. I'll be released. We'll head back to Y Knot. Even do some hunting along the way." That scenario sounded better with each word and yet didn't bring a smile to Colton's face. "But on the off chance we do have more problems with Jack, I want you to be at that leather shop before sunup. We can't chance missing Trent's departure. Tell him what's happened and ask him to get word to the Heart of the Mountains as soon as he reaches Y Knot."

Colton nodded. "But the trip back in a wagon will take him a good five days." His eyes grew large. "That's a long time. Can't he do something here to help?"

That's a good question. "I don't think so. Jack won't listen to anyone. He likes the power he wields, especially against me. I'd rather know that word was heading toward the ranch hands.

They'll know what to do." *At least, I hope they do.* With his pa, brothers, and Brandon all down in Cheyenne, Luke wasn't quite sure yet what that help might be. Roady was at the ranch with Sally and their new two-month-old daughter. Still, he'd think of something.

"I won't let Trent get away, Pa. Not without talking with him first." A wobbly smile appeared. "You can count on me."

"I know I can. Now, go back to the hotel and get some sleep." Luke straightened and glanced out the door. "Wait. You haven't had any supper. Those little portions at the wedding weren't enough to feed a mouse."

"You didn't either."

Under the circumstances, Luke hadn't even noticed he'd missed a meal. "I'll be fine." Luke reached into his pocket for the silver room key, which he was surprised Jack had missed. Unfortunately, the implement hadn't worked on the cell door. "I know you already have a key to our room, but take this one too. See if Mr. Kasterlee at the hotel can find you something for supper. Be sure and ask. He can charge that, and whatever else you might need, to our room. Do you have any money left?" He placed the key into Colton's palm as his son nodded. "Good. Jack took my money clip when he grabbed my gun."

Colton wasn't saying anything, but even in the semidarkness, Luke could see the apprehension lurking in his eyes.

Luke grasped his shoulder and gently squeezed. "Go on, the time's gettin' late. Everything will be all right. We just have to be patient. Get some sleep and then get over to that leather shop bright and early. Catching Trent before he heads out of town is important. He may be going at dawn."

Colton just stared.

"Later tomorrow, I'd appreciate you bringing me my trail clothes." He didn't have to look to know his dress clothes were rumpled and stained. "I'll be more comfortable." Colton looked young and frightened. His eyes drooped with fatigue. Luke longed in the worst way to pull his son into his arms and assure him of their future. Problem was, the bars prevented that, and he wasn't all that sure himself what tomorrow would bring.

Chapter Seven

Denver, Colorado, one month earlier

Judge Harrison Wesley pushed back his heavy captain's chair from the supper table, satisfied by the hearty meal weighting his stomach. "That was wonderful!" He patted the waistband of his woolen suit as he looked at his five-year-old daughter, her big blue eyes pulling at his heart. "What do you think, Carlie? What was your favorite dish? I don't think I've savored a better Sunday supper in my life."

Pauline lifted her brows. "You say that every week."

"My favorite will be the chocolate cake, Papa. I helped Mrs. Drier with the mixing. We stayed up until eight o'clock."

Ignoring the soft tsking sound coming from his sister-in-law sitting to his right, Harrison reached over and stroked the underside of Carlie's chin. "Then I can hardly wait. Did you stick your finger into the batter as sweetener?"

Carlie giggled, causing her chestnut curls to bounce around her small shoulders and the lace collar of her dress. "No, Papa, the sugar did that." She scooted out of her chair and reached for her plate. "May I help take our plates to the kitchen? We'll get to dessert quicker."

"No, my dearest," Pauline scolded as she patted her lips with the linen napkin.

Carlie's smile fell.

"Let Mrs. Drier clear the table," Pauline went on. "That's what she's paid to do. You're a lady. Ladies wait to be served. She'll be in shortly. Sit and put your napkin back in your lap."

Pauline. My sister-in-law. The bane of my life. She hadn't been so controlling when Agnes was still alive, but since Harrison's wife passed, she'd become downright insufferable. Controlling Carlie all the time. He knew the grief from losing her much-younger sister was to blame, but Carlie was grieving, as well. His little girl needed time, patience, and love. The nine months since Agnes's death felt like ten years. Time had finally arrived to make a change.

"Nonsense." He looked at his daughter's dinner plate—the fine china he'd given Agnes, his second wife, as a wedding present six years ago—practically wiped clean. "I think your helping Mrs. Drier tonight would be very thoughtful. Just be careful with the serving pieces."

"Harrison!"

His stern look halted Pauline's next words as Carlie gingerly lifted her plate with both hands and headed for the kitchen.

"You're ruining that child."

He pulled a toothpick from his front pocket and put the implement into his mouth. "Please don't start—not tonight."

"Agnes would be horrified if she thought Carlie was clearing a table like a common servant."

He struggled not to frown. "I asked you to stop."

Carlie returned, followed by a slow-moving Mrs. Drier carrying a large white tray.

The housekeeper and cook had been in the household since he'd married Agnes, and a pleasanter woman he'd never met.

She was good medicine for his daughter. Pauline had been living with them as well since the week after the wedding. Unmarried at thirty-one and both parents buried in the graveyard at the church, she had had nowhere else to go. Now, at thirty-eight, she was still a handsome woman but far from the beauty her sister had been. If she'd just smile once in a while or laugh, their lives would be a lot happier.

"That was a fine meal, Mrs. Drier," Harrison said. "Thank you." His comment brought a wide smile to the cook's wrinkled face. Getting into the spirit of what was to come, Harrison himself stood and took up Pauline's plate, the empty bowl of green beans, and reached for the potatoes.

Mrs. Drier's eyes went wide. "Sir?"

"I want to help as well. Before I became a circuit judge, I was a lawman. And before that, a simple cowboy. I feel better doing something than sitting on my backside. I hope you won't mind, Mrs. Drier. We want to get to the cake a little faster."

With an armful of dishes, he headed toward the kitchen, whistling a jaunty tune and thinking how excited Carlie would be when she heard the news. Pauline's face flashed in his mind, and he steeled his nerves. She was a formidable woman, but he held the winning hand.

A half hour later, the three, now finished with their dessert, sat quietly at the table. This was when Agnes would read some poetry or share an interesting article she'd seen in the *Rocky Mountain News* or at times play a piece of music on the piano in the corner of the dining room. His heart squeezed. Would there ever be a time that her memory didn't color every moment of his life?

He glanced at Pauline's dour face and then slid his attention to his daughter, who was flicking at a cake crumb on the tablecloth.

Mrs. Drier's clinking and clanking in the kitchen was the only sound in the room.

Seemed everyone was lost in memory. He gently tapped his spoon on the side of his coffee cup. "I have some news."

Carlie's face brightened, and Pauline looked over.

"I've had a letter from Justin."

"Justin!" Carlie said.

Unable to contain her excitement, his daughter bounced up and down in her chair. She adored her older half brother. To her, he set the moon and stars as well as everything else in the universe.

Because of Harrison's circuit judge position and being gone much of the time, Justin had spent more time with Carlie than he had. That was about to change. "That's right, sweetheart. A few days ago. He likes his new position as deputy sheriff in Y Knot. Says the country up in Montana Territory is remarkable. I couldn't agree more. He's excited to see what life brings next."

Pauline's eyes narrowed to a slit. "Is the boy ready for a job like that? Think about the outlaws. And Indians."

"He's hardly a boy any longer. I've taught him everything I know about sheriffing. Y Knot is just rustic enough Justin will get the experience he needs without facing danger night and day as he would in a more populated place—like Denver. The town is a good starting point for his career."

"I hope you haven't just signed his death certificate."

Carlie cringed, her eyes large.

Harrison sent Pauline a threatening look. "I've spent enough time in the Y Knot sheriff's office to know the checkerboard doesn't get dusty. And Crawford is a good man. Honest. He'll teach Justin well. Justin will be a much better deputy sheriff than Jack Jones ever was!"

"Oh, Papa, Justin's wanted to be a deputy for so long." Carlie clapped her hands. "Can we go visit?"

Pauline pushed back in her chair, her mouth pinched. "Certainly not, young lady. That's a man's world up north. No place for a sweet little princess like you. I'm sure he'll come here to visit just as soon as he can."

His sister-in-law would not be happy with his next statement. He should feel guilty about the happiness that thought brought him. "Actually, Justin has invited *us* to join him, if we have a mind to. Move to Y Knot. I've been contemplating my retirement for some time now." *Since Agnes's death. I want more time with Carlie—before a disgruntled relative of some outlaw I've sentenced to hang shoots me down in cold blood. Has happened to more than a few of my friends.* "The day has arrived, Carlie, Pauline. We're moving to Y Knot."

Pauline's eyes went wide. The cup she'd been raising to her lips returned to her saucer with a loud clank.

"You can't be serious, Harrison! That's... that's totally ridiculous. You're talking north. Much farther north than Denver. Think of the winters." She flipped her hand in front of her face. "The snow. The hardships. The Indians. No! I won't allow you to put Carlie in such danger. Agnes would never agree to a move to Y Knot. I must act as the child's protector until you come to your senses." She glanced over to the liquor cabinet where several crystal decanters sat with a variety of bourbons and whiskeys. "Have you been drinking? You're taking Agnes's death harder than I was led to believe. You can't mean a word of this crazy outburst."

You're the one with the crazy outburst. He waved off her concern. The only reaction he was worried about was Carlie's, and she seemed delighted. "Indians aren't much of a problem these days, Pauline, but you're correct about the hardships. We won't have a house like this. Or paid staff. We'll be on our own."

Like when I was a young man. I like the idea. Getting back to a simpler life.

"Please, Papa. I want to live with Justin. I won't mind cooking and washing and stuff."

He smiled at her obvious delight.

Pauline's hands trembled. "What will you do? You're forty-four years old. Not a young man anymore, by any stretch of the imagination. To be starting over at such an advanced age…"

He held back the retort he felt and, for Agnes's and Carlie's sakes, put a smile on his face. "As of yet, I don't really know what I'll do, Pauline. Maybe a little ranching. Or work in a shop. I've done my time laying down the law as a sheriff and then as a judge. Let someone else do the heavy lifting. I'll take up the slack. Sounds just about perfect for this time in my life."

Pauline shifted in her chair and repositioned her napkin. "Think about Mrs. Drier. What will she do? Where will she go? She's not a spring chicken either."

He had thought of the cook. Had found a friend who was in need of her services. But what about Pauline? She didn't have anywhere to go, except with him. And unfortunately, that was the outcome he was expecting. Then again, if she really was too frightened to go north, she might find a way to support herself here in Denver. "Mrs. Drier has been taken care of. I've discussed the possibility of other employment with her, but at that time, I hadn't made my final decision."

"And you have now?"

Satisfaction settled in his chest. This was the correct decision. He couldn't wait to get started. "Indeed."

Chapter Eight

Barely past sunup, Francis busted through the door of the sheriff's office, uncertainty burning his gut. When he'd first learned Luke's predicament from Trent, hot anger made him set out for Priest's Crossing without returning to the ranch. "Luke," he bellowed, looking around.

Jack Jones leaped from his chair, knocking a stack of books and papers from a foot-tall mess on his desk to the floor. "Francis!" he barked. "What're you doing here?"

Now as tall as Jack, Francis charged forward and grasped Jack by the shirtfront. He jerked his face close. "You know what I'm doing here, you lily-livered skunk! Do you still have Luke locked up? I ought to beat the you-know-what out of your cowardly skin for a stunt like this." His gaze cut to the door to the cells beyond the thick oak wall. With disgust, he pushed away Jack and started over.

"Hold up!"

Francis glanced back to see Jack had a gun leveled at him.

"You want to speak with my prisoner, you leave your gun with me. As a matter of fact, *anyone* here to see McCutcheon has to check their weapon. When you leave town, you'll get back your Colt."

"You're out of your mind, Jones," Francis said stiffly. Trent had warned him that, after leaving Y Knot, Jack had gone to Priest's Crossing and somehow landed the sheriff's job. Francis still found that fact difficult to believe—but here he was, standing right in front of him.

Jack motioned with the barrel of his weapon to the gun belt around Francis's hips.

Disgust tightened Francis's throat. "You're serious?"

"Dead serious." He slowly nodded. "I've never been more."

"Oh, yeah, you're talking big, Lawman. I'm scared."

Jack's eyes narrowed. "Set your gun belt on my desk. No fast moves, you hear? I wouldn't like to shoot you."

"This is ludicrous." He looked at the desk. "Where? There's not a clear spot anywhere."

Jack frowned. "How old are you now?" he asked, eyeing Francis. "All of eighteen?"

"That's right. And I'm more man than you'll ever be." Feeling hobbled, Francis slowly unbuckled his holster, took two steps, and set his weapon and belt on top of a stack of books. Without another word, he strode to the door and went inside.

In the second cell, Luke waited by the door. "Thanks for coming, Francis."

Taken aback by Luke's unkempt appearance, Francis swallowed down the objection he'd almost blurted out. By what Trent said, Luke had been locked up now for five days. That was a hell of a long time when you didn't know if anyone was on their way to get you out. Black whiskers covered his jaw, and his rumpled clothes were out of character for his boss. The air in the room was thick with all kinds of disgusting smells. This place wasn't fit for an animal, let alone a McCutcheon. Francis had never seen such deep lines fanning out from Luke's eyes.

"I have to admit," Luke went on in a teasing tone. "You're a sight for sore eyes. And I can tell you, mine are sore." His gaze went expectantly to the door.

"They're on their way. I was out a day's ride from the ranch when I ran across Trent on his way back from Priest's Crossing. He'd pushed his team hard and shaved off a day. I set out from there."

Luke thrust his hand through the bars and grasped Francis's. "Thank you. You set out without even your camping gear or food. You must be starving."

That was an understatement. He'd ridden as hard as he could push Redmond and then lain on the ground at night with only his saddle blanket for a bed. Cold water and sunshine had been all the sustenance he'd needed to get here as swiftly as he could. "I'll take care of that as soon as we talk. Where's Colton?"

"He'll be in anytime. Poor kid's lost. He'll be happy you've arrived. Took me two days to convince Jones to give him my money clip."

Francis bit off a few choice cuss words. He didn't miss the hard line of Luke's mouth or the disdain in his voice when he mentioned Y Knot's disgraced deputy, fired last year. Francis still couldn't believe the slacker had ended up here as sheriff. Who would trust a man like that?

"That swine's butt. I'd like to…" Francis grasped one of the steely cold bars between them and rearranged his thinking. Luke didn't need him adding to his troubles. "What's this about, Boss? All Trent said is some woman accused you of murdering her husband and roughing her up. That's the most ridiculous thing I've ever heard. Surely they can't have any proof."

Dropping his head, Luke pushed splayed fingers through his shaggy hair.

Francis watched him sympathetically. The whole situation must feel like a nightmare.

"I'll tell you everything you want to know." Jack strode into the room. "I wouldn't arrest McCutcheon without a positive identification from the victim, no matter how stupid you think I am. I knew there'd be repercussions, but what else could I do?"

Francis swung around to face Jack. "Start at the beginning. Don't leave anything out."

Looking almost contrite, Jack came closer, his gaze tracking between the two. "Mrs. Blanche Van Gleek lives a quarter mile out of town with Benson, her husband. The fellow was a freighter and often gone. The day Luke and Colton arrived, she claims Benson had just returned from a pack trip. Luke came to her house looking for something to eat. After they gave him food, he demanded what money they had. He killed her husband and beat her up, but she fell and pretended to be dead until he was gone. Look at his knuckles. There was blood on his trail clothes."

Luke thrust out his hand. "I explained about that. I skinned 'em getting wood for our campfire the previous night. And the blood was from game we killed along the way. We had to eat!" Luke glared at Jack. "Jack believes after I killed Benson and *thought* I'd killed the woman, I waltzed into town and went to Joe's wedding. Oh, alongside my young son too? Where's the logic in that? I'd like to know."

Jack shrugged. "I can't say. But after you left, and when Blanche was able, she dragged herself into town, battered and bruised. When she saw Luke, she recognized him." He raised an eyebrow at Luke. "That's when Blanche and her friend, Miss Adair, came to me, and I arrested McCutcheon."

Francis made a sound in his throat. "That's hogwash! That's the stupidest thing I've ever heard—even from you, Jack."

Disgust filled him. "Even from you! Luke, you were with Colton. Jones can't keep you locked up if you have an alibi."

Luke cleared his throat. "The day before arriving in Priest's Crossing, Colton and I camped at the spot Pa took me when I got my first deer, even though we could have easily made the short distance to town that afternoon. Colton was excited about that, since we'd talked the subject to death on the ride." Sucking in a deep breath, Luke's gaze sought his. "The spot has sentimental worth, and I thought Colton would like the small lake as much as I had as a kid. After making camp, we did a little scouting that evening and found sign of deer. The next morning, before daylight, Colton up and snuck away with his rifle hoping to get his first buck on his own."

"Well-thought-out story," Jack mumbled.

Luke's mouth flattened into a line.

Francis felt Luke's growing frustration as his own.

"When I woke up and found Colton gone, I wasn't that surprised because that's what I'd done at his age, as I'd told him many times. He had a new rifle and a burning need to prove himself. After some time waiting for him to return, I got angry. Then worried. We had Joe's wedding to attend, and I didn't want to be late. We'd been on the trail for several days, doing what men do when they're alone. We both needed a bath, and I needed a shave. So, I went looking. I admit I did happen on Mrs. Van Gleek's cabin. I knocked on her door, and she came out. I asked if she'd seen Colton. When she said no, I asked if I could water my horse at her well and get a drink. She agreed. She was fine at that time. Not a scratch or bruise on her. I never saw her husband, but three or four mules stood in the corral, as well as a horse. After I watered my gelding, I left. But because of Colton's sneaking off and me being alone, I don't have an alibi. It's my word against hers."

A small sound made Francis turn to see Colton in the doorway. Apparently the boy hadn't put two and two together until hearing the words from his pa's lips. Francis flinched at the stricken look in his eyes. He'd been doing for himself for five long days, and the consequences showed.

Still, his chin lifted, and he stepped forward.

"Colton," Francis called, putting out his arm.

"Good to see ya, Francis." He squared his shoulders and stayed out of reach. "Are the others here too? Roady, Smokey, and the rest of the boys?"

The grown-up talk sounded so strange in his quavering voice. "On their way." Francis turned back to Jack. "So what's your plan? We both know Luke would never murder anyone in cold blood—for any reason."

"Blanche Van Gleek is a longtime citizen of this town." Jack shifted his weight from one leg to the other. "What am I supposed to do, call her a liar? That wouldn't sit well with anyone, or me either. Law's the law. She identified McCutcheon as the culprit. My hands were tied well and good. They still are. Besides," he added, his eyes narrowing at Luke. "How do we know for sure McCutcheon is innocent? He may have a side he's been hiding all these years."

Francis just stared. "How the heck did you get to be sheriff here? They must have been hard up, to say the least. You didn't answer my question, Jack. What's next?"

"We're waiting on a circuit judge to have a trial."

"When do you expect him?" In Y Knot, they could go months without seeing a justice to settle a case. The time frame must be about the same, or worse, for a small town like Priest's Crossing.

Jack's face flamed red. "Not exactly sure. He was here two weeks ago, and the telegraph's gone. I sent a letter—"

"A *letter.*" Francis smashed his palm against one of the bars. "You're not keeping Luke for months in this stinking cell. How long have you been sheriff?"

Jack stuck out his chest where the star was pinned. "What difference does that make?"

"A lot. Doesn't take too many days for your stupidity to surface. When that happens, the citizens may be more apt to listening to another side of the story. That woman is lying, Jack. All we have to do is learn the truth."

A loud gasp echoed around the room.

Turning, Francis saw a young woman clutching the side of the doorway. Chestnut waves cascaded around her shoulders as her pretty emerald eyes, lined with thick lashes, flashed angrily. Slender and of medium height, she reminded Francis of a fine yearling filly feeling her oats. His insides stirred, and he actually sucked in a surprised breath. Without a word, she spun on her heel and was gone.

"Mrs. Blanche Vanderdick?" Francis uttered, still captured by the sweet beauty of the young woman.

"*Van Gleek*," Jack corrected. "And no, that's not Blanche. That was Miss Ashley Adair, Blanche's friend and the town's schoolteacher. You've just offended her by calling Blanche a liar."

Francis shoved his hands on his hips. "I don't care who I offend. I'm telling the truth."

"Colton," Luke said. "Why don't you take Francis out and find some breakfast? By now, I'm sure you know what's good in the restaurant." He winked at his son. "Am I right?"

Colton looked around. "What about you, Pa? Have you eaten?"

"My meal should be arriving soon."

Jack stepped back. "And I need to go see what Miss Ashley wanted."

Francis didn't miss how Jack's face lit up when he said the young woman's name. He supposed that was only natural for such a pretty girl. "You're right, food sounds good about now. But we'll be back as soon as we're finished."

Luke sat on his bunk. "Don't rush on my account. I'm not going anywhere."

Francis pointed a finger. "That ain't funny. Joke all you want, but me and Colton are plenty worried. I'll be glad when the others show up. Getting you out may take some doin'."

And then some. How did you call a woman who's suffered a horrible attack and lost her husband a liar? But she had to be, didn't she? Luke *was* innocent. A sick feeling roiled around in Francis's gut, making his stomach pinch. After a strong cup of coffee, he'd be better able to figure this out, or at least he hoped he would. His good friend, Luke, was in a world of trouble.

Chapter Nine

With Colton beside him, Francis ambled down the dusty street, Redmond's reins dangling in his fingers and his boots kicking up the dry earth. He was dead-boned tired. "Where's a restaurant and livery? I need to take care of my gelding so I can get some grub. Don't think I've ever been this weary before or this hungry."

Colton pointed forward. "Down there's where we have our horses. And right across the street is the food." He took the reins from Francis. "I'll stable him so you can get started on the eats."

Francis lifted a brow. "Thank you. I appreciate that. You sure have grown up. Last I remember, I was giving you orders."

"Yeah, well, I've been in Priest's Crossing alone for enough days to feel pretty old."

"I guess that's true." He lifted his hat and scratched his head. "But you weren't alone. Luke was with you."

"Locked up." Colton started away, his shoulders slumped.

Wasn't difficult to see the boy's hope was all but gone. The kid must still be thinking about his pa's statement he'd overheard in the jail. If Colton hadn't gone off without permission, Luke would have an alibi. The sight needled Francis, making him frown. His small friend was his shadow.

Where Francis went, Colton followed. He'd helped teach Colton to ride and tend cattle. Showed him what bait to use to hook the largest fish in the brook. "I'll meet ya inside," he called to Colton's retreating back. "And thanks, little buddy. Be sure they rub him down and feed him some grain."

Making for the eatery, Francis stepped inside a bustling room. He was so famished, the aroma on the air was a mixture of heaven and hell. He aimed for a table by the wall, passing the counter where a plate of several kinds of muffins were piled high. Unable to stop himself, he snatched up a blueberry and what looked to be a lemon, maybe, as he passed, imagining how good the treats would taste with his first sip of coffee. His mouth watered.

A sturdy fella working the kitchen side of the room glanced his way. Several plates ran up the man's arm as he headed to a table across the eatery. After placing the dishes in front of each customer, he acknowledged Francis with a nod. "I'll be right with ya, stranger."

"Thanks. I helped myself to these." He held up both muffins so the man didn't think he was stealing.

"Not a problem. That's why they're there."

He's friendly enough. Francis broke apart one of the goodies and put half into his mouth as he opened the menu and glanced down the first side.

"Just makes my stomach turn," one of the women at the next table said. "He was such a good man, and in his prime. A hard worker, polite, and God-fearing. I wonder how Blanche is doing."

Francis stopped chewing when he realized their topic of discussion. He glanced over.

"She'll never be the same," the one facing him replied, the bright pink bow in her hair looking too young for her age. "You don't live through such an ordeal and come out unscathed. Have either of you seen her since *it* happened? I wonder if more is involved with the story she's not saying. Something that may have happened to *her.*" The woman took a bite of a muffin and chewed, both eyebrows raised high.

The wobbly skin of her neck reminded Francis of a Thanksgiving turkey.

The oldest-looking woman leaned toward Turkey, her expression dark. "Don't go speculating. That's as good as gossip." She rubbed a shaky hand over her mouth. "Such a heinous act. And to happen right here in Priest's Crossing." Granny, as he immediately nicknamed her, raised her teacup to her lips, took a drink, and then replaced the cup on the table with a little clink of finality. She must have felt his gaze, because she slowly turned her head until they were eye to eye. Quickly he returned his attention to the menu in his hands.

The third woman pointed her spoon at the others. "I haven't seen Blanche or Ashley since. I hear Blanche is living with the Adairs for now. She can't bear to go back to the cabin alone. And I can't blame her in the least. I'm just glad she has somewhere to stay."

She reminded Francis of a months-old pumpkin because her large noggin was covered in curly orange hair. From the corner of his eye, he noticed a quiver in her shoulders as she moved one hand to her throat.

"Benson murdered in cold blood." Pumpkin moaned low, sounding like a specter from a haunted house. "And by a half-breed Indian. If I were Blanche, I don't think I'd want to go on living. They'd only been married a little over a year." She patted her forehead with her napkin. "I can tell you one thing; I've begun bolting my doors every night—with no exceptions. I don't care if the animal responsible is locked up. The world is changing. Men are fast and loose. Heathens, all of 'em."

Animal? Heathen? Luke? He was the best man Francis knew, as were all the McCutcheons. Hearing such talk cut deep. Why had Luke's words of denial been so quickly disavowed? Because of Jack Jones, that's why. The man was out for revenge for being fired by Luke's best friend, no matter what he said.

Granny nodded. "It's a good thing school is over for the term, or Ashley would be forced to be out and about before she's ready to face the people, poor dear."

"Don't be silly, Mildred. Nothing has happened to Ashley."

Pumpkin sighed loudly. "She's Blanche's dear friend and is caring for her. They're extremely close. I'm sure she's living the tragedy just as Blanche is."

When Colton came through the door, Granny, who Francis now knew was named Mildred, saw him first thing.

She nudged Turkey with a pointy elbow. All three looked askance when Colton joined him only one table away from theirs.

By now, everyone in town must know who Colton was. Son of the accused heathenistic, Indian animal.

"Order yet?" Colton asked.

"Naw, not yet." Francis looked around for the waiter, aware the old busybodies had stopped speaking and were undoubtedly listening to his and Colton's conversation.

"He's sorta slow," Colton went on. "I wouldn't want to count on him if my barn was on fire." He picked up Francis's menu.

Colton, unaware of the hostility wafting over from the women, browsed the contents. His mouth pulled down in a frown, and his heavy-lidded eyes were things Francis wasn't used to seeing.

Colton glanced up from the menu. "I've pretty much tried everything. Not as good as the Biscuit Barrel."

The spark of life that usually infused Colton's voice and face was missing. He'd been shouldering this burden alone for days. Francis was glad he was here to help. "I'm trying the batter-fried steak." He pointed to the item at the bottom of the paper menu in Colton's hands.

Colton nodded. "It's good." He closed the menu and laid the list of options on the red-checkered tablecloth, fingering a small snag close to his hand. "Sorry I got Pa in this trouble," he said low. "I didn't mean to. If I'd stayed put where I was supposed to, none of this would have happened. I wish we'd never came for Joe's wedding."

Horrified to see Colton's teary gaze, Francis reached out and touched his arm. "You didn't cause this trouble, Colton. Trouble found you in the wrong place at the wrong time. Things happen. And your pa would be the first to say so." He sat back and glanced at the women, who abruptly buried their gazes into their plates. "This is gonna get straightened out. Then we'll all head home. No one gets away with falsely accusing a McCutcheon. You have to have faith."

"But Grandpa and Grandma are away in Cheyenne. I'd feel a whole lot better about things if they were here to help."

"I know what you mean, but we won't need them," he said, forcing a smile on his lips. "Truth is on our side. All we have to do is make our case to the judge. Luke is innocent. Period. Nobody can change that."

The man with the dirty white apron he'd seen earlier was back. When he saw Colton, his steps slowed. For a moment, Francis wasn't sure he'd speak.

His eyebrows creeped up. "You with him?"

"I am," Francis said, feeling overly protective. "And also with the innocent man your sheriff has locked up in your jail."

Colton's eyes grew round.

The man snorted. "We'll see about that when the judge arrives, won't we?"

"I'm sure you've heard by now that he's a McCutcheon," Francis stated matter-of-factly as he felt his own ire rising.

The waiter shifted his weight, his face a stone mask. "McCutcheon or not, he's gonna pay for killing Benson in his own cabin. And then roughing up Blanche. Benson was a good friend, and I don't take that lightly." He pulled the pencil from behind his ear and nailed Francis with an angry stare. "You want to eat or not?"

Do I trust this man with my food? "That's why I'm here. Give me a batter-fried steak plus three eggs over easy and potatoes"—he turned over the white porcelain coffee cup already on the tabletop—"and coffee. I already ate two muffins, and I'm going for more."

"They're two cents each," the waiter stated and then looked at Colton.

"Bacon and eggs," Colton said quietly, not meeting the man's gaze. "Coffee too."

Francis could understand Colton feeling shy, being he'd been an army of one for a good five days. Under the scrutiny of these people, anyone would crumble. Not many nasty looks and harsh words were needed to feel like an outcast. Well, things were about to change. Francis waited for the man to leave. "Is there anyone in town who believes your pa?"

"Tilly, the old saloon girl from Y Knot, and her husband. Not sure about Christine Meeks." Colton pushed away the hair that had fallen into his eyes. "She runs the mercantile. She's been real nice to me though. She's Joe's sister."

"That's right." Francis straightened. "I remember Tilly. I haven't heard her name mentioned for a long time. I'll look them up next. What's Joe been doing to help?"

Colton leaned back in his chair. "He doesn't know yet. Once the wedding was over, he and his new wife took a honeymoon trip. I think they're set to get back to town soon."

Francis nodded. "That's good."

"One thing," Colton added, still picking at the tablecloth snag.

"Yeah?"

"Benson Van Gleek, the man who was murdered, is Joe's new wife's brother."

A rock of disappointment hit Francis's stomach like spoiled meat. *Blood is thicker than water.* "That might be a problem."

Colton lifted a shoulder. "That's what I think too."

"Well, we know your pa is innocent. For now, we'll sit tight and wait for Roady and the rest to arrive. Having reinforcements will help." He wadded his napkin and tossed it, hitting Colton playfully in the face.

The boy looked up and grinned.

"Stop fretting," Francis ordered. "Make yourself useful and go get me two more muffins. They're tasty, and my stomach is aching."

The boy jumped up. "Sure thing."

The second Colton turned away, Francis smiled at the ladies who were still conspicuously quiet. Not one cup had been raised since the boy returned. "Luke McCutcheon is innocent," he said politely. "He didn't kill that man, and we'll prove that fact. Just wanted to give you ladies something to talk about."

They gasped in unison.

The fluster, patting, and babbling to have been caught in the act of eavesdropping was almost funny. Chuckling, Francis gave a good-mannered nod and reached for the plate Colton held out, questions in his eyes.

"What was that about?" he asked quietly, slipping back into his seat.

"Just meeting some of the locals. No telling how long we'll be here. May as well be friendly."

Colton took one of the muffins, his eyes narrowing.

As the waiter poured two cups of coffee, Francis acknowledged to himself that this straightening out wouldn't be as easy as saying the McCutcheon name a time or two. A man was dead, and the eyewitness had accused his best friend. *She must be in on the crime.* He hoped, for Luke's sake, they could clear his name. And then set him free.

Chapter Ten

Ashley moved around the guest room, dusting, plumping, and folding.

Blanche had refused to get up again today.

Ashley wasn't asking her to take a walk around town, merely come out to the parlor. Setting the feather duster on the highboy, she went back to the bedside and gazed down at the side of Blanche's face. Thank goodness the largest bruise, the one that covered her right cheek and eye, had faded. Each time Ashley saw the damage the murderer had inflicted on her friend, she flinched inside.

"Blanche," she whispered, touching her shoulder. "Please, let me help. Mother is worried about you." *And so am I.* "You'll feel much better if you get out of bed and bathe. I can fix your hair, and we'll sit in the parlor and have a drink of apple cider. Or better, we can make a batch of cookies. Any kind you'd like."

Blanche rolled onto her back, her gaze darting to the door.

"Don't worry. I'm alone. I'd never let anyone in without your permission. No one's been here since the sheriff a few days ago. No one will ask you about anything. They'll have to come through me first."

A small smile wobbled Blanche's lips.

Everyone in Priest's Crossing knew Blanche loved cookies. That's how she made her extra money now that she'd given up teaching to marry Benson. Baking cookies and selling them to the mercantile, the restaurant, and to anyone who suddenly had a sweet tooth when they saw her walking down the street with her basket. The aroma of freshly baked cookies followed everywhere she went, making her very popular.

A pang of sadness wrung Ashley's heart, seeing her friend's sparkling energy dimmed by pain and grief. Blanche wanted so much out of life, and she was willing to work to get ahead, even though she'd no longer been a teacher.

"Is that a yes?" Excited, Ashley reached for the lightweight cotton robe draped over the wooden footboard. She held up the garment and looked away as Blanche crawled out of bed, going slowly because of her bruised ribs. Ashley had seen the extent of her injuries when she came limping into town after the wedding. She'd been in the mercantile when Blanche passed the window. From that time on, the new widow had been living with her and her mother.

After Blanche washed, Ashley brushed her long, dark hair, twisting the tresses into a bun on the back of her head. "There, you look nice. Mother'll be happy to see you up and about." She threaded her arm through Blanche's elbow and reached for the doorknob. "I may have to run to the mercantile for another sack of flour, but that won't take long. You can visit—or just sit," she amended when Blanche suddenly pulled back.

"If you're sure you don't mind?"

"What? Going to the store?" Ashley smiled. "Of course not. I'm happy to." *I'd do anything to help you get over the trauma you've suffered. Anything at all.*

Chapter Eleven

Stepping out of the restaurant behind Colton, Francis felt a satisfying fullness to his stomach but ignored the heaviness of his eyelids. "You take those over to your pa while I go to the mercantile and meet Joe's sister. I'll be there in a few minutes."

Colton held a napkin with three crumbly muffins. The boy nodded and headed across the street.

Francis crossed the road as well but angled to the left. Pulling open the door to the small building, he stepped inside. The interior was well organized and had a good amount of supplies and offerings on the shelves. A large window on either side of the main door let in plenty of light. Narrow stairs in the back led to the second story.

A woman looked up from her ledger. "May I help you?"

"I hope so." Francis went to the counter, passing a shelf of baked goods he'd be sure to look through on his way out. Find something to take to Luke himself. "I'm from Y Knot and work at the Heart of the Mountains. I'm here because my boss, Luke McCutcheon, is locked up in your jail."

She set down her pencil. "Yes, I've heard. I met Mr. McCutcheon at the wedding. Such a shame this horrible travesty has happened."

Holding his hat, Francis dipped his chin, resisting the urge to attest to the fact that the horrible thing had nothing to do with Luke. "My name is Francis, and I believe you're Christine Meeks, Joe Brunn's sister. Am I right?"

"You're absolutely correct." Her smile grew warm. She was a sturdy woman and resembled Joe in the wideness of her eyes and the shape of her face. A white apron covered her brown dress. "I've written to my new sister-in-law's family to let them know about Benson's untimely death as well as to inform my brother. I know he and Luke are very good friends, and he speaks highly of him and his family. Still, I don't know what he can do, if anything at all. The letter will take some time as well. Even without the news, they were slated to return within a few days." Her lips pressed tightly together. "An unfortunate turn that our telegraph operator was such a deceitful scoundrel."

"Hello, Francis," a voice said from behind. "I've been waiting for reinforcements to arrive. Did everyone from the Heart of the Mountains come too?"

He turned to find Tilly, the saloon girl he remembered from the Hitching Post, standing a few feet away. He'd know that silky voice anywhere. She looked different. Her lips were devoid of the color she used to wear, as was her face from war paint. She wore a starched white blouse and black skirt that went all the way to the wooden floorboards and swirled at her ankles when she moved, which she did now to set a few cans on the shelf. If one didn't know her past, a person would never believe she'd once been a soiled dove. "Tilly! I heard you were working here. How're you?"

Tilly went to the counter to stand beside Christine. "I'm happy, Francis. Faith declining this job turned out to be my greatest blessing. I never knew what life could be like outside the saloon walls. Or what self-worth was. The Hitching Post had been my world." She laid a gentle hand on Christine's arm, her eyes glowing. "And now I do. Life's very good, to be sure."

Liking the sound of that, he smiled again.

"I feel for your boss," Christine began. "But I feel worse for poor Blanche. Her husband was murdered right in front of her eyes, a horror she'll never forget. And she received an awful beating as well. I can't even imagine how she's holding up." She placed her fingers over her lips.

Frustration made Francis look away for several moments. "But that doesn't have anything to do with Luke. He's innocent."

Tilly nodded, her expression in complete agreement with Francis, but Christine didn't look quite as sure.

"Blanche was there," the store owner said, her voice steely. "Surely she couldn't make a mistake such as you're suggesting."

This was a battle he'd not win in one conversation.

Chapter Twelve

The door to the mercantile opened, and Ashley Adair, the pretty young woman he'd seen earlier, stepped inside. For a few moments, she didn't notice him at the counter speaking with Christine and Tilly. Then shock registered on her face. She turned toward the door.

"Wait," Francis called, surprising himself. "Please don't go yet. I'd like to speak with you."

Her gaze traced to the women and then back to him.

He slowly stepped closer. "Jack Jones said you're close friends with the woman who's accusing my boss, Luke McCutcheon, of murder. Can I ask you a few questions?"

"It's all right, Ashley," Christine called. "I'm here, and so is Tilly. I believe speaking with this young man is the least we can do. Ashley Adair, this is Francis."

The young woman nodded and followed Francis toward the back of the store.

"I came as soon as I learned Luke had been arrested for the murder. I just want to piece together the way the incident happened."

Her mouth firmed. "You mean the murder? You were speaking with the sheriff. I'm sure he told you."

"That's true enough. But your sheriff, Jack Jones, can't be trusted. He used to be the deputy in Y Knot and was fired last September by Luke's best friend, the sheriff. He's been caught in more than one lie since I've known him. He's not fond of the McCutcheons. I wouldn't trust him with—"

Her face blanched. He'd given away too much information too quickly. Perhaps she liked Jack Jones. Maybe he'd saved her dog from a fire or rescued her kitten from climbing too high in a tree. Francis had never been very good at bluffing at poker or hiding his feelings.

Miss Adair crossed her arms over her chest, and her expression hardened. "Sheriff Jones has proven himself a good lawman since his arrival. Sounds like you've already tried the sheriff and found him lacking. I don't appreciate your attitude."

"Maybe I have, miss, but I can't help that. Can you just give me an accounting of the details as you heard them from the witness? I'd greatly appreciate your rendition." He smiled, remembering Lucky, the bunkhouse cook, telling him he could get better results by being nice. Besides, her face was pretty, and he liked the sound of her voice. Why shouldn't he be nice? "Miss Adair?"

She gave a little huff. "Blanche told me your boss showed up early in the morning looking for something to eat. After she and Benson gave him most of the food they had, he demanded money. He got angry when she told him they didn't have any savings. They argued. The quarrel escalated. When Benson turned away to the door after demanding he leave, your boss picked up the fire poker and hit him across the head. After that, he took to her with fists until she pretended to be dead."

"Pretended to be dead?" *This is the stupidest story I've ever heard. Like Luke couldn't tell the difference.*

She took a deep breath. "Blanche is a good person who was very generous to me. She was a marvelous teacher as well, knowledgeable and funny. Without her help, I'd never have become a teacher myself. I owe her *everything*, and in the very least my trust and loyalty. Benson was a kind man." Her lips wobbled. "They'd only been married a year…"

Tears sprang to her blue eyes. Moved by the sound of sadness in her voice, he pulled out his handkerchief.

She waved it away. "I'm all right. I just hate to think of Benson being murdered like that. Such a horrible thing. And now Blanche is a widow." She heaved another deep sigh. "So you see, the case is pretty clear. All that's left is waiting for the judge and your boss will get his due."

Francis digested her story. Nothing made a lick of sense. Luke didn't have to demand money from anyone. The whole family was the richest in the territory. Why would the woman, Blanche, say such a thing? Maybe someone else was passing through who looked like Luke. More details had to be involved. "You've heard of the McCutcheons from Y Knot?"

She ran one finger slowly over her lips.

He could tell she didn't want to answer that question as she avoided his gaze. No one in their right mind would think any of them capable of murder. "Miss Adair?"

"Of course I have. Everyone was shocked when they learned Benson's murderer was a McCutcheon."

"How about Blanche? Was she shocked too?"

"Why, yes, actually…" Her mouth snapped closed. She glanced around the store.

"Doesn't that seem strange, a McCutcheon killing a man for money?"

"I'm not on trial, sir," she said softly. "And neither is Blanche. I would appreciate if you'd remember that. I feel as if you suspect me. Maybe McCutcheon was so angry about something he snapped. You say he was looking for his son. Perhaps Mr. McCutcheon has a black temper no one knows about." She straightened and lifted her chin.

Francis admired her strength and loyalty. Those qualities made a person, in his way of thinking. She was searching for some explanation to validate Blanche's cockamamie story, more interested in defending her friend than looking logically at the situation, and he could understand why. She must be in a real dilemma. Ashley had to know the story had holes you could drive a stagecoach through.

He stayed his first impulse to reach out and touch her arm. Since Charity, Luke's younger sister, this was the first woman he'd felt so strongly about. He'd flirted with Fancy, the saloon girl in Y Knot, ever since Charity married Brandon. He'd begun to think a woman for him didn't exist in the world. Maybe a man with no blood kin to call his own would never find a woman to love. But this young schoolteacher made him feel different. Even though he didn't know her well, she gave him just a tiny glimmer of hope.

He stepped back, knowing he'd pushed her about as far as he should at this point. He was anxious to get back to the jail and speak with Luke. And Colton was waiting. "Thank you for your time, miss. I can't help but notice that everyone in town is shooting daggers with their eyes. Not you though."

When a ghost of a smile appeared on her lips, the hat dangling in his fingers fell to the floor. He quickly picked it up.

"You're welcome. I know you're not the enemy. I'm sorry if the citizens of Priest's Crossing haven't extended a warm welcome. But I'm sure you can understand, under the circumstances."

"I do." He nodded. "I best get back to the jail." Francis held her gaze. "And visit my innocent friend. We need to work though the facts and figure this mess out." As he walked away, Francis stopped at the counter. Muffins, breads, and some small fruit pies that made his mouth water just looking at them sat on a tray. He wanted to take something to Luke. Make him feel better.

"Every baked item is exceptional," Tilly said, coming to his side. "He has a true touch. Can make the mundane taste like gold."

"Who?"

"Daniel Clevenger. Owner of the restaurant."

Francis nodded. "I ate there this morning. The fare was quite tasty."

Tilly pulled back, her eyes opened wide. "Just tasty? Did you have any of his muffins? I have to have one every day, and sometimes twice, now that I'm expecting."

He laughed, keenly aware of Miss Adair watching from the center of the store. He glanced at the pies one more time, then turned slightly and caught her eye.

She blushed and pulled her gaze back to the bag of flour in her hands.

"I ate several, and Colton is taking a couple to Luke as we speak. Knowing Luke, he probably wolfed them down," he joked. He couldn't believe he was actually flirting with Tilly. She was a married woman and an old friend. He'd only been a boy when she'd moved away from Y Knot, and he hoped she'd forgive him for milking this opportunity in front of Miss Adair. "I'll take this pie, as well."

"He'll thank you later," she gushed as she took his dime.

Settling his hat on his head, Francis stepped out the door after one more backward glance at Tilly and Christine Meeks, as well as the pretty Miss Adair. Had his questions made her think twice about trusting Mrs. Van Gleek's trumped-up story? He'd spotted the mistakes in the tale right away. Blanche Van Gleek hadn't known Luke was a McCutcheon when she'd pointed the finger. A tasty bit of information to chew on. He would have liked to see her face when she'd learned the truth. Much more was involved with this story than Blanche was saying. Figuring that out would be up to him and the rest of the boys.

Chapter Thirteen

Luke paced a circle in his cell before he remembered Colton was sitting quietly on the long bench opposite, watching his every move. Luke looked over and stopped. His son's fretful gaze hurt. What had happened in the Van Gleek cabin? That was the winning question. All he'd done was ask the woman if she'd seen Colton, watered his horse and himself, and left. He needed to figure out the puzzle because Jack wouldn't. His gaze narrowed on the wood grain of the dry-looking oak above Colton's head.

Francis came through the door and pulled up. "What're you thinkin'?"

Luke turned and gave him quizzical a look. "What do you mean?"

"I've known you long enough to recognize when you've got something important on your mind. Your forehead crinkles and your head tilts to the side. Just like now. Something has struck you. What?"

Luke straightened his head.

Colton got up and came over to the bars, the worry lines still deep in his forehead.

Luke reached out and placed his hand on Colton's shoulder, but only for an instant. His son didn't like to be treated like a baby. And he shouldn't be. He could help. Be Luke's eyes and ears.

Francis tipped a pie he'd purchased somewhere to one side and slid the pastry through the bars.

"Thanks. This looks good." Luke retrieved the dirty fork from his breakfast dishes sitting on the cot and dug in. "I sure miss Faith's cooking, I can tell you that."

Francis nodded. "I'm sure that's not all you miss."

"You're right there," he said enjoying the sweet taste of the apples and tangy cinnamon. The butter-laden crust crumbled in his mouth. He brushed a few morsels away with the back of his hand and kept eating. "I miss my home, the laughter of my children and wife, and tucking everybody in at night." He glanced at Colton and smiled. "And spending quiet time speaking with Faith after everyone is asleep. I'll never take those things for granted again."

Deputy Clark came through the door, the heavy iron key ring, with a key for each cell, dangling in his fingers. He stood for a moment and then turned to leave.

"Hold up," Luke called.

The heavy-shouldered man turned back.

His tangle of short brown hair reminded Luke of a shaggy buffalo. He looked about Luke's age, with a hard glint to his eyes. Crossing his arms over his chest, he waited for Luke's question. This man would give as good as he got, Luke figured, not like the faint-hearted Jack Jones. Priest's Crossing had put the two men in the wrong positions. "What's the status of things? Is anyone investigating who else may have killed that fella? I'm innocent. Do some detective work."

"Who says we're not?"

"Me. I haven't heard a peep out of either one of you." Luke grasped the bars. "I won't be a scapegoat for anyone."

Clark chuckled nastily. "You don't have much say in this, McCutcheon. How does being on the other side of the bars feel?"

"That's uncalled for," Francis barked. "He's only asking a logical question, considering the circumstances."

"Leave the law to us." Clark punctuated his words with a pointed finger first at Luke and then Francis. "You'll get a fair trial, when the time comes." Without another word, Deputy Clark stamped out of the room.

Yeah, a trial would be held all right, and the jury would find him guilty if they didn't have any other possibilities to consider. His appetite gone, Luke set the pie on the cot.

"What now, Pa?" Colton asked.

"I've been thinking."

"Yeah?" Both Francis and Colton moved closer to the bars.

He motioned with his hand to keep their voices low. "What if Mrs. Van Gleek's husband was already dead when I rode up? She wasn't very friendly or keen on inviting me in. She stood like a warden with feet planted and hands on hips as if guarding the door. Didn't move from her spot when I asked about the surrounding area." He gave Francis and then Colton a long stare.

Francis's eyebrow lifted. "Maybe so," he said just above a whisper.

"But she wasn't beat up, yet, Pa."

"You're right, she wasn't." She looked a bit disheveled, like maybe she'd been sleeping late and I'd disturbed her." He looked straight into Francis's eyes conveying a silent message.

Francis gave a slight nod.

"Say she and her husband had a fight," Luke went on. "And she killed him in self-defense?"

Francis scratched his chin and whispered, "Self-defense is hard to prove. Men don't like thinkin' women can get away with nothin'. Some don't consider using their fists to discipline their spouse a crime."

"That's sadly so. But how could she blacken her own eye and bruise her ribs? I'd say that's impossible." He didn't like speaking about such unseemly issues in front of his boy, but Colton was growing up. He'd said so himself several times.

Colton glanced around. "Then someone had to help her. Maybe he was inside waiting to kill you if you came in and discovered the crime."

Nodding, Luke pointed to the door.

On silent footsteps, Colton walked as quietly as a cat and glanced into the outer room where the sheriff had his desk. Quickly returning, he mouthed the word "Empty."

"Good." Luke leaned one palm on a shiny metal bar. "I know I didn't kill him or beat her up. And yet she claims I did. My first thought was they'd had a fight, he beat her, and then she smacked him on the head when he wasn't looking. Now I'm not so certain."

"Are you talking premeditated crime?" Francis asked, still leaning toward the bars.

"Could be."

"Well, we better get busy." Francis straightened. "I met Joe's sister, Christine Meeks, at the mercantile. She said she met you at the wedding and knows how close Joe is to you and the family."

Luke lifted a shoulder. "That's pretty much common knowledge."

"She didn't appear all that sympathetic to your plight. I told her you were innocent, but she's feeling pretty bad for her friend becoming a widow and about Benson. You'll be going up against the whole town if this goes to trial. If we can't even get the support of Joe's sister, we may have trouble convincing anyone else."

Luke scratched the side of his face, fingering the unfamiliar whiskers. "You're right on that account, Francis. Then we better get cracking. If I didn't kill him, and she didn't kill him, who else was in that cabin that morning? Had to be somebody."

"If the judge arrives tomorrow, Pa, what'll happen?"

That was a very good question. He respected the law as much as, if not more than, most men, but he wasn't hanging for a murder he didn't commit. If what Francis said was true, he wouldn't find much understanding in Priest's Crossing.

"Would they hang ya?" Colton's voice quivered unsteadily.

"Maybe." *How difficult to admit to my own son.* A hot despair clawed at Luke's throat. *He's trying to be so brave. But better for him to know the truth than paint an unrealistic picture.* "For now, you'll have to continue being my eyes and ears. Make note of everything. Go places and hang around. Someone might let something slip." Luke reached out and ruffled Colton's hair, not caring if he got mad. Luke wished with his whole heart he could pull his son into his arms and tell him everything was going to be all right. He'd like to be a little more sure about that himself. "Francis, I'm thankful you're here, but I'll feel a lot better when the rest of the men arrive."

Chapter Fourteen

The man glared at his hands with revulsion as he walked down the side of the street, still disbelieving what he'd done only five days prior. Even the midmorning sun that had chased away the fog couldn't lighten his mood. He felt like a fool for letting Blanche catch his eye. She'd chased him. Hadn't given him a chance to say no. This situation was all her fault. Why had he trusted her at all? He should've looked out that window himself. He knew Luke McCutcheon. Almost everybody in Montana Territory knew Luke McCutcheon. Grubby clothes and whiskered or not. Everyone but Blanche.

How stupid! The woman was a moron. Now he'd have to be very, very careful. The story they'd concocted reeked of a lie. No one would believe McCutcheon killed Benson for money—at least, not for long. If things got hot, would Blanche hold up? Or would she crumble and sing like a bird, accusing him of killing Benson without her knowledge? Twisting the story so all the blame fell onto him. Keeping an eye on her would be difficult, but he'd not hang for a crime of passion that should be laid at her feet. If things didn't conclude quickly, he'd have to find a way to silence her. He needed a judge and fast. Before someone wised up enough to ask real questions. Since Blanche was living with Miss Adair and her mother for the time being, getting access would be near impossible.

And then he faced the mystery of his missing money clip. Where had he misplaced the thing? So much for his distracted mind. He needed a rest. Somewhere he could get away from these troubles.

A woman shouted his name. At the same moment, he heard the rumble of wagon wheels. Jerking around, he stumbled back the instant before being rundown by a fast-moving buckboard. The driver's attention was turned toward his passenger and hadn't seen him.

Across the street, Christine Meeks was on her toes, waving her bonnet back and forth. "That was close!" she called. "You scared five years off my life."

Busybody. Go away. He smiled as he lifted a shaky hand to his head, pushing his fingers through his hair. "I didn't see that coming! Thanks for the warning." Feeling a prickle on the back of his neck, he glanced behind him.

Standing at the jail, Francis, a young cowhand and McCutcheon's boy watched.

He stretched his shoulders, shaking off the scare. He had more important things to think about.

"We've already had too much sorrow around town without adding more," Christine said. "Be more careful."

With a nod, he continued as if his only care was the fact he'd almost been killed by the wagon. In reality, Benson's funeral was held two days ago. Most of the town turned out, teary-eyed, whispering at the horrible way one of their own had been murdered right in their midst. The undertaker wanted to wait for Benson's sister, Pearl Brunn, to get back to town since she was his only blood relative. But the warmth of the days made waiting any longer impossible.

The cemetery was on a small rise overlooking the town. He kept his gaze trained far away from Blanche. That was easy. The sight of her made him sick. He'd been looking at the clouds when he got that feeling of being watched. He'd spotted that boy, the McCutcheon kid, watching him from the alley. Did Luke McCutcheon's son suspect him? How could he?

He rubbed a hand over his face and kept walking. The thought of Blanche disgusted him. He hadn't meant to cause so much damage when he'd roughed her up, but his anger had welled and his fists seemed to have a mind of their own. In actuality, he'd been tempted to kill her. That would have solved the problem he had now. Accusing McCutcheon. He still couldn't believe she'd gone and done something so stupid. Because of her, he'd now have to live with another grisly murder on his conscience for the rest of his life. And just when he'd put the past behind him. He rarely thought back to that time long ago and his brother's begging words.

Chapter Fifteen

The thunder of hooves pounding the dirt road outside brought Ashley running to her front window.

"What's that sound?" Mrs. Adair asked from the kitchen.

A group of riders galloped by so fast Ashley barely had a chance to discern who or what they were. "I... I don't know." But she did. They must be from the McCutcheon ranch. All the cowboys, with the exception of one, were large men, their faces stony masks of anger. When they'd gone by, she noticed a long ponytail of dark hair trailing out behind the smaller rider. A woman! Who could she be? Ashley turned and met her mother's worried gaze. "I'll go find out." *I don't like the thought of all those men. They could make trouble. More trouble than we already have.*

Her mother looked to the hallway that led to the guestroom where Blanche still rested. After the noon meal, her friend had complained of a headache and lain down for an hour or so.

"You don't think they'll try to break out the prisoner, do you?" her mother asked. "I don't want to see any more killing in our town."

Still so skittish and frail. Even a whisper of confrontation put her poor mother into a panic. The only place she felt truly safe was among their apple trees. Ashley ran her hand comfortingly down her arm. "No. Sheriff Jones won't let anything like that happen. Or Deputy Clark. We're well protected here." Both the lawmen's faces popped into her mind. Jack Jones, with his engaging, yet a bit sneaky, smile and his deputy's more calculating expression. Hoss Clark was a quiet man most of the time, but that didn't mean he was stupid. Ashley had the impression he was exactly the opposite.

"Are you sure you should go? If there's trouble, Jack or Hoss will come tell us."

"Nothing will happen." She thought of Francis, the handsome young man who'd taken the time to speak with her yesterday about his boss. He'd seemed kind and sincere. She barely knew him, but already she liked him better than the sheriff. And the stranger liked her. But then, the sheriff had liked her too… not that she'd felt any desire for Jack Jones. He'd been too persistent. She wondered what Francis would do in his place. "I'm going to the mercantile to see what I can find out. I'll be back as soon as I can."

Finally in town, Faith practically jumped out of her saddle and ran into the jail as the others dismounted and tied their horses to the hitching rail. She passed through the vacant outer office to the jail cells, where Luke stood at the bars as if he'd heard them coming. Francis and her stepson Colton were there too. At the sight of her husband, her heart slammed painfully against her ribs. His ragged clothes and unkempt look didn't bother her, but the beaten look in his eyes—that frightened her to death.

"Luke!" She rushed to the bars that kept her from her love. At the same time, she put out her arm to Colton, but he didn't fall into her embrace as she'd expected. He did come forward a few inches, and she pulled him to her side, thankful to see all of them alive. Horrible thoughts had played through her mind ever since Trent Herrick brought the shocking news to the ranch. Francis gave a nod when she looked his way, and then his gaze darted to the door where Roady Guthrie, the ranch foreman, Smokey, Pedro, Shad, and one of Shad's younger brothers, Nick, followed.

Luke's hands were already through the bars, holding hers.

"What's this arrest about, Luke?" She worked to keep her voice from shaking but wasn't being successful. Since marrying into the McCutcheon family, her life had become stable and good. These last few days reminded her all too much of her time on the run from Ward Brown and the few days before Dawn was born. "How can anyone believe you're guilty of murder? That's not possible."

Luke's hard gaze cut from her to Roady.

"She couldn't be stopped," Roady responded. "We tried our best. All of us did."

Seeing Luke alive did little to quell the anxiety pinching her insides. How long had he been locked up? The entire ride here, she'd prayed that by the time they arrived Luke would have been cleared. Set free. Seeing him like this reminded her of the angry caged eagle a band of gypsies had brought through Y Knot last year. He didn't belong here any more than that huge, wild bird belonged in a show. His Indian heritage was more pronounced than ever. Black hair swept back haphazardly, long and ragged. Whiskers covered his strong jaw. Deep lines cupped his mouth and fanned out from his eyes. Would Jack Jones let her inside with him? *All I want is to feel his strong embrace.* She didn't think so. "Luke, please, tell me what's going on?"

"You shouldn't have come."

His sharp voice reminded her of broken glass.

"You belong at home with Dawn and Holly." His gaze dropped to Colton, who had yet to speak. "I'm sure they're frightened. This jail and this town is no place for you."

At his angry tone, she took a small step back but lifted her chin. She couldn't remember a time he'd ever spoken so harshly. And never in front of anyone else. "Don't you order me around, Luke McCutcheon. Not now, not ever. I'm your wife, and I'll be any place I want to be, do you understand? I don't need protecting."

Roady came to her side. "See what I mean, Luke? And that's toned down, I can tell you that."

She saw appreciation in Luke's eyes as he took in the faces of his ranch hands all crammed in the small, dark area. The first thing she would do is bring more lanterns. This place felt like a tomb. She swiveled and looked at the door. "Where's Jack Jones? I want to speak with him."

"Haven't seen him for a couple of hours now," Francis said. "Not since he was in here asking again what Luke was doing out at the Van Gleek homestead, as if his answer would be different this time." Francis hooked his thumb over his shoulder toward the door. "He goes off somewhere in the afternoon."

Smokey scoffed. "Probably takes a nap with his binky and blanket."

The ranch hands laughed, but Luke and Faith didn't, nor did Francis or Colton.

The reality was far more serious than any of them had thought. If Jack hadn't released him on his good name as of yet, surely her showing up with the ranch hands wouldn't change his mind now. She turned and started for the door. "Well, then, tell me where he lives. I'll go to his house. Luke has to be released. He's been in there far too long already."

"That won't help, sweetheart," Luke said.

His tone was finally back to something she recognized. A simmering burn constricted her throat. She'd been angry and strong during the ride here. Now she just wanted to fall into Luke's arms so he could tell her everything would be okay. She needed to feel his kiss on her lips. This was bad. Very bad. And the scary part was, she didn't know what to do.

Chapter Sixteen

Francis stepped out of the jailhouse into the midafternoon light, shading his eyes against the sun that beamed through the western trees. Inside, Luke was still filling in the others and answering questions. With so many men in the small area, the place felt like a coffin. Francis didn't like small, confined spaces. When only Colton and Luke were there, he'd been fine—but seven large men, plus Colton and Faith, made the walls feel like they pushed on his lungs. He needed air.

Besides, no new information had surfaced that Luke could share. They needed to start digging. If Luke didn't kill Benson Van Gleek, somebody else did. Since yesterday, they'd tossed around ideas, but they needed cold, hard facts. If his wife didn't kill him, someone else had been in the cabin that day. Period.

Across the street, the man who'd served Francis breakfast yesterday as well as supper a few hours later came out with a bucket and tossed what looked like plain water into the street. Since then, Francis had learned his name was Daniel Clevenger and he pretty much ran the restaurant on his own. When he saw Francis and all the new horses, he plucked the dangling cigarette from his lips and held the smoke in his fingers. His gaze went over the scene slowly, and then his eyes narrowed.

Almost a week had passed since the killing. Francis didn't like this fellow's challenging regard. He was burly and looked like he could fight. Could Jack and his deputy fend off the townspeople if they didn't want to wait for a judge and took matters into their own hands? Francis had his doubts.

Their guns. The men needed to stash them away before Jack or Deputy Clark returned to confiscate them. His hand slipped down and felt his thigh where he normally wore his weapon. He felt naked without it.

Down the same side of the street and across an open lot, Miss Ashley Adair stepped out of the mercantile, stopped, and looked down at the jail. When she noticed him leaning on the side of the building, she jerked her gaze away but stood there as if waiting on something.

"Colton," he called inside.

In a moment, Colton came out.

"Go tell the others to hide their guns before Jack or Clark shows up to confiscate them. Like they did mine." He wanted to speak with Miss Adair.

Colton followed his line of sight.

"Tell 'em to stable their horses at the livery and put their guns under the hay in the loft of the outbuilding. When I was there, the place looked deserted. This time of year, the stock aren't needing much feed. The weapons should go unnoticed until we can find a better place. They need to go now, before it's too late."

"Fine," Colton replied. "But how come you're not?"

"I'm looking for evidence."

"With that girl?"

"Her name is Ashley Adair. And yes, I'll look wherever the evidence takes me. The Van Gleek woman is staying at her house for the time being. I'll be back shortly."

Colton nodded and disappeared.

Francis made his way over the dry, dusty earth to the porch of the mercantile. The small overhang gave them relief from the hot sun. He stopped when he reached Miss Adair and tipped the rim of his hat. Her curious green eyes studied him a moment as her high-set cheeks took on a rosy hue.

"Your name is Francis," she said clearly. "But I didn't catch a last name."

"Just Francis. I was a foundling. I make no bones about my past. The McCutcheons took me in, and I do just fine with my first name." The family treated him like one of them, but he wasn't *really* a McCutcheon. He'd never expected to be fully adopted. Things in an untamed territory weren't that formal. He was grateful for what he had. He lifted his chin and glanced around. *What is that sweet scent? Does she smell like apples?*

Her brows shot up, and she blinked a few times. "Ah, no, I didn't mean to be rude with my question. Was wondering, that's all. I didn't know."

"Good. I just wanted to have that out there right off. My lack of a name can be a stumbling block, I admit that, but most times, I shrug off the matter. Now, if someone teases me about having a *girl's* name, that's a different story entirely. I might get angry over that."

She actually smiled.

A very pretty one too.

"No, I won't do that. Actually, my great-great-grandfather was named Francis Melbourne Adair. He was born in Australia and came over on an America-bound ship when he was sixteen. I'm told he was a bit of a scamp, but was devilishly handsome and had his pick of wives." Her pleased expression deepened.

"If he had a smile like yours, I can see why."

Her cheeks bloomed scarlet, and for a moment, she glanced away.

Maybe he was rushing things. "I'm sorry. I didn't mean to embarrass you. Just stating a fact."

For the first time in days, Francis felt a surge of happiness. He'd never met another man named Francis. A handful of women, yes, but never a man or even a boy. "Pretty remarkable—to know so much of your history." Awe filled him at the thought of an overseas adventure. And this Francis sounded like a good man—strong-minded and hardworking. He'd had a family, despite all the challenges he'd faced. "I'd enjoy hearin' more about him sometime if you don't mind. He sounds like a determined fella."

Her blush-kissed cheeks darkened even more. In a nervous gesture, her glance traced to the sheriff's office once before returning to his face. "I'd be happy to tell you more if we have a chance. Are you still working on the murder? I'll try to help if I can."

Surprised, he tipped his head. "Yes, I am. Why're you willin' now? Do you think my boss is innocent, like I said?"

She thoughtfully met his gaze. "No, I don't. I have no reason to believe Blanche would lie. But I'm a teacher. I believe in open communication. The sooner we clear up this case, the faster Priest's Crossing can get back to normal. This situation isn't easy for Blanche, or the children of the town, hearing the whole grisly story rehashed over and over. The murder seems to be the only thing people talk about when I come into town. I hope we can soon put the whole ordeal to rest."

She certainly has a lot to say. A long conversation with a young lady was not a daily occurrence for him. He was happy, and a bit surprised, to hold his own so well. "Has Mrs. Van Gleek been back out to her homestead since she's come to live at your place?"

Ashley laced her fingers together in front of her dress. "No, she hasn't. She's mourning Benson and stays in her room most of the time, crying and staring out the window. I'm sure weeks will pass before she's ready to face their home."

"I see." He scratched his chin, thinking tomorrow he'd shave more carefully. "Anyone you know of been out there?"

"I assume the sheriff and his deputy would have looked around after they removed the body. But other than that, not that I know of. Blanche said they locked up the cabin tight, waiting on the judge and the trial."

Before Francis knew what he was up to, he let a disbelieving grunt escape his lips.

Her eyes instantly narrowed.

"I didn't mean anything by that sound," he quickly said. "Just thinking out loud."

Across the street, next to the jail, Jed Kasterlee, the hotel proprietor, stepped out onto the boardwalk in front of his establishment and began sweeping. A white apron was tied around his waist, and his hair was slicked back.

A moment passed before he spotted them in front of the mercantile.

With his excellent eyesight, Francis noticed a slight tremor in his hands, and then his mouth pulled angrily to one side. Every few seconds, he dared another glance in their direction. Kasterlee wasn't happy to see him speaking with Miss Adair. Why? Did he know something Francis didn't?

Chapter Seventeen

Ashley knew she needed to stop fostering these warm thoughts toward this cowboy from Y Knot. He was on the wrong side. Blanche's enemy, so to speak. And especially now, with the ardent widower, Jed Kasterlee, watching her and Francis's conversation as he swept clean his boardwalk kitty-corner across the street. Last year, the hotel owner had set his sights on her, but since she'd turned him down, he hadn't said more than boo in passing—which suited her just fine. But now that didn't stop his glances from under his small-brimmed brown hat. She avoided him whenever possible, but today his chore out front had him close enough she could feel his intent gaze. "Francis, your thinking out loud puts me off. As much as you believe your boss is innocent, I think the same of my good friend."

"Sorry, Miss Adair, that isn't my intent. I appreciate your willingness to help me work through my questions. I really do. Jack Jones and Deputy Clark have been noticeably closed-mouthed about any evidence. I wonder if that's why Jack's been disappearing. I don't see him around much during the day."

"He's working on his house, a deserted shack he claimed soon after he came to town. Making improvements. At least, that's what he does with most of his time after he comes into town in the morning and returns again in the late afternoon. Deputy Clark sees to most of the lawbreaking matters."

"Where is the place?"

She pointed past the jail. "A quarter mile beyond my house." Was she giving away too much information? A niggle of apprehension swirled inside. Telling the truth couldn't hurt. But if what Francis said about his boss was true, then some sort of blame for Benson's death might lie at Blanche's feet. That just wasn't possible. Blanche Van Gleek had been nothing but sincere and morally upright for all the time Ashley had known her. She had been full of energy and maybe a little restless, but that was only natural. Before she'd arrived in Priest's Crossing, she'd probably been used to a more exciting life than people led in this little town. When Blanche fell in love with Benson and he asked for her hand in marriage, Blanche spoke to the town council in favor of Ashley taking over her position, even though she was only seventeen at the time. She owed Blanche so much. Ashley would never turn her back on her.

One by one, the men she'd seen galloping past her home stepped out of the sheriff's office. They glanced slowly up and down the street, as if committing every small detail to memory. Four large white men and a dangerous-looking Mexican made up the group. The woman must be McCutcheon's wife, for she remained inside.

"Those are the ranch hands from the Heart of the Mountains," Francis said when he saw the men emerge. "The remainder stayed back at the ranch to watch over things there. The operation is large."

"It appears so. That many ranch hands bespeaks great wealth."

He captured her gaze. "Exactly my point."

He didn't have to say any more. She wondered if something was amiss with Blanche's story of how things happened, but she'd not tell him that.

The men collected their horses and proceeded down the street toward the livery. As they approached, they stared at her and Francis.

Embarrassment turned to anger. Had they no manners? Just as that thought was about to pass her lips, the men nodded and touched their hats.

"Francis," a bowlegged, leather-skinned fella called out. "We'd like to speak with you, when you can tear yourself away."

"On my way, Smokey." He didn't make a move to go.

Flattered, she dropped her gaze to the boardwalk and felt a tiny smile on her lips. She liked his attention and conversation.

"I have one last thing to say."

Francis held her gaze longer than was proper. The fact that she didn't look away troubled her conscience. "Yes?"

"Be careful."

"Careful?" Her heart did a summersault. "Why?"

"I know Luke is innocent. That means whoever killed Benson Van Gleek isn't locked up. That person is out there— somewhere. Who knows what might spook 'em?"

When she opened her mouth to object, he held up a silencing finger to his lips. "Just consider what I've said. Please." With that, he turned on his boot heel.

She watched him walk away, catching sight of Jed Kasterlee still snooping. Angered, she looked directly at the hotel owner.

He snapped away his gaze.

A plausible explanation had to exist why a rich McCutcheon would come to Blanche and Benson's home and demand money. Perhaps he had a secret history with Benson, the money was owed him from a past debt, and he was angry Benson hadn't yet paid. Or he'd found himself in financial troubles and was too embarrassed to tell his family. Several different situations not yet explored were possible. She'd not turn her back so quickly on her best friend just because Francis made her feel all warm and fluttery. Or that his sincerity and claims had merit. She wasn't a warm and fluttery type. She thought things through. Looked for evidence in every situation, and that's just what she would do here, before things got out of hand.

Chapter Eighteen

Francis strode into the livery under the suspicious gaze of Pink Kelly, the proprietor. Thick blond hair covered the stable owner's head, and a blue kerchief was tied around his neck. Instead of the usual clothing of denim overalls most stable hands liked, Pink Kelly wore close-fitting jeans that hugged a slim waist. His shirtsleeves were rolled midway up his arms and a pair of gloves were looped over his leather belt.

Francis smiled and passed through the barn into the rear breezeway that led to an outbuilding, the one where he'd told the men to store their guns. As he grew closer, the voices he heard quieted at his approach until he turned the corner to find them circled up close. Francis glanced up the ladder. "Up top?" he asked, keeping his voice low.

Shad nodded. "But I don't like leaving them there for long. We may need 'em."

Nick's brows drew down. "You think a gunfight is certain?"

Roady, his arms crossed over his chest, said, "'Course not. We're not here to break the law. If we wanted to take Luke out of the jail that way, with all of us, the doin' would be easy. But then we'd have a chase on our hands, and someone might get killed. Francis was smart to give us a heads-up about our weapons being seized. Once darkness falls, we'll find a better place to store them. But for now, under the hay will do."

The men tightened their circle around Francis.

"What do you know?" Roady whispered, his tone deep in all seriousness.

Francis had never seen the ranch foreman so grave. "Luke thinks someone else, besides the woman, must have been inside. I'd say that's a good hunch unless she's the one who killed her husband." He glanced over his shoulder and out the door to be sure they were still alone. "Her cabin is locked up tight. Clark and Jones aren't saying much. I'm not sure they did any investigating at all. Just learned Jones is renovating his house, of all things. I guess he feels like his job is done now that he has an eyewitness and a suspect locked up. He's waiting on a judge."

Pedro's jaw clenched and released several times. "He knows Luke's innocent. He knows and yet keeps the *jefe* locked up like an animal." The Mexican's eyes formed into slits. "Jones is a *tonto del culo*. Needs a visit to the anthill."

Smokey gripped Pedro's shoulder and gave a little shake. "Don't let your temper get the best of ya. We need to keep our wits about us, to help the boss, not make things worse."

Francis nodded. "Smokey's right. The townsfolk have been watching me as if they think I'm Longabaugh of the Wild Bunch and just broke out of jail in Sundance. There're never less than six sets of eyes on me at all times. Feels eerie. At other times, I feel sort of famous. They're even suspicious of Colton. Poor kid has been shouldering the scorn until I arrived. He's not said much but feels responsible for what's happened to his pa. If not for sneaking off, Luke would have an alibi." He heaved a deep sigh, thankful the men had arrived. With everyone working on the case, they'd clear Luke. He glanced at the foreman. "I didn't think I'd see you here, with Sally giving birth so recently."

"She insisted I come. She's staying with Heather while I'm gone and has a lot of help. She's worried about Luke, just like the rest of us. That said, we have some investigatin' to do. Tonight at the cabin. See if we can't come up with something Jack missed."

"Evening, boys," Deputy Clark said, stepping into the shed. His eyes narrowed. "What's going on out here?"

The strong-armed liveryman was only one beat behind. His shoulders filled the doorway.

"Just catching up on events without the town listening in," Roady said evenly, his tone friendly. "We arrived a little while ago. We're just sorting things out and wanted someplace quiet where we could talk. You must be Deputy Clark. I'm Roady Guthrie, the ranch foreman."

The deputy's nostrils flared when his gaze traveled to each man. "You came unarmed."

His skeptical tone said he didn't believe that for a second.

Roady smiled, then glanced at Francis and the others. "We're a friendly bunch."

"Yeah, right. You've already been at the jail. You know all you need to know."

"Just hearing Francis's version."

Francis shrugged and gave his best innocent face. Clark was a big man. Looked hard of arm and strong. Not a pushover like Jack Jones.

"Did you leave your guns with Jack?" the deputy demanded.

"You'll have to ask him," Roady replied calmly.

The liveryman's chin jutted out. "You're paying me to keep your horses. Not give you a place to plot more killin'. You best get outta here!"

Nick straightened and his face turned hard.

One thing Francis had learned about Nick was that he had a fuse shorter than an eyeblink long. If a man was being square with him, he'd take orders fine, but he didn't cotton to being on the squat end of sass. And especially not from a stranger. Shad had to intervene a few times in Y Knot when things had gotten rowdy in the Hitching Post.

Roady tipped his head toward the door. "Let's go get a few rooms and then find something to eat, fellas." He rubbed his stomach. "I'm plumb empty."

Smokey played along with a smile, and the rest only nodded as they filed past the two.

The liveryman's lingering aroma of horse manure made the air heavy, and Francis was only too happy to comply. The look Deputy Clark gave him said he knew exactly what had transpired, but maybe he wouldn't take the time to search the place. Possibly he'd think the men had stashed their guns somewhere out of town. One could only hope.

Chapter Nineteen

"What'll we do, Luke?" Faith asked, her gaze searching his face.

The worry in her eyes twisted his gut. She glanced over to Colton asleep on floor. Poor kid was exhausted and had been unable to keep his eyes open a moment longer. She'd brought Luke clean clothes as well as soap and water.

"You're taking Colton to the hotel and getting some supper, and then you're going to bed. I can't believe you rode all the way from Y Knot with the men. I'm sure they pushed their horses—"

"What're you talking about?" she said, cutting him off. "You did the same for me when I was in trouble. I'm not any different from you. I love you, Luke. I'll never abandon you."

His jaw muscles strained as he gritted his teeth. Being locked up had hobbled him completely. At least the last time Faith had been in danger he could do something to help.

She was right. He'd ride to the ends of the earth for her, without question. He guessed he shouldn't sell her short. Her tone, almost angry, sounded the way he felt. He hated having her see him like this. Locked up, unshaven, in need of a bath. And worse, over the past few days, his astonishment over being accused and placed behind bars had turned into apprehension.

He never would have believed this farce could have gone so far. Would a judge really put him on trial for murder? What was Jack thinking? Surely he didn't actually believe he'd killed that man. Now, after so many days, he'd begun to doubt. Here he was dragging down the McCutcheon name—*again*. Just like when he was a kid. Old hurts and memories surged in his mind.

"Joe should be back from his honeymoon any day," he said to reassure her. "Things'll change as soon as he arrives. He'll be a word of reason in this crazy town. At least, we'll have one of the townsfolk on our side." *He'd better be on my side.* "Joe'll help the boys dig around and uncover the truth. Until then, we just have to be patient." *Patient?* Doing that would be much more difficult than he would have ever believed.

She blew out a breath, disturbing a few loose hairs that had escaped her ponytail. Her dusty, worn clothes were something he wasn't used to seeing.

Reaching through the bars, she cupped his whiskered cheek. Her worried gaze captured his. "I have a very bad feeling about this. What will Joe accomplish that others haven't? I don't know. We shouldn't pin too much hope on him."

Does Deputy Clark have something to do with Jack's obstinacy?

"This reminds me of when you traveled to Kearney to clear my name," Faith whispered. "For weeks, my life spun out of control. I thought all was lost. Ward was determined to make sure we never married. You were shot, rode out wounded, and weak from the loss of blood. Let me take care of you now."

Her downy-soft voice was a balm to his ragged nerves. In her eyes were truth and love. Needing to feel closer, he cupped her hand with his, pressing her warmth more firmly to his cheek. After a moment, he gently pulled away and paced the length of the cell. "I don't know this town, Faith, and who's friend and who's not. I didn't kill that man, but somebody did.

Since I'm the one locked up, a killer is walking free. I don't like to think of you and Colton in danger. I'd rather you take him home. That's the prudent thing to do."

Her shoulders pulled back. "I won't."

"Faith, please, be reasonable. Think of Holly. She's so young. And Dawn must be wondering where her mommy is." His throat constricted, thinking of his little honey pies. The bars, the miles, and the uncertain future had him missing them more than ever.

"The men will keep us safe."

He stepped onto his cot and looked at the darkening sky. Behind the jail was an open field. All he could see was the road leading away, and some trees with what looked like a dilapidated chicken coop. The first star of the evening twinkled over the aspens. He wiped his hand across his moist brow, thinking about a cold bath. This was the hottest July he could remember. He cringed to think of how he must smell.

"What are you thinking?"

He stepped down and returned to the bars between them. "Until I'm out of here," he said low, glancing back at the window and then at the door. "I'm assigning Smokey to stay with you at all times. I don't trust Jack Jones, his deputy, or anyone else."

Her eyes opened wide. "Luke."

"Roady needs to lead the investigation, or else I'd give him the job. Smokey's the right man. He'll stay in your room, as well, Faith. I don't want you to argue with me over this. My mind is set."

She huffed out a sound of disagreement.

Deputy Clark came into the room carrying Luke's supper tray.

Jack Jones was by his side. His flushed face looked like he'd been working out in the heat, and his shirt had sweat rings under his arms.

Luke couldn't fathom what he'd been doing all day.

"Jack!" Faith blurted. "How could you? How dare you lock Luke behind bars? He's innocent. This is low, even for you."

Colton sat up and rubbed his eyes. He climbed to his feet when he saw Jack and the deputy.

Jack halted in his tracks.

Deputy Clark, his face as hard as stone, took the round key ring from his pocket and unlocked Luke's cell. He handed Luke his meal and relocked the door.

"Mrs. McCutcheon," Jack began, a waver in his voice. "I had no choice. We have an eyewitness who was with her husband when Luke killed him."

"This whole thing is absurd! Luke's no murderer!" She planted her fisted hands on her hips. "I'm ashamed of you."

Jack grasped the back of his neck, his mouth a tight, hard line. "Mrs. Van Gleek pointed out Luke without any help from anyone. She didn't even know his name. Locking him up is the law. I can't go against procedure just because I've known Luke for years. Brandon would never bend the law like that." He tapped the star pinned to his vest. "I have a duty to uphold. Unfortunately, I don't have a lot of time to listen to all your grievances. I'm sure I'll hear enough of them when I see the others from Y Knot." He actually looked around when he said that, as if he expected the ranch hands to appear out of thin air.

Luke hadn't seen the men since they'd left a couple of hours ago. Good. The less conspicuous they were, the more they might find out on the sly.

Faith crossed the small room to where Jack stood. "Who's this woman accusing my husband? How long has she lived here? What do you know about her?"

Jack's mouth hung open.

"You're new to town, Jack." Faith's back was ramrod straight. "You couldn't possibly know much."

"It's Sheriff Jones, to you," the deputy interrupted.

When Clark addressed Faith and stepped closer, Luke grasped the bars on either side of his face, gripping them with all he had. Razor-sharp heat shot through him, and he realized he was totally helpless to protect his wife.

Colton lunged forward between Clark and his mother, his arms close to his chest and hands fisted.

"Stay away from her!" Luke said low, feeling as if he *would* commit murder if he wasn't behind bars.

"I'd suggest your wife leave this business to us," Clark responded.

Luke didn't like the way the deputy's gaze openly roamed over Faith.

"She should get the hell out of town," Clark said. "Things could get ugly if frustrated townsfolk decide they're not waiting on some trial."

Faith's gasp sliced his heart.

Colton lifted his foot and brought his boot down hard on the deputy's.

The man bellowed in pain and grasped for Colton, but he jumped away.

"They wouldn't!" Faith shot back. She glanced his way.

The fear in her eyes wrenched his gut even more. Clark had said the exact thing that would keep her here, damn him. Now she'd never go home.

"Mrs. McCutcheon." Jack reached out, his palms up. "I'll not let anything unlawful happen. We're waiting on a judge. Once he gets here, you can present a case. If Luke is innocent, like he says, he'll be set free."

Luke noted Clark's stance never relaxed. He didn't want to reassure his wife; he wanted her frightened. If Luke were out of this cell, he'd wring that man's neck with his bare hands and enjoy the task. Since Luke had been locked up, Clark had kept his cards close to his vest, not really letting on what kind of a man he was. But Luke had had a feeling, and now his intuition was playing out right before his eyes.

Roady and Smokey, divested of their guns, took that moment to walk through the door. In an instant, they both assessed the situation and came to flank Faith on either side with Roady and Clark standing eye to eye. "What the hell's going on here?" Roady asked.

As much as Luke wanted to feel relieved, he couldn't. And wouldn't, until he was out of this cell.

"Nothing," Jack said, his chest puffed out. "Just discussing the best recourse for Mrs. McCutcheon. And that is she take her boy and go back to Y Knot. Leave this work to me."

Clark glanced over his shoulder at Luke and then to the food tray on the cot. "Let me know when you're through. Now that your men have arrived, one of us'll be sticking close, so don't get any stupid ideas about breaking out." He turned to Jack.

Luke couldn't see his face but thought he must be challenging Jack to dispute his direction. The deputy was obviously running the show.

"That's a good idea," Jack parroted. "I was about to say that myself. If you need anything, Mrs. McCutcheon, you let one of us know, and we'll be happy to oblige. That is, until you leave for Y Knot."

Luke held back any more comments until Jones and Clark exited the room. He signaled Roady and Smokey closer. Faith and Colton followed. "You get rooms at the hotel?"

Roady nodded. "We did. And we found a place to move our weapons to tonight, where they won't be discovered and we can get to them quickly. Clark has already searched our rooms." He glanced at Luke, Faith, and then Colton. "But I'm not saying where. The fewer who know, the better."

Good thinking, Roady. "Smokey, I want you to stay with Faith at all times. Don't leave her side. That means sleeping in her room and walking her to the necessary. Colton, you stay with your ma. I mean that, son. I don't like the feel of how things are progressing. This farce may get worse before it gets better."

Smokey nodded. "Will do, Boss. You don't have ta worry. I won't let nothin' happen."

"I know you won't." Luke's blood still rushed in his ears, his muscles tensed. "I don't like seeing you without your guns. You're defenseless. They could claim anything and shoot you down. You're putting your lives on the line for mine."

"No one's complaining, Luke," Roady said. "Every man here knows what he volunteered for. And everyone back at the ranch wanted to come along. Lucky sends his thoughts and prayers for a fast resolution. Says they better be feeding you right."

His friend's voice brought a calming effect to Luke's soul. They'd been through rough spots before. Roady had his back. He just wished he were out so he could have his. This whole state of affairs stunk to high heaven. The sooner the mix-up was sorted out, the better.

Roady leaned closer. "We're going out to the cabin tonight. See what we can find. Francis has struck up a friendship of sorts with the female friend of Mrs. Van Gleek. Her name is Ashley Adair. Van Gleek is living with her while she *mourns*."

Luke couldn't stop his brows from arching at that word. "Be careful." He searched Roady's face. The man was dearer to him than he ever let himself think. "And, Smokey, you'll stay behind with Faith and Colton."

Smokey rolled the rim of his battered old Stetson in his hands. "'Course I will, Boss."

The tan felt was a murky brown from constant wear and tear. When this was over, he'd buy Smokey a new Stetson. Hell, he'd buy all the men a new hat. He swallowed, feeling the tightness back in his throat. His men showing up was a very good thing. For his spirits, if nothing else.

Faith nodded and reached through the bars to caress his arm. "We'll get through this, Luke. None of us will let anything happen to you."

He looked her straight in the eye, needing to be sure she understood. "And you'll stay inside tonight, you and Colton, with Smokey."

She nodded, the corners of her lips pulling up just slightly. "Yes, we will. I'm not stupid, Luke. My talents aren't sneaking out in the dark. I'll know when and where to move."

He tamped back his frustration. She loved him, wanted to help. He could understand that. "I just wish you'd go home."

"You can keep wishing, but that's not a wish that'll come true. I'm sorry."

Chapter Twenty

That evening, after darkness fell, Francis relaxed in the restaurant, projecting the picture of ease. The hotel claimed the kitchen stove's flue was clogged and couldn't serve the group of ranch hands any supper, so they'd ventured across the street to the restaurant. Since the arrival of the others, Jed Kasterlee, the sullen-looking hotel clerk, had turned almost hostile. The man said few words unless asked a direct question. If Colton hadn't spoken up about the empty rooms, Kasterlee would have turned them away. He wouldn't be of any help, and he may even be a hindrance. Hadn't anyone ever heard of innocent until proven guilty?

Faith moved in with Colton. Smokey would throw his bedroll against their door. Francis had been booted out and took a bed in Roady's room, while Pedro, Shad, and Nick shared another.

Roady leaned over the table in Francis's direction. "You speak with that girl any more? That Miss Adair?" he asked softly.

Francis glanced up from cutting his steak. "Not since you saw us talking when you rode in earlier today." He put the piece into his mouth, chewed, swallowed, and then glanced at Shad and Nick, eating at their table as well. Smokey, Faith, Pedro, and

Colton were across the room. A few other diners were in the eatery, but not many. Daniel Clevenger, the same grumpy waiter who had been serving Francis since he'd arrived in town, glared at him from the kitchen area.

"She's pretty," Nick said, a suggestive grin stretching his face. "Good thing you saw her first."

Francis stabbed another chunk of meat with his fork. *So this is the way the wind is blowing.* "You're right, I did see her first. You best remember that."

Nick chuckled and then shrugged while his older brother cut him a watchful glance.

Roady's eyebrow crept up. "I don't want any trouble between the two of you here in Priest's Crossing. Save your grievances until later, if you must. I'd rather you learn to get along."

Nick was older than Francis, but they were about the same size. Since last summer, Francis had bulked up plenty. Not from any one thing he'd been doing intentionally, just Mother Nature kicking in. He smiled politely at Shad and then his brother. Today, when Ashley told him about her great-great-grandfather's name being Francis, something inside him changed. His heart had grown a mite larger, and his confidence multiplied. He hadn't stopped thinking about her since that moment.

"Maybe you can find out some more," Shad said, forking in a mouthful of mashed potatoes and gravy. He took a sip of his coffee and set the cup back in its saucer. "Being that she's close friends with the Van Gleek woman. I hear they're living in the same house."

Nick smiled. "Sweet talk her a little. Gain her trust."

Francis didn't like being asked to spy. And especially not by Nick Petty. He wouldn't playact with Ashley. He'd ask her questions, and possibly for help, but he wouldn't hoodwink. Her gentle laughter lilted through his mind. "Keep your voice down," he muttered, cutting his gaze to Clevenger, filling salt and pepper shakers at the end of the counter. The man's ear was turned in their direction and his hands were barely moving. More was going on here than met the eye.

Roady took a forkful of potatoes.

One thing about Clevenger, he served a man's meal. Nobody would go away hungry tonight when they were out sneaking around.

"Don't get defensive, Francis," Roady said, barely over a whisper. "Miss Adair looks like a nice girl. Nobody's asking you to do anything deceitful. But if we could speak with the witness, Mrs. Van Gleek, then maybe we'd get somewhere. Jones gave us nothing, and Clark even less. I need to have a few words with her, that's all. You're really the only one who can approach her. Can you do that first thing tomorrow?"

They did need to talk with the woman accusing Luke, and that was a fact. This biscuit-crumb-sized town didn't have a lawyer, and Francis was sure Roady would take that role. Asking a few questions couldn't hurt. Answering them was the least she could do, in mourning or not, when another man's life was on the line. "Sure. I can do that. First thing in the mornin'."

"And maybe we'll find out something important tonight," Shad said under his breath as he watched Clevenger take the coffeepot over to Smokey's table.

The large metal coffeepot would be heavy for anyone else, Francis thought, but for Clevenger the cast-iron appliance looked as light as a feather. He filled Smokey and Pedro's cups, but Faith turned him down. Colton could use some cheering, but Francis didn't know how to accomplish that with his pa still locked up.

Clevenger stood next to Roady. "More coffee?"

All the men nodded. Tonight would be a long one, and everyone needed to be alert and at their best. They'd quietly retrieve their horses from the livery and skedaddle out of town to the place Luke had described. They'd break in and search the place with lanterns. Was there anything Jones and Clark had missed? If the murder had been Brandon's case, Francis knew that lawman wouldn't miss a speck of dust on the ceiling if it pertained to the incident. Not so for Jones. And he didn't know Clark well enough to say.

Clevenger silently filled their cups.

"This steak is mighty tasty," Roady said with a smile, meat on the end of his fork.

Clevenger grunted. "Want to warn you that if you make trouble for the sheriff or the deputy, they'll have plenty of backup from us merchants."

"Who's making trouble?" Nick asked, an edge to his voice. He straightened in his chair. "We've been perfect gentlemen since riding in."

Roady shot Petty a glare. "We're not looking for trouble. Just answers. That's the least we deserve."

Clevenger gazed at them for a long moment, lifted a shoulder in answer, and then walked off.

Tonight would prove interesting. But they'd all best be on their guard.

Chapter Twenty-One

The time was close to one o'clock in the morning, and Ashley was unable to fall asleep. The sight of all those cowboys wearing guns as they rode into town kept making her toss and turn. She didn't want to hear of any more bloodshed.

And then there was Francis. He was never far from her thoughts. Imagine, having great-great-grandpa's name. Was that in some way significant? She didn't want to read her feelings into something that wasn't there. Still, she couldn't deny that his eyes moved her deeply. She couldn't figure out why that might be.

And what about Blanche? Ashley thought she'd known everything there was to know about her older friend, and yet, since the killing, everything felt off. Out of whack. Like a broken fingernail that had yet to slough off.

Indeed. Blanche was a mystery. She was being so offish to everyone, even to her. Ashley couldn't tell what she was thinking. Ashley had to keep reminding herself that yes, her friend's husband had been murdered in a very troubling way right before Blanche's eyes. That would change anyone. Her mood swings were understandable. But she was snappish, jumpy, and started at every little thing. This evening, when the house was dark and they were going to their rooms to go to bed, she'd met Blanche in the shadowy hallway, making her shriek in fear. Seemed she was afraid of her own shadow.

Ashley assumed she'd be crying her eyes out. And she was, at times. But mostly she just stared out the window. At other moments, she had the most troubling expression in her eyes. Something Ashley had never seen before.

Frustrated with her lack of sleep, Ashley swung her legs out of bed and stood, then pulled on her light robe, firmly tying the sash. As usual this time of year, her window was open, but no whisper of breeze stirred. She reached for the damp cloth by her bedside and ran the cool rag over her face.

What she needed was a glass of water. Anything cool. The fried chicken her mother prepared for supper had been delicious but now weighed heavy in her stomach. Perhaps that was adding to her sleeplessness. Retrieving the empty glass on her nightstand, she quietly opened the bedroom door, detecting a slight aroma of smoke.

Frightened, she padded quickly down the narrow hallway to the front room, but pulled up short. Blanche stood in the dark, gazing out the front window. A tendril of smoke trailed up to a cloud hovering at the ceiling. She must not have heard her approach for her friend didn't turn around. What she should do? Would she be intruding? Perhaps Blanche wanted time alone.

"Please, join me."

The voice was unusually deep, sending a shiver of uncertainty up Ashley's spine.

Blanche turned.

The moonlight through the windowpane gave just enough light that Ashley could make out a strange smile twisted on Blanche's lips. She said the first thing that came to her mind. "I don't want to intrude."

"You're curious about me, I'm sure." A throaty laugh followed. "And you've caught me smoking. For shame, for shame."

Ashley had smelled something on Blanche before but hadn't put two and two together.

"I hope you're not too shocked. The school board would have fired me immediately if they'd known. I'm lucky they never discovered my one weakness. And now—because of *me*—*you're* the teacher, lucky girl. A very good job too, I'd say. I'm sure you'll keep my guilty secret for me—since we are best friends. With Benson dead, I'll have to find work somewhere."

"I won't say a word," Ashley responded, coming farther into the room. She stopped by Blanche's side and looked out the window as well. The smell of the smoke heated her lungs and burned her throat. She resisted the urge to cough.

"Actually, I couldn't sleep," Blanche said, rubbing her side. "No matter how I turn, my ribs ache so, I thought I'd go mad. They'll be healed soon though, and I'll never again suffer like I did at the hands of that horrible man. McCutcheon will pay for what he did."

Ashley swallowed nervously, keeping her gaze trained on the land that sloped down to the road and the trees on the far side. Blanche had changed. Goose bumps prickled Ashley's arms. Movement across the road in the brush caught her attention.

"What?" Blanche asked, looking over.

"I don't know." Her grip around the glass tightened. "I thought I saw something, but in the darkness, I'm not sure. Maybe a coyote is lurking about."

As they stared, a rider passed by several feet off the far side of the road, winding through the brush and keeping to the trees. After he was gone, another rider came on his heels.

"Not hard to guess who's out there. Or where they're going," Blanche snapped. "Those cowboys are out to prove me a liar. I have half a mind to walk into town and tell the sheriff."

Ashley thought of Francis. The guns she'd seen on the ranch hands when they'd first ridden by her house on their way to town. The anger in Deputy Clark's eyes resembling a smoldering keg of dynamite ready to go off. "No, don't do that. In this heat, the mountain rattlers may be out searching for someplace cool. Tomorrow will be soon enough to report what we've seen."

Blanche stared at her for a long time.

They were close enough that Ashley could see her friend was none too pleased with her remark. Did she think she was siding with the McCutcheons?

Blanche leaned in, her eyes dark and unreadable behind the smoke. "I should just let them break into my home?"

A trickle of sweat slipped down between Ashley's shoulder blades. "We don't know for sure they're headed to your cabin. That's our assumption. And if they are, I don't think they'll hurt anything. They'll just hunt around for clues. Since you have nothing to hide, they won't find anything." She'd been about to say *if* you have nothing to hide but bit her tongue at the last moment. For whatever reason, she wasn't as sure about her friend as she'd once been. She kept thinking about Francis's pleading tone to keep an open mind. To be careful. She couldn't fathom him a liar or cheat.

"And you know this how?"

The cigarette had burned low, but Blanche didn't seem to notice the amber hot end so close to her fingertips. "It's just how I feel. But do what you want. I can't stop you. If you really want to walk to town now, I'll dress and go with you." She studied her friend's face. "I'm here for you, Blanche, come what may." With that, she turned back to the window and focused her attention on the low hanging moon.

One last rider slipped by her house in complete silence.

If she and Blanche hadn't already been awake, no one would have been the wiser. The horses were too far away for her to identify any of the riders, and she wondered if one of them was Francis. He was so sure Luke McCutcheon hadn't murdered Benson. Because of that, he was a very compelling witness. She chanced a glance to her side to find Blanche staring at her again.

She swallowed. "I guess I'll go back to bed." Ashley wondered if she'd stay upright on her shockingly weak knees. She pressed the glass against her middle to keep it from trembling.

"Don't you want a glass of water? That's what you got up for."

"Oh, yes, of course. The cowboys made me forget. I'll get that now." She was chattering like a frightened schoolchild. Before Blanche could say anything else, Ashley turned and hurried to the kitchen, a drink of water the very last thing on her mind.

Chapter Twenty-Two

"**H**old the light closer," Roady whispered, hunkered down by the back door of Mrs. Van Gleek's cabin.

Francis moved the lantern as close to the side of Roady's face as he could get without burning the foreman. The other men waited on their horses twenty feet away, hidden among the trees. No use having them all out in the open in case somebody else showed up with the same idea they had.

Roady delicately probed the lock with a long, bent nail, his ear pressed to the door. "There she is," he said with a gentle twist of his wrist. "Easy now, sweetheart. Come to daddy." He glanced up at Francis and smiled. "We should be in shortly."

Francis heard the click. He let go of the breath he was holding and waved to the others. Soon everyone except Pedro, who stood watch a few hundred feet down the road, concealed between the rocks, silently moved through the door. The *amigo*, who had the eyesight of an owl and the hearing of a wolf, wouldn't let anyone take them by surprise.

Inside, the furniture was sparse and rustic. The dry sink at the end of a counter on the far wall was still stacked with dirty dishes, and the floor was none too clean. A skittering sound behind a handful of logs on the stone hearth told Francis the home wasn't rodent-proof—Lucky would have something to say about that if he were here.

Shad went to each window and pulled closed the coarse brown curtains as Nick, with a lantern of his own, scanned the room. Roady took the lamp from Francis as soon as they came inside and began a meticulous search of the place with Francis close behind. What one man missed, another might see.

"What exactly are we looking for?" Nick shifted his weight from one leg to the other.

Francis couldn't believe he was already asking questions. His attention span was that of a gnat. Roady had given detailed instructions before they'd retrieved their weapons and ridden out. Now here was Shad's younger brother already needing direction.

"Anything that looks out of place," Roady said quietly. "Anything that looks wrong. Anything that brings a question to your mind."

Nick lifted his hat and scratched his head. "Like why didn't this woman do her job? This place is a mess."

"Hush," Shad said irritably. "Just get to lookin'. You'll know it when you see it."

Nick shrugged and then smiled. "I suppose."

Heck, the place is so small we've already looked everywhere in the first three minutes, Francis thought. *What more can we find?* Frustrated, he smacked one fist into his palm. Something had to be here. A clue that would clear Luke. He wasn't leaving until they found some evidence. Francis lifted a small rug in the middle of the room. A brownish stain resembling a three-quarter moon, of all things, marred the wooden floor. "Here!" he called excitedly. "Here's where Benson fell."

The men crowded around.

Francis tried to visualize how Van Gleek would have lain. Which way had his feet been pointing? Had he just entered, or come out of the bedroom? He took a long step to the door. "Say he came inside like this." He walked to the middle of the room. On his left was the fireplace where the rock chimney climbed the wall by the front door. He reached out a hand. "If I lean far enough, I can touch the fireplace tools." He did.

Roady's brows creeped up his forehead. "That's good, Francis. Pick up the poker."

It wasn't as heavy as he'd expected. He stared at the mark on the floor. "That's a lot of blood in one place," Francis said.

Shad hunkered down, staring at the stain. "Didn't she claim Luke and her husband had a fistfight?"

"She did," Roady answered. "Over money, of all things." He scoffed. "Ending with a blow to the side of his head that killed him. If that were the case, more bloodstains would be splattered around. I've never had a fight where I didn't break the skin of my knuckles or get a bloody nose or lip." He glanced around. "Anyone see any other spots? Look close. They could be tiny."

After a few moments, everyone shook their heads.

"Not a thing," Francis said. *The crimson spot will tell its own story.* "Heads bleed a lot. I remember getting that tiny cut on my hairline over my forehead and thought I'd bleed out." He fingered the small scar and then chuckled.

Like granite sculptures, no one moved.

"We don't know if this stain is from the back of his head or his face." Nick pushed up to his feet and the others followed.

A hoot of an owl sounded, followed by two more short hoots.

"Pedro. He's spotted something. We better go."

"Look!" Across the room, Francis thought he saw something almost covered by a chair. Shad quietly moved the furniture to the side, revealing the print of a boot.

Roady stared a long time.

Francis felt sweat break out in his palms. This was something important. A chance find that might be the difference between life and death.

"Someone stepped in the blood," Roady said, even though that fact was obvious. He carefully considered the marking.

"Not someone. By the size, the print belongs to a man. We've just cut the field by fifty percent," Francis corrected. "No woman I've ever seen has boots that large." He gave a long whistle. "If I'm wrong, and she does, you can tar and feather me." He pointed closely at the heel. "And look at this. One side's uneven, worn down differently."

Roady nodded, still gazing at the print and then glanced up at Francis. "Good work."

As Francis stood, he spotted a glimmer of silver wedged between the chair's cushion and the base of the armrest. He palmed a money clip fashioned in the shape of a gun and holding two one dollar bills. "Might be Benson's. Might be the killer's. Who knows?"

"Bring it," Roady barked. "Something that unique has a history." Before making for the door, Roady placed his boot over the print, checking the size. His boot covered the print completely. "Everyone, hold your foot over the mark."

The men followed orders. Shad's boot overshadowed the stain. Same with Nick.

Francis's fit the mark to a T. "Just like Cinderella." He chuckled as a small amount of relief passed through him. He replaced the chair over the boot print hiding the evidence and Roady threw the rug back over the brownish bloodstain.

Whoever was here must have been in such a panic to leave they didn't notice the print. Or had the bloodstain been covered on purpose?

Nick blew out their lanterns, and then Shad went around the room and opened the curtains. The place looked exactly like when they arrived; except for the fact the bloody boot print was now completely hidden. If no one had noticed before, they'd definitely not find the mark now unless they moved the furniture.

In total silence, the men exited the cabin, and Roady clicked the door closed but was unable to lock it without a key. "Can't be helped," he said as they hustled to their horses. "Doesn't matter anyway. We got what we came for. They'll know we've been inside."

Pedro rode into sight. "Sheriff Jones coming over the ridge. Still a few minutes away."

"Good work, Pedro," Roady said, swinging his leg over Fiddlin' Dee. "And good work to the rest of you. I have a feeling we're on to something." Roady reined around.

The men followed. Francis brought up the rear. Knowing Roady as he did, he was sure the foreman would take them in the opposite direction for some time, circle around, and then reenter Priest's Crossing on the other side of town after finding a new spot to cache their guns. They'd have their horses back in the corral before sunup, and be warm in their beds if anyone came looking.

Francis thought about the coming meeting with Ashley and wondered if he'd get an interview with Mrs. Van Gleek. As much as he hoped he would, only time would tell.

Chapter Twenty-Three

The dark night was a glove wrapped around Luke's throat, keeping him from sleep. The silent burst of cool air that randomly issued through the small window was his lifeline in the stuffy cell. Everything was silent in the sleepy town. The inky darkness was wholly quiet except for the soft hoot of an owl.

Just to see the mountains. Smell the fresh air. If I get out of here, I'll never take my freedom for granted…

Luke stretched out on the cot, crossed his boots, and then pillowed his head on his woven fingers as he gazed up at the small square patch of black high on the wall. The bars glimmered in the moonlight. He was glad Faith had finally gone to the hotel so he could drop his façade of calm. In truth, his insides had been clenched in a death grip since the first day he'd opened his eyes to the bars and locked door.

He wasn't a good prisoner. He'd been playing nice for Faith and the others, but his blood ran hot—simmering like the mineral springs at Yellowstone, ready to erupt. Might be his Indian heritage. Might be his McCutcheon upbringing. Whatever the reason, with each passing day, staying calm and collected behind these bars became more of a challenge. The McCutcheon name wouldn't get him out of this one. A murderer was out there, somewhere, willing and ready to make sure Luke took the fall for his deeds. He wouldn't be happy until the hangman slipped the noose around Luke's neck and pulled the lever. Until then, he'd be sure to incite others against Luke's Cheyenne blood. It behooved him to make sure nobody listened to, or believed, the words of a half-breed.

In the outer room, Luke heard the squeak of the door. He held his breath to see if he could make out any conversation. Had Faith come back in the middle of the night? Luke didn't trust Clark at all.

"Your prisoner awake?"

A man. The voice familiar. Relief that the visitor wasn't Faith washed through him.

Luke closed his eyes when steps hesitated at the open door between the rooms. He wasn't in the mood to talk to anyone. Or be stared at by Jack or anyone else. After a moment, whoever was there moved away.

"Don't know. Haven't looked in since his wife left. I suppose so."

Deputy Clark taking his position to heart. Now Luke knew how a caged cougar felt. He reached up and slapped something off his neck.

"You're out late, Neil," Clark went on. "What've you got under that cloth-covered plate? Something to share? You've tickled my curiosity."

Yeah, mine, as well. The deputy's insolent tone was off-putting.

"Oatmeal apple cobbler made by Tilly. For McCutcheon and his son."

The sounds of a chair sliding reached the cell.

"Let me see."

Luke turned his head to look at the doorway and then silently swung his legs to the floor, sitting up. He'd guess the time to be one o'clock in the morning. What was Neil Huntsman doing delivering a care package at this time of night? Did he have a hidden motive? Kill off the suspect before he had a chance to prove his innocence and send the law looking for someone else? Not a half-bad idea.

"That looks good. And she made plenty. Would you mind if I had some? McCutcheon will never know."

"It's for McCutcheon only," Neil snapped. "Not for you or Jack. She expressly told me that. Said Luke's been locked up for a good long time and needed some home cooking. Hoss, you don't want to anger Tilly. You know how she gets if crossed. You best not go looking for a fight."

"Yeah, I do know. Only all too well." He gave a halfhearted chuckle. "But who's gonna tell her? You?"

Huntsman didn't answer right away, as if he were weighing his options carefully.

"If she asks, and she will, I won't lie. I don't lie to my wife. I won't start now."

Good for you, Neil.

"Killjoy," Deputy Clark drawled. "I know who wears the pants in your family. That said, you're not waking McCutcheon tonight. He's asleep and peaceful. Leave the dessert, and I'll make your delivery first thing in the morning."

A laugh.

"Hey! Where you going with that?" Clark barked.

"I'm not stupid. I don't trust you. Tilly can bring it back tomorrow."

"Why, you…"

Luke heard the door close, and then the place was quiet. Huntsman apparently left with his poisoned baked good. That had been interesting. He wondered if Neil Huntsman could actually be a killer. Or if he'd been alone out at the cabin with the Van Gleek woman. That would be a bitter pill for any woman to swallow. The man had seemed very much in love with his wife and soon-to-be child.

He lay back and stretched out. No sleep would come tonight. Too much speculation and worry about the activity at the Van Gleek cabin. His men were in peril every minute they stuck around Priest's Crossing. Roady, a new father. Luke had been surprised to see him arrive from the ranch. And Francis too. The young fella had his whole life ahead of him, as well as Shad, newly engaged to Poppy Ford, and the short-fused Nick Petty. When Pedro's faithful face flashed in Luke's mind's eye, he actually sucked in a breath. He scrubbed a hand over his face, fatigue making his arm heavy. He didn't like any of his men risking their lives to clear his name. Jack Jones was liable to shoot first and ask questions later.

The thought of trouble propelled him back to his feet to pace the cell. Thank God he had Smokey to make sure Faith and Colton stayed put in their room. He didn't trust either of them to follow his orders. He wouldn't if either of them was in danger as he was now.

Chapter Twenty-Four

Colton gazed out the hotel window at the darkness below. A wisp of air felt good on his skin, cooling him and easing his troubled mind. The second-story room he shared with his mother and Smokey had an excellent view of the street but also collected the heat from below. The building out the window was straight down. No chance to climb out.

Look at all the trouble he'd caused. He wasn't even Luke's real son. Just a stepson. A hanger-on, coming into his life because Luke had married his stepmother. Faith had recounted to him many times how his real ma died when he was just a baby and had asked Faith to look after him.

A rattling snore reverberated from Smokey, stretched out on his bedding in front of the door, not minding the hard flooring in the least. Anyone coming in would have to push him out of the way or go over. He had a derringer hidden under the rolled-up towel he used as a pillow. Even if the sheriff thought so, they weren't completely unarmed.

And his ma? Was she asleep? The fact he didn't hear any breathing made him think she was awake too, just lying there thinking about Pa. He'd been careful sneaking out from under the sheet, antsy, too wound up to sleep. He set his elbow on the windowsill and pillowed his chin in his palm.

He should be looking for clues. He was old enough. And he was the one who had started all this trouble in the first place. If only he hadn't been so anxious to use his new rifle. If only he could go back and do that day over. He sighed. Wishing was no use. He'd have to think of something else. Something that would make a difference.

Movement on the street below caught his eye, perking up his senses. Streetlamps were placed about, making seeing possible.

Tilly's husband walked up the other side of the street toward the sheriff's office, carrying something large in his hands.

As far as Colton could see, he was the only person out. No, that wasn't true. Looking straight down the side of the hotel, he noticed the clerk, Mr. Kasterlee, leaning against a porch post. The golden end of his cigarette brightened when he drew in the smoke.

Mr. Huntsman looked across his way, but the two didn't exchange any words. Tilly's husband stepped into the jail but reappeared a few minutes later, still holding whatever he'd carried inside, and returned up the street toward the mercantile, the way he'd come.

That was when Colton noticed Daniel Clevenger with his broom on the porch of the restaurant next door. Colton had to stick his head out the window a ways to see him, but if he was on watch, he needed to see everything that was taking place. Didn't anyone in this town sleep?

"Colton, what're ya doing up, boy?" Smokey whispered in a groggy voice. "You should be asleep."

"It's too hot to sleep."

"I hear you there."

The cowhand was on his way over to the window when a group of horsemen came into view on the west end of the street by the livery. They walked in slowly. Silently. "Look! They're back." Colton tried to keep the excitement from his voice so he wouldn't wake his mother. She was heartbroken. He'd never seen her so sad before. "That has to be them."

Smokey stuck his head out the window. "Indeed. Let's hope their maraudin' paid off. I don't like seeing your pa in that jail cell, no sir, not at all. The quicker he's out, the sooner I'll be able to sleep."

Colton didn't even try to hide his smile. Smokey had been sleeping just fine. "Sure they found somethin'. They're smart," Colton replied. "I've a good feeling about tonight. They'll be back soon to fill us in."

"I doubt that. They're avoiding suspicious eyes. Besides, it's late. They'll want ta get some sleep."

Colton knew if he were out looking for clues, sleeping would be the last thing on his mind.

"Now, get ta bed before we wake your ma. She has enough on her mind without being droopy-eyed tomorrow. If she hears us talking, she's bound to want to know what's going on."

At the sound of boots coming quietly up the stairs, Colton rushed to the door. Without even asking who was out there, and before Smokey could stop him, he threw it open and stepped out—right in front of Jed Kasterlee, the hotel clerk.

"Some reason you're awake at two o'clock in the morning, son?" the man asked tersely. "I'd think, with all the trouble your family has already, they'd keep you on a shorter leash."

Smokey stepped past Colton, meeting the man in the hall.

Kasterlee lifted his lantern, making the lamplight flicker.

"Ain't none of yer business, Kasterlee," he said. "What're you doin' wandering the halls this time of night, yourself? The question works both ways."

Smokey's firm palm on his shoulder felt good. Colton was thankful for his friend.

"What's going on?" Faith called from inside the room. "Colton, are you out there?"

"Ain't nothing, Faith," Smokey replied then directed a glare at the clerk. "Get inside, Colton," he bit out.

Colton knew better than disobey.

"You best watch out for the boy," Kasterlee said. "Keep the doors locked. Once I turn in, I don't hear nothin', so to speak. I won't be responsible if any harm should come to him or anyone else."

Smokey didn't seem intimidated in the least.

"Is that some sort of lame threat?" Smokey asked. "Because I've seen women who looked more dangerous than you, my friend. You're the one who best watch yourself." He pulled back his work-hardened shoulders.

Kasterlee eyed him. "Is *that* a threat?"

Smokey laughed then glanced back at Colton, who now watched from inside the room through the open door. "Naw. It's a promise. One I look forward to keeping. I don't take kindly to full-grown men scaring a boy."

Colton bristled. *Boy.* That word again. Boy or kid. Well, kids could get things done just as well as some grown fella. He could and he would, maybe even better. He'd show them all.

Chapter Twenty-Five

Getting out of bed the next morning was torture. With the little sleep she'd managed, Ashley's eyes felt bloodshot and her head woozy. Still, noises and aromas from the kitchen taunted her. Mother was up, working, putting kettles on to boil. Without further ado, Ashley pulled herself from her soft mattress, briskly washed her face, brushed her teeth, and absentmindedly ran a brush through her thick hair, not bothering to do more than plait the mass down her back. Dressed in her overalls and apron, Ashley laced her battered black boots and tromped into the kitchen.

"Good morning, lazybones," her mother greeted with a smile. "Ready for your breakfast?"

She was and then some. She nodded.

"Good. Everything is ready and warming in the oven. We have a good day's work ahead of us, and I didn't want to waste any time with extra cooking. I made yours and Blanche's when I made mine."

"Why didn't you wake me?" Shame filled her at her mother's weary countenance. "I could've made breakfast."

"I didn't have the heart. I peeked in and you were sound asleep. A summer grippe is going around, and I don't want you to get sick. The next week of harvesting is crucial. Last year when we lost half our apples to frost was hard enough. I don't want to suffer through another winter with so little."

"I'm teaching now, Mama. Things will never get that bad again."

Her mother turned to face her, her eyes serious. "I hope you're right, God willing." Her mother went to the oven and, with a thick folded cloth, withdrew a plate of scrambled eggs, bacon, and toast.

The two strips of bacon stacked over the eggs smelled delicious. Blanche's staying with them was a bit of a hardship, but they didn't mind. As long as they didn't run out of supplies, they were both happy to share.

Ashley ate everything on her plate, knowing hours would pass before she'd get another chance. The day would be exhausting. The early summer apples that had ripened over the week needed to be harvested quickly. Leaving them on the branches for long risked losing them to the birds and squirrels. "There, I'm finished." She stood, went to the sink, and was just putting down her plate when a knock sounded on the front door. She looked at her mother. "I'm not expecting anyone. Are you?"

Her mother's posture tensed. "No, I'm not."

"It's eight in the morning. Who would come calling this early? Maybe Sheriff Jones or his deputy have more questions for Blanche." She hurried into the living room, trying to get there before whoever was there knocked again. She pulled open the door.

Francis. His hat dangled in his fingertips. His hair had been combed back, and he held a small bouquet of the tiny yellow buttercups that grew wild along the road. The width of his shoulders made his slim hips and strong legs all the more noticeable. His face brightened when he saw her.

She gaped down at her overalls, scandalized to be caught wearing men's clothes. What would he think?

"Morning," he said politely. "I hope I'm not stoppin' by too early. Been up for hours and sort of just forgot about the time." As he spoke, a red line crept up his face. He held out the flowers.

She gently took them from his hand. "Thank you for these." She briefly held them to her nose.

"They were everywhere. Just thought you might like some."

"Who's there, Ashley?" Her mother came into the room, drying her hands.

Ashley stepped back, a silent invitation for him to come inside. "Mother, this is Francis. He's one of the men from the ranch in Y Knot. Francis, this is my mother, Angelia Adair."

Her mother's gaze went from Francis's face to the flowers in her hand and then back again. "I see. What does he want?"

Warmth crept up into her face when she realized he hadn't even said. Surely his motive must have something to do with Blanche. He wouldn't be here for any other reason. She looked up into his face, seeking answers as the little buttercups bobbed in her hand.

"I've come to see if Mrs. Van Gleek feels strong enough to speak with Mr. Guthrie sometime today. Since the town has no lawyer for Luke to hire, our foreman is taking on that job. He's real smart and would like to hear from her how the murder happened."

"Hasn't Sheriff Jones spoken with you?" Mrs. Adair asked. "Told you the details?"

Francis nodded, followed by a long, drawn-out sigh.

Ashley had the urge to reach up and brush away the stray lock that had fallen forward onto his forehead and flirted with his left eyelashes.

"He has. Just the barest details. Jack can be stubborn. And Clark is no help." He shifted his weight from one foot to the other while his fingers worked the edge of his hat brim. "When a man is accused of murder, Miss Adair, Mrs. Adair, a good man, a man who is clearly innocent, we"—he placed his palm on his chest, making his brown plaid shirt flatten against his body—"his friends, his family, take the accusation seriously. Luke's been locked up now for eight days. The longer this draws out, the more people's minds close down. He's a convenient solution for Jones. We aim to make things more difficult for whoever actually committed the crime."

His tone was sincere and low, and she was glad. After last night, the sight of Blanche standing in the dark still had her agitated. Her friend would be up soon enough. Why begin the day on a stressful note?

Her mother came closer, her mouth pinched in opposition. "Isn't your boss an Indian?"

"Half Cheyenne, ma'am," Francis replied, squaring his shoulders.

"A wild, no-good half-breed." Mrs. Adair's eyes had narrowed. "Just like the man who scalped my husband. Ashley's father. But only after he'd had a drink from our well at my invitation. When killing's in their blood like that and the mood strikes them, they can't stop themselves. Nature takes over."

Francis blinked several time. "That's foolishness."

"The scalping didn't happen here," Ashley said quickly, needing to explain. Mother held on to that ten-year-old memory and blamed all Indians for her father's death. Ashley wished that wasn't the case, at least for a day or two. Mother was eaten up with hate. Ashley had been so young, the memory had softened over the years. "At the time, we lived much farther north, in Canada. Mother and I moved here to escape the memories."

Francis looked at her mother from under a lined forehead. "Luke's blood don't have a thing to do with this, ma'am. Not one thing. You can't lump all men together because of the color of their skin."

Her mother's chin tipped up. "I can. And I do."

Mother would be so much happier if she'd let go of the past. It's sad, really.

Francis looked down and softly cleared his throat. "I guess we best get back to the reason I'm here. That talk with Mrs. Van Gleek. Is she around?"

Ashley nodded. "She has yet to awaken."

He rubbed his chin and glanced out the still-open door at his horse tied to the front tree. "It's getting on in the morning, and I'm sure she'll be up soon. Do you mind if I wait until she is? The men and Roady are waiting on her answer. I hate to go back and disappoint them."

Ashley felt her mother bristle without having to see her expression.

Mrs. Adair returned to the kitchen without another word.

Francis's dark, sensitive eyes were on her face again, making her stomach roll in a pleasant way.

"Yes, you may wait. But I have to warn you." She gestured to her overalls. "I was just on my way out back to our orchard."

His face brightened. "Are you harvesting?"

"Yes. If you're willing, I may put you to work." She felt her lips twitch and then pull up at the corners. "I can't imagine how fast the chore will go with a man's help."

A full-blown smile grew across his face, revealing a row of straight, white teeth. "It would be my pleasure to help you, Miss Adair. I'm at your service."

She clapped her hands together. "Wonderful. I told Christine last week I'd soon have apples, as well as some baked things, for her to sell—and then Benson was murdered, and everything went awry. He was our freighter who took our harvest all over the territory. I'm not quite sure yet what we'll do now. But one bridge crossed at a time." She led the way into the kitchen, where her mother was carefully dropping apples into a stewing pot of hot water to make into applesauce and apple butter. "Mother, Francis has agreed to help for a few hours. Isn't that nice?"

Her mother nodded but didn't manage her normal smile. "If you say so. The baskets are out back and waiting to be filled."

Ashley preceded him through the back kitchen door, smiling over her shoulder at her tall, handsome visitor. How blessed they were he'd shown up today. A job that normally took days would be cut in half. *But that's not the only reason you feel like you're walking on air,* she scolded herself. *You like Francis. You may as well admit the fact. He makes a bevy of butterflies flutter in your stomach each time he glances your way.*

Chapter Twenty-Six

From the top of a tall, wobbly orchard ladder, Francis stretched his arm to grasp the greenish apple with crimson stripes. He was used to seeing plain red, so when they'd first arrived at the small two-acre grove and the first trees they'd picked, he'd thought they were harvesting too soon. The sweet, tangy scent of the fruit tickled his nose, and the warm morning sun already had him sweating. Insects hummed and chirps of birds filled the air. On the walk out, he'd kept an eye out for tracks in the dirt in case the killer who'd left a print in the cabin was prowling around. If the man had been carrying on with Blanche before, reasoning said he'd seek her out again.

He looked over to the tree next to him as he placed the apple into the satchel he wore around his shoulder. "What did you call these again? Some fancy-pants name, to be sure." Soon he'd look like a lopsided camel.

Her laugher gave him a dizzy, light-headed feeling that he'd better cast away if he didn't want to end up on his head and embarrass himself.

"Duchess of Oldenburg. They're one of the oldest breeds in the Montana Territory. They came from Russia and ripen earlier than most. Mother and I were blessed to find this quaint house that came along with the original orchard, all planted and bearing fruit each year. We even have twenty good-sized saplings started. A small stream runs all year, just over that rise." She pointed. "Can you see?"

Francis searched through the branches and nodded. "From my bird's-eye view, quite well."

"The harvest helps us get by. And now that I have the teacher's job in town, we're humming right along."

Francis liked the picture she made in her overalls with a red bandanna wrapped around her pretty chestnut hair and tied at her nape. The majority of her thick waves were woven into a braid that tumbled down her back in an enticing picture. Her face was shiny from the exertion and warmth. When he'd first met her, she seemed so prim and proper he'd felt beneath her. But now her suntanned arms, lean and strong, were perfect in his mind. He liked that she was tough and hardworking and still pretty as a picture. Her smile was as playful as a spring breeze.

She laughed again. "What're you thinking, Francis? I can't figure out that look on your face. I'm just a farmer's daughter, and nothing more." With raised brows, she glanced at the ladder beneath his feet. "You better be careful or you'll fall and hurt yourself."

She was more than all the girls he'd ever known wrapped up in one. She was a princess in disguise. He'd once overheard Faith telling Dawn and Holly a bedtime story about a little girl raised by the gypsies who turned out to be a long-lost princess. She was fair to behold and had a musical voice. All the swains fell at her feet each time she was near.

That's how Ashley looked today, just like a long-lost princess in her blue jean overalls and short-sleeved shirt. He couldn't look at her enough.

Ashley yelped and batted at something in her face.

"What?"

"A bee. Won't leave me alone."

Francis was mesmerized by her beauty. Even though she'd never said so, she must have a suitor. They were little more than acquaintances, he reminded himself. He shouldn't let his imagination run wild. She needed his help, and he was lending a hand while he waited to speak with Mrs. Van Gleek. Who, by now, must be up and dressed.

He looked once more at the stream. "Do you carry water buckets from over the hill?"

She flexed her arm while holding a large piece of fruit. "That's how I've gotten so strong. We moved here nine years ago, when I was nine. These apple trees are like my family. The brothers and sisters I never had. I love each and every tree, as does my mother. I get a lot of enjoyment seeing to their needs."

Francis took a moment to wipe his arm across his sweaty brow. "Hasn't anyone ever dug you an outlet to bring some water closer?"

Her eyes brightened.

"I can do that. Just like we do at the ranch. Won't take long, especially if I corral Nick and Pedro to help."

"I could never ask that of you. But thank you, anyway."

Nonsense. When he got back to town, he'd ask Roady. Maybe the request would be out of line, but he'd ask anyway. If they said no, he'd find time to dig the ditch himself.

He pulled away his gaze and glanced down at his basket of apples on the ground by the tree trunk. The container would need to be emptied soon. He'd finish this branch and then carry both baskets to the back porch where he'd dump them into several large barrels.

The very top of the tree had numerous plump pieces of fruit. If he picked those now, this tree would be done. He went up a step, then one more to the second to the top of the ladder.

It didn't feel steady. Sweat broke out on his back, and he gripped a sturdy nearby branch for balance.

"You needn't go that high, Francis! We usually leave those at the top. I don't want you to get hurt."

He dared to glance her way causing a shiver of apprehension to run down his spine. He tightened his grip on the tree branch. "What? This isn't high. You should see me on the bunkhouse ro—"

Suddenly the ladder quaked violently, forcing him to grasp for the top step, as he swayed back and forth. *That hard ground is going to hurt!*

Ashley gasped, and even though she was ten feet away, her arm shot toward him as if she could steady his position.

Laughter rang out.

A moment passed before Francis's footing was steady enough to look down.

Still holding the ladder, Nick grinned up innocently. His eyes twinkled with mischief causing a hot anger to burn in Francis's chest.

Nick planted his fists on his hips, looking much like a swashbuckling pirate. "Francis, we've been waiting on you. Roady sent me to make sure you didn't get lost somewhere along the way." He turned and eyed Ashley longer than he should.

Resentment shot through Francis. "Petty! I'm gonna—"

Ashley beat him to the ground, a scowl planted on her pretty lips. She marched to Nick's side. "What on earth were you doing!" She pointed an accusing finger at Nick's chest.

On the ground, Francis stepped in front of Ashley, happy the time had finally arrived to give Nick his due. A few fists to his own face would be worth punching out his aggravation on Nick.

Ashley grasped his arm just as he heaved a punch, throwing off his aim and landing her on her backside. Shocked, he reached down, grasped her hand, and pulled her to her feet.

"Don't fight him, Francis. Please. It's not worth it." She scowled at Nick. "And you can just wipe that smile right off your face. I've never seen anything so irresponsible! So stupid! Ladders are not playthings. They're dangerous! Francis could have broken his neck or his back."

Nick laughed. "Or his skull? Naw, the bones are too thick."

"You should be ashamed of yourself!"

By the contrite grin on Nick's face, he was enjoying the dressing down more than he should.

"I'm sorry, Miss Adair," Nick finally said. "Francis and I have this ongoing competition, you know, between friends. By the way, my name is Nick Petty, and I ride for the Heart of the Mountains, just like Francis here."

Yeah, but you're a newcomer. Who knows how long you'll last?

"Let's be friends." Nick stuck out his hand, but she just stared. When she didn't take it, he shrugged and turned his attention back to Francis. "So did you make that appointment yet?"

"Which one of you is the young man who came asking to see me?"

Francis turned, as did Ashley and Nick. A woman with just the shadow of a black eye stood in the bright sunlight not twenty feet away. She was of average height and looked about thirty years old. A few strands of gray glittered in her black hair.

Ashley's mother stood a few steps behind.

Francis walked forward and put out one hand. "That'd be me, ma'am. I'm…" He glanced at Nick. "We're from the McCutcheon ranch, and our foreman is asking for the privilege to speak with you for a few minutes." The way she held herself was surprising. He'd expected someone timid, especially after what had happened to her and her husband. Not Mrs. Van Gleek. Her stance was challenging, if not confrontational. "Today, if you could."

Mrs. Van Gleek's gaze strayed over to Ashley and then returned to him.

"Won't take long." *If you have nothing to hide, you'll accept.*

"Today will be fine. Tell him to come here at two. I don't have anything more to say that I didn't already tell the sheriff."

Ashley's mother nodded.

The words she'd said about Luke kept pricking his mind. Luke never seemed to outlive the stigma of being a half-breed. Well, Francis didn't care, and neither did the other fellas. They were loyal to him and the brand. Nothing could change that— ever. "Thank you, ma'am." He glanced back at Ashley. "I'll take these apples to your porch, and then I best get back to town. The morning is long past."

She nodded, her eyes sparkling. "Thank you for your help, Francis. You've already taken a big bite out of the chore. I appreciate your kindness."

"I'll be back again to help finish the job, but that might not be today." *And I'll come without Nick Petty to poke fun at me every chance he gets.*

Chapter Twenty-Seven

Harrison Wesley sat on the wagon seat next to the freighter he'd hired to transport their possessions from the train stop in Waterloo to their destination in Y Knot. A second wagon followed, loaded with the belongings the judge had collected throughout his life. Approaching the east end of town, they would enter Y Knot and pass the Biscuit Barrel, then travel down Main Street to the sheriff's office where he'd meet up with Justin.

Seated on the bench behind his, Carlie could hardly contain her excitement. She'd been a chatterbox the entire journey, first on the train and then again during the wagon ride. Her questions might be many, but they were intelligent, and he wondered where she'd learned so much. She was a joy, and he'd never tire of answering her animated queries or hearing her soft voice.

"Are we almost there, Harrison?" Pauline whined. "My bottom has taken a beating. The journey in this dilapidated buckboard has ruined my health. At least the seats in the train had padding, albeit cracker thin. I don't think I have the strength to climb down."

When she moaned loudly, the freighter next to him scowled and snapped the lines.

He was probably more than ready to be rid of the faultfinder. His sister-in-law was the exact opposite of Carlie. Where his daughter was cheerful and excited for the move, Pauline was dour and walked around with a scowl. She'd cried the whole week before they'd left Denver. A scowl was frozen onto her lips for the majority of the trip, which in return had kept his gut in a knot.

Did any possibility exist that here in Y Knot she might meet a nice fella and fall in love, move out, and leave him and Carlie in peace? She wasn't that old. The thought had merit, but the gent would be a country fellow, a cowboy, or a miner. With those choices and her fussiness, Harrison didn't see a marriage happening.

Mr. Simpson, nailing a flyer to the mercantile post, caught his eye. With a big, toothy smile, the elderly, hard-of-hearing clerk lifted a large hand in hello. Harrison smiled and waved back. Nearby, Mr. Lichtenstein was deep in discussion with Chance Holcomb. Old Mr. Herrick, the leather shop owner, sat in a rocking chair outside his front door, a blanket folded over his lap. Harrison was surprised at how much the man had aged since his trip last May, but that was understandable with the horrible winter they'd suffered. Trent came out of the building and handed his father a cup, laying a hand on the back of his chair. Yes, this was a good town. Moving here was the right thing to do.

"Papa, look!" Carlie screeched, pointing at Mr. Tracy, the telegraph operator. "He's so tiny. Why is he so short?"

Turning, Harrison caught Pauline as she pushed Carlie's arm down before Mr. Tracy saw his daughter pointing. Harrison didn't think the man had heard her innocent question over the rumbling of their wagon wheels and the buckboard behind.

Tracy did look up, a handful of mail in his palm. He smiled and waved. "Heard ya was moving to Y Knot, but I didn't believe my ears," he called out in a loud voice. "Welcome ta town! You've arrived just in time. We're in a predicament and need your help."

What did that mean?

The man's eyes went wide when he spotted Pauline.

Everyone knew Harrison had lost his second wife and that he was again a widower.

The telegraph operator nodded politely.

Pauline's indignant huff reached Harrison's ears, and he didn't have to turn to know what she looked like. "Thanks, Tracy," he called. "I have to say being back sure feels good. Especially since I won't be riding out tomorrow. A new experience for me!"

The wagon had reached the telegraph operator and was now moving past.

"Don't count your chickens…"

Confused, Harrison tipped his head. "I'm just one of the regular folk now," he called back. *With a target on my back.* He drummed his fingers on the edge of the wagon. No. He'd not let morbid thoughts ruin his new life. Months would pass before anyone from his past cases would hear that he'd moved away. He had plenty of time before he had to worry. "I'm retired."

The small man's wide grin made him chuckle.

Harrison put an elbow on the back of the seat and turned to Pauline. "I think you have an admirer."

"Oh, *please*. That just tickles your fancy, doesn't it? You like to see me miserable."

His smile faded. "That's not true."

Carlie looked up. "Who, Papa? That funny little man?"

Harrison chomped down on his bottom lip. He'd have to have a talk with his daughter and point out a few things. "Never you mind, sweetness. This is our new home." *Where you'll be safe, and life will be uncomplicated. Getting lost in the slowness will feel good.*

The air was sweet and clean, quite a difference from Denver. Harrison took a deep breath, holding the air in his lungs for several seconds. Moving to Y Knot would not only be good for him but Carlie and Justin as well. Maybe even Pauline. Today was the first day of the rest of their lives.

"Pa!" Justin hurried from the jail.

He must have heard them coming. The freighter behind called to his animals as he parked his rig behind the lead.

"Good to see you, son." Harrison jumped down and embraced his boy, feeling a deep, abiding love surge between them. Justin felt good and hearty in his arms, and by the expression on his face, his son was genuinely happy. They stepped back, identical smiles between them.

"You've arrived early. I didn't expect you until suppertime."

Harrison glanced at the drivers. "They could feel my need." He reached up and easily lifted Carlie from the back of the wagon. Extending a hand to Pauline, he helped his sister-in-law to the street, ignoring her pinched face.

"Good to see you, Aunt Pauline," Justin said, kissing her cheek. "I hope your trip was pleasant. You'll like Y Knot. I'm sure life will be slower than you're used to, but the quiet grows on you."

Harrison gauged the interchange between his son and his sour sister-in-law. He hadn't wanted to put a damper on their arrival, so he'd kept Pauline's reticence about the move a secret.

"Yes, I'm sure I will," she had the decency to say. She patted her shiny forehead with her hankie.

Carlie bounded up and down on her toes. "Justin! Justin!"

"There you are, little mouse." He picked her up and twirled around, the skirt of her prairie dress billowing out. "I thought you decided not to come and stayed in Denver," he teased. Setting her back on her feet, he gave her a good long look and then glanced at Harrison. "What have you been feeding my sister? Carlie's grown a whole foot since I saw her last." He rubbed his hand over his jaw, his brows bunched. "Whatever the mash, I'll sell it to the McCutcheons and Chance Holcomb to feed to their cattle. I'll make a fortune."

"You're teasing me, Justin," Carlie sang with happiness. "I only eat people food."

He nodded. "Really? Say, how about before taking this stuff out to the house and unloading, we walk down to the Biscuit Barrel and get something good to eat? You must be hungry. I wouldn't want Carlie to stop growing. My treat." For a moment, his smile faded. "And, Pa, Luke McCutcheon has some trouble, but we can talk about that after you get a hearty meal, and not a moment before."

Harrison's intuition said maybe he had indeed arrived at the correct time as they ambled toward the Biscuit Barrel. He'd taken this walk to the café a hundred times, if not one. But today was different. A sense of wonder lifted his chest as he held Carlie's warm hand in his own.

In front of them, Justin pointed out the businesses to Pauline.

Harrison wondered if Justin noticed his aunt barely responded to his observations. The warm air felt good. The blue sky, filled with puffy white clouds, reminded him of the ice cream social at Denver's National Bank where he'd taken Agnes on their first outing.

He pushed away his hurt. This was their new beginning. His new beginning. From this day forward, he wouldn't look back. Only forward.

"That you, Judge Wesley?" a tottery voice called. Old Mr. Herrick made to stand.

Harrison released Carlie's fingers and rushed forward, gently setting his hand on the man's shoulder to ease him back into his chair. "You're absolutely correct. Harrison Wesley, at your service." He hunkered down to chair level, and the leather shop owner's eyes brightened in his wizened, timeworn face. They'd shared some good times over the years, sitting in his shop by the woodstove, drinking coffee and sharing conversation. Even out here in the fresh air, Harrison imagined the leathery scent bringing a smile to his lips. This dear friend wouldn't be around much longer.

"Well, I'll be." Mr. Herrick looked around and just now caught sight of the others. "That boy of yours is sure helpful ta me. Ya should be proud. Followin' in his ol' man's tracks."

Harrison cut a quick glance to Justin, who stood there smiling. Herrick was right, he couldn't be prouder of his son if he tried.

"And who's this sweet young thin'?"

Harrison looked at Carlie, but when she didn't move or step forward and a disgusted look appeared on Pauline's face, he glanced back at Mr. Herrick to see him casting a sparsely toothed, come-hither grin at his sister-in-law. Seemed she'd have all the attention she wanted here in Y Knot.

"What's her name, Harrison? Or are you keepin' her all to yerself?"

Behind him Justin chuckled.

He reached back and took his sister-in-law's hand, slowly bringing her forward. "This is my beautiful sister-in-law, Pauline. She's moving to Y Knot with us."

"Well, I'll be," Mr. Herrick said again, a sense of wonder filling his voice. "She married?"

"Nope."

"I never expected this. All the mail-order brides that show up in Y Knot are far too young for me. This one looks more my style."

Chapter Twenty-Eight

Priest's Crossing

Blanche mentally forced the tremors from her hand as she reached for the cup of tea only a few feet away on the pinewood table. Bending low, she took a shallow breath to hide her rattled countenance from Mr. Guthrie. He sat opposite in a straight-back chair, and the other men had politely asked if they could stand quietly along the side wall, the young man Ashley was taken with being one of them. Thank goodness McCutcheon's wife hadn't come too or his boy. Ashley sat beside her on the small sofa, giving her courage.

"You may only have ten minutes of her time." Angelia sent her a compassionate smile.

Little did Angelia know Blanche couldn't stand her simpering ways and just put up with her for propriety's sake— and for a roof over her head that wasn't hidden away on the outskirts of town like her cabin.

Angelia looked at Mr. Guthrie. "Her ribs are still healing."

Why am I sitting here as if I'm the one on trial? She hadn't killed Benson. That moron had. Now that she'd had time to go over that fateful day, surely she could have thought of *something* that would have satisfied Benson's angry questions. Maybe Mr.

Romantic was delivering a package to the homestead and twisted his ankle. That was why he was lounging in their chair where she'd tripped and fallen into his lap. That amusing thought almost made her smile. Convincing Benson might have been difficult, but he was a simple man—or had been, she should say. After he got over his anger, he'd have forgotten and forgiven, especially with the extra attention she would have given. Could she get through these next few days without breaking down?

Mr. Romantic, ha! That stupid nickname now only made her laugh. If she never saw him again, that would be too soon. But she would, on every trip into town.

"Ten minutes should be fine, ma'am," Mr. Guthrie said. "My questions won't take long. But before I begin, first let me say again thank you for agreeing to see me, Mrs. Van Gleek. The fact you've been though a trauma and are in mourning isn't lost on me."

Now, *here* was a man who would make any woman proud to call her own. His large, rough hands sent a delightful quiver down Blanche's spine, thinking about how they might feel on her skin. "You're welcome, Mr. Guthrie. It's the least I can do. Once you know the truth about your boss and realize he's been lying ever since you've arrived, the sooner we can stop all this foolishness."

He looked over to his comrades and then back at her. "Can you please tell me, in your words, how that morning took place?"

She swallowed. Remembering exactly what she'd said to Sheriff Jones was critical.

"Don't be nervous. Just state what happened."

Easy for you! She felt like sneering but kept that impulse to herself. "Thank you. The sun had just crested the mountain.

Benson had returned from his last freighting trip only minutes before. He'd barely come into the house when we heard a horse whinny. Looking out the window, he said someone was coming. Someone he had never seen before."

"He'd never seen Luke McCutcheon? From what I learned, your husband was born and raised here. Not knowing Luke seems strange."

To fortify herself she took a sip of her tea. "Strange or not, that's the truth."

"Go on when you're ready."

"Benson opened the door when the stranger knocked. He asked for food. I had some leftovers so I gave him those, but then he wanted more. When Benson told him we weren't a restaurant, he got angry."

Ashley's mother nodded from her chair. "That Indian blood. Makes a man crazy."

Thank you, Angelia.

Mr. Guthrie nodded for her to continue.

"Lunging forward, McCutcheon wrenched Benson's arm behind his back," she whispered in a shaky tone, "demanding money or gold—whatever we had." She glanced away, made her lips tremble. "We aren't rich people by any stretch of the imagination. We don't have money lying about. We live day to day."

Taking her handkerchief from her pocket, she twisted the material in trembling hands. *Is anyone buying my story?*

"When Benson told him that, McCutcheon got irate. He began shouting. Said he'd give Benson one last chance, and then he would hurt me. Thinking we were both dead, I pushed McCutcheon from behind giving Benson a chance to pull his gun. But that didn't happen. That heathen picked up the fireplace poker and smashed Benson on the side of his head.

Benson fell to the floor right before my eyes and that madman turned on me." For a brief moment, she clenched her eyes closed before continuing. "He hit me in the face, breaking my lower lip, and punched me in my ribs more times than I can remember. He would've killed me too, if I hadn't played like I was dead."

Forcing several hot tears from her eyes, she brushed them away with her handkerchief.

Roady sat back and placed his hands on his knees. "You already knew your husband was dead?"

She stiffened. *Did I slip up?* "I *thought* he was dead. H-He looked dead."

The foreman nodded.

But she could see deep in his eyes he didn't believe a word she was saying. Who would? Now that she'd learned the drifter was Luke McCutcheon, no one would think him capable of such brutality. And especially not over money. She was in deep trouble and had only one person to blame. She'd not take the fall for him!

"Is there anything else you'd like to say, Mrs. Van Gleek?"

"Isn't that enough?" She gently blew her nose and then put her linen away. Her gaze went to the listeners along the wall. The whole time, Francis had been staring at her feet, of all things. Like he was afraid to look into her eyes. She carefully pulled them back under her skirt.

Why on earth did I agree to this interview? I should've made them wait until the trial. But to refuse would seem like I had something to hide. I must remember I didn't kill Benson. I am innocent.

"Can you tell me what you did when Luke left?"

His tone was soft, solicitous, but anger burned deep in that hawklike gaze. A knifelike jab to her heart almost made her gasp. She dared not reach for her cup again, because her culpability would give her away. Beneath her clothing, her body flushed. These next few minutes might be the most important of her life.

"Heartbroken, I... I lay on the floor next to Benson's dead body for about twenty minutes after I heard him ride away. I was in pain and frightened he'd return to kill me off so no one could tell what he'd done."

"Question," Mr. Guthrie said, raising a hand. "Did Luke ever get close to your husband's body once he was lying out on the floor? After he was hit, and perhaps dead?"

What did they know? This was a trap! She dropped her gaze to the small bouquet of buttercups on the center of the table. What should she say? Through her lashes, she could see all the men waiting. Waiting to hear her blunder. Swallowing, she wet the inside of her mouth. "Remembering is difficult."

His regard hardened. "Take your time. There's no rush." He rocked to the side in his chair as he took a breath, gave Ashley, sitting beside her, a brief smile, and then his gaze tracked back to her. "Mrs. Van Gleek?"

The fool! Did he think he was smarter than her? "No, he didn't go near the body. After Benson fell, he turned on me and beat me like an animal, like I said before. When I fell to the floor I closed my eyes, but I remember he was by the front door. He waited a few moments and then left. He never checked to see if either of us were indeed dead."

Mr. Guthrie glanced at his men, victory in his eyes.

The young man that had followed Francis out today struggled to keep a grin contained.

The wrong answer! What did they know that she didn't? She took a steadying breath and cast her gaze at Angelia, wanting out of this room. Out from under their scrutiny.

"Odd he didn't search your place for money. That is what you said he demanded. Or that, after he murdered your husband, he headed into town as if nothing was wrong. Most men would take to the hills. Disappear. He and his son went into Priest's Crossing and attended a dear friend's wedding."

Again she glared at Angelia.

Angelia stood. "That's more than enough. Blanche is tired."

Roady nodded and stood.

"One last question, if I may," Mr. Guthrie said, his hand out in offering. "And then we'll get out of your hair for good. You said Luke arrived early in the morning and killed your husband. You said you pretended to be dead for approximately twenty minutes before you moved from the spot he left you. You didn't point out Luke until after Joe's wedding, and that was in the late afternoon. Was anyone else in your home between the time of the murder and you identifying him?"

Another trap! Her heart slammed against her ribs. The cowboys could hardly contain their grins. She'd been such a fool. A bloody, stupid fool! She'd told Jack she'd been alone. No one else there. She had to stick to her story.

"Ma'am?"

"No one. Just me. I was in shock. I got to town as soon as I could pull myself together."

"So, almost a full day passed."

His tone didn't hold near the caring as when he'd begun. She nodded.

Mr. Guthrie smiled politely. "Thank you, again, ma'am. This interview couldn't have been easy—given all your memories. Condolences over your husband. Everyone has said what a good, honest man he was."

Another jab! Her stomach churned as she hid her fisted hands in the fabric of her skirt. He'd skillfully boxed her into a corner in front of a handful of witnesses. What a fool she'd been.

Chapter Twenty-Nine

From the corner of his cell, Luke watched Faith pace from one wall to the other as they waited for Roady and the men to return. Early this morning, Roady had filled them both in on the bloody boot print as Colton listened sullenly from the bench against the far wall of the jailhouse. Now the boy was off with Smokey, fetching coffee from the restaurant across the road.

Faith turned, her expression hard. "What's taking Roady and the men so long? Why aren't they back yet?"

"I doubt a half hour has passed since they left. You may as well sit and relax. Who knows what kind of resistance Mrs. Van Gleek will give them?"

"She won't tell them anything. I'd like to question her myself. And I would if she'd ever come into town. She's hiding out, Luke, not mourning. I have no doubt in my mind that she's been carrying on behind her husband's back. Mr. Van Gleek came home and discovered them, and that was that."

Pretty much what I'm thinking too. "You're probably right."

"Luke, how can you be so calm at a time like this? I'm scared to death, and you act like being locked up for days is nothing. I wish your parents and brothers were here. And Brandon. We need to send for Justin. With Brandon in

Cheyenne, he's the next best thing. Having some law on our side would be comforting. At least having Y Knot's deputy will pull some weight with Jack Jones."

His wife's frustration was feeding his anger. "I wouldn't count on that, sweetheart. Jack has his mind set, at least for now. If he gave in without reason, he'd look like a fool. We'll get the evidence we need. You don't have to be frightened."

Her lips gripped together, going white.

His words weren't helping in the least. Faith was rattled. Maybe she had good reason to be. "Come here," he said, going to the bars and putting out his hand.

She quickly crossed the room and laid her cheek against his palm.

The feel of her skin always reminded him of a thunderstorm on a dark night, one of his best memories. She was his rock, but now he could feel her quivering with fear. The anger he tried to keep tightly in check ratcheted up a few more notches, making him want to punch his fist through the back wall. "We'll see how things go over the next few days," he said, as calmly as he could. "Justin can't leave Y Knot with Brandon and my family away. His duty is there."

"Hayden can watch over the town. And Chance and Tobit. Trent Herrick, Morgan Stanford, a lot of good, responsible men. I can think of several handfuls of more names if you'd like to hear them. We can send Nick for him as soon as—"

"No, we can't." He ran his thumb over her cheek to soften his curt interruption. "With last winter's devastation and so many ranchers wiped out, we've had more than our fair share of lawlessness this spring. Men are hungry, and that will move them to do anything to feed themselves and their families. For now, Justin needs to stay put in Y Knot. Period. If things here get bad enough, I'm sure Roady will send for reinforcements and also send a telegram to Cheyenne to the family and Brandon. For now, we're doing just fine. Investigating takes time. The guilty person won't jump out and say hello."

He put his face as far through the bars as he could manage and pulled Faith closer for a kiss. Jack Jones wouldn't railroad him. He had a wife to love and children to protect. If push came to shove, he wouldn't go down easy. But until they exhausted all the legal ways to circumvent this situation, they had to play by the rules. And that was difficult for Faith. All she could see was a bad end coming. He wouldn't let that happen.

Gazing deep into her eyes, he silently made a promise to her and himself. Nobody would use him as a scapegoat and get away with the deed. Not while he was still alive.

The screech of a hawk sounded outside. He drew back and turned his head, listening.

"What?" Faith asked.

Luke put his finger to his lips and cut his gaze to the door to the outer office. Jack and the deputy had been there when Faith arrived a little while ago, and they'd heard the sounds of their voices in conversation. Now all was quiet, but Luke had the strangest feeling something was up.

"Keep talking low, like we just were," he said close to the bars. "I'll climb on my bunk and look out the window."

She nodded, and her pupils dilated. Blinking, she cut a glance back to the door and then watched Luke.

"Go on, sweetheart," he whispered, slowly moving to the cot.

She nodded. "I can't wait to have you home," she said, unhurried and loud enough that they could hear her if they were listening. "Holly and Dawn miss you terribly. I can't even imagine what they're thinking. They miss their daddy tucking them in bed each night."

Faith's words moved softly around the room, the truth of her statement about the girls making his stomach tighten, and then anger blossomed hot. He was innocent. He hadn't killed anyone. Jack Jones would pay for his stupidity when Luke was free.

He didn't know what to expect outside. One foot up, he leaned to the wall, feeling the coolness beneath his palm. Grasping one bar, he pulled himself farther up. Nothing out by the broken-down chicken coop. He looked down and received the shock of his life.

Chapter Thirty

"Fox Dancing!" Luke blinked, wondering if he was hallucinating or if his young Cheyenne sister stood beyond the bars on the grass outside. A year had passed since he'd learned of her existence. The night was burned firmly in his mind. She had been unconscious in the loft of his new barn, fighting for her life the night of Brandon and Charity's engagement party.

Roady discovered her and climbed down the ladder with her in his arms, a picture Luke would never forget. Until that day, he'd been ignorant of her birth. Her beauty and strength, as she stood proud before him now, sent a surge of joy through his heart. Knowing she was alive and well was a gift all in itself.

"Luke," Faith whispered, from her spot on the other side of the room. "Is someone out there?"

Turning, he was unable to hide his happiness. "Fox Dancing," he whispered, knowing his wide smile must look absurd. Since she'd departed the ranch last year, he had no way of tracking her whereabouts. Or knowing whether she was alive or dead. What her people were going through. He turned back to the window.

She looked well, and better, strong and fit. Confident. Her dark eyes flashed rebelliously, and she held her frame straight and fearless. A warm breeze lifted a colorful feather attached to the bottom of a narrow braid, almost lost in her thick mane.

Her appearance in his life then had been a huge surprise, as it was today. Why was she here? And what would transpire if anyone from this town saw her? He pushed his arm through the bars.

She reached up, touching his fingers.

Her impish smile made him chuckle. "Fox Dancing," he whispered, the gravity of the situation returning. "If you're seen, I can't help you."

"I'm happy to see you too, important white brother," she replied quietly. "You have no words of greeting for your long-lost Cheyenne sister?"

Oh, how he wished he were out of this jail. The sound of her voice was enough to move mountains of sentimentality through him.

"Of course I'm happy," he whispered. "I'm thrilled to death. A year is much too long between visits. But I fear for your safety." He looked around behind the jailhouse, imagining all sorts of trouble. Deputy Clark running forward with his gun, taking aim. A mob of angry townsfolk. "You need to leave now. You can do nothing to help."

"It is *your* safety you should be worried about," she replied with all confidence.

He realized that she was probably right.

"Not mine. I am free, where I'll remain. Stupid white dogs want you to hang. They don't care if you're guilty or not. Your Indian blood is all the reason they need."

She's dead-on again. How can I make her understand her being here makes things worse for me? If something happened to her, I'd never forgive myself. "If anyone sees you off the reservation, they'll lock you up or worse. You must go."

"Save your breath, brother. We hear my white brother in trouble. We come swiftly."

Luke jerked his gaze from her face and searched the landscape until he spotted Painted Bear Stone hidden in a thicket of trees, a rifle cradled in his arms and a bow draped over his shoulder. Luke could feel the brave's defiance from where he watched. Over the year, Painted Bear Stone had grown stronger. Taller. Luke was sure his gaze missed nothing as he kept guard. He wouldn't let anything happen to his love.

"I see him," Luke said quietly, feeling a growing despair. "Painted Bear Stone."

Her eyebrow peaked. "My husband."

Luke smiled again. The rightness of the union calmed his soul. "Congratulations. I'm happy to hear that news. Be sure to tell my new brother-in-law I fervently approve. I just hope he doesn't regret his decision after you start bossing him around."

Again the eyebrow, but this time with amusement playing on her lips. And love pouring from her eyes. They were a good match. "How did you hear I'd been jailed?"

"We have our ways. Since I returned from Y Knot last year, everyone knows of my Luke. Not everyone lives in the white man's camps. We—" She glanced over her shoulder at Painted Bear Stone. "We come and go. Can't stand to stay on reservation for long. We live on land, *our land,* unseen and unheard."

She was avoiding his question. He asked again.

"Like a bird flying across country, word found me. I will never abandon you, Luke. Our spirits are connected, more so than just our blood. We think alike. Feel alike. I've lived your frustration since you've been caged."

He let out a deep sigh. As glad as he was to see that she was still alive, fear for her life was stronger. "You can't fight the whole town."

"Who says I'll do that?"

Anger welled. She was being foolish. "Me. I know you better than you think. You're right about our spirits. I can tell what you're thinking now."

Her chin tipped in defiance.

"Listen to me, Fox Dancing. You and Painted Bear Stone are only two against many. Get whatever you're thinking out of your head."

Her brow arched as if she hadn't heard a word he'd just said.

"Luke?" Faith asked more insistently. "How is she? What is she saying?"

He kept hold of the bars but turned to look at Faith. "She and Painted Bear Stone are married," he whispered, then chuckled at her smile. "Just like us, they're tied together for life." He liked the way that statement lit up Faith's expression.

Luke sobered. The seriousness of the situation loomed. He turned back to his sister. "The McCutcheon name has no pull in this town. The best way to help me is to go home now. As your older, responsible brother, I expect you to respect my wishes."

At the sound of someone approaching, Luke quickly stepped off the cot and spun. Leaning his shoulder to the wall, he looked at his fingernails. Stupid to be sure, but that was all time allowed.

"Mrs. McCutcheon..."

Luke lifted his gaze.

Deputy Clark strode into the room and pulled to a stop.

His eyes narrowed. He looked back and forth between Luke and Faith; most likely discerning what the strange sense in the room was all about.

Faith stood by the cell, one bar grasped in each hand, her face flushed and her eyes wide.

Luke strode over to the bars and took one of her hands. "What do you want, Deputy?" he barked. "Can't you see my wife is upset? Do you have to pester us every minute of the day?"

Faith blinked several times, and then moisture sprang into her eyes. "What now, Deputy Clark?" she said in a shaky voice. "I'm just so tired of this. You need to come to your senses. My husband didn't kill anyone."

Clark looked between them again, his nostrils flaring.

Did the man suspect something? Faith was playing her part to the hilt. Luke needed to stall Clark a little longer so Fox Dancing and Painted Bear Stone could get out of sight.

"You've been awfully quiet in here for the past few minutes," he said, walking closer. Clark sucked on his upper teeth. "What's going on? Care to let me in on the big secret?"

"How can anything be going on?" Faith replied, her tone turning icy. "I'm just wondering about Smokey and Colton. Did they run into trouble at the restaurant when they went to get coffee? The way the citizens of Priest's Crossing have turned against good, law-abiding people is not right. You'll see when we prove my husband's innocence."

Good girl, keep Deputy Clark busy.

Faith straightened. "I'll go check on them. I don't trust this town where my son is concerned." She looked at Luke. "They even pick on a small boy."

Luke reached for her arm. "Oh no, you don't," he said in his no-nonsense voice. "You're staying right here until Smokey returns. You know my rule. You don't go anywhere without him. I'm sorry I let him go. Maybe the restaurant was out of coffee and they had to perk a new pot. Any number of things could be keeping 'em, but you're not finding out."

"Whatever you say, McCutcheon," Clark said. "You're a strange pair. I don't even remember what I came in here to ask you. Something of Mrs. McCutcheon, but…"

The tall man scratched his head, but Luke didn't buy his stupid act at all. He'd seen the way the deputy watched and listened. His gaze strayed to the window one too many times, and the way he gnawed on the inside of his cheek meant he wanted to get to something else. He was suspicious. And if he wasn't, he should be. Or did he have something to hide, as well? That was an interesting thought. Luke wished he was free to investigate the town himself.

The man spun on his heel and left.

Luke heard him talking low to Jones in the outer room, even though he couldn't make out their words. When Faith opened her mouth to say something, Luke quickly held a finger to his lips.

Jones' chair scraped on the floor. A few more whispers and then the outer room was quiet.

"They aren't as dumb as they look, or that we think they are," Luke whispered. "We need to be very careful. Fox Dancing is playing with fire showing up." He fisted a hand and stared at Faith. "We need to take action soon. The longer I'm in here, the longer she and Painted Bear Stone are in jeopardy of being discovered. Of course, she wouldn't think of going home."

"She loves you, Luke." Faith reached into the cell and tenderly stroked his arm. "We all do. I understand her motives. Besides, you didn't really think she'd leave, did you?"

He gazed at her, wondering where she was taking this.

"The two of you have the same blood. What if she'd told you to go home that horrible night in Pine Grove when that horde of fired-up men wanted to hang her? I'm sure you'd have just ridden out because she asked you nicely."

His gut tightened. That was a terrifying night. "It's not the same thing. She's a girl. Younger than Charity."

"A young *woman*. She and Painted Stone are married. All her life she's been fighting to stay alive. You might be surprised at how clever a young, helpless woman can be."

Faith had him there. A day didn't pass that he wasn't surprised by his wife, Charity, or now Fox Dancing. Even Dawn and little Holly were turning out to be forces to be reckoned with. He might as well give up trying to get his younger sister to comply.

"Good. I can see you've come to your senses."

Faith might be right that he didn't have any power to protect Fox Dancing, but that truth didn't make him happy. No sir. Not one little bit.

Chapter Thirty-One

The heat in the kitchen rose by several degrees, and not because of the weather. The expression on Blanche's face had Ashley terrified. Ever since Francis and the other men rode off ten minutes ago, her behavior had been frightening.

The words that spewed from her mouth were enough to shock a sailor, let alone her and her mother. Had seeing Benson murdered right before her eyes caused her friend to lose her mind? Blanche was calm and collected before and during the interview with Mr. Guthrie. Ashley thought the whole process had gone well.

And yet a niggle of doubt had already sprouted last night when she'd found Blanche smoking alone in the dark. That behavior was so unlike her. Did Blanche have more alarming aspects Ashley wasn't aware of? Were there more parts of Blanche's life that her friend kept safely hidden away—from everyone?

I mustn't think these things. They're shameful and wrong. Blanche needs my support now more than ever. Poor thing is distraught and doesn't know what she's saying. Or doing.

"How dare he act like I'm some criminal!" Blanche cried out, her right fist clenched before her face. "I know where his questions were leading. I saw the speculation in his eyes. How stupid does he think I am?" She kicked out in anger, sending a small stool clattering across the room. Ashley winced and turned to the stove. *She's innocent. She's scared. She feels backed into a corner. Perhaps I'd act the same.*

The picture of Blanche alone at the window in the dark room had Ashley spooked. Ashley didn't like the direction of her thoughts. As much as she liked Francis, and felt in her heart that he wouldn't lie for his boss just to get him off a criminal charge, she also owed loyalty to her friend.

If only a judge would show up soon. Or even if Joe and Pearl would return. A new viewpoint on the situation couldn't hurt. The town seemed to be rallying behind Blanche, and Ashley wasn't sure that was the right place to be.

"So, you like that young man? Think he's handsome and nice?" Blanche said from behind her.

Ashley almost dropped the peeled apple she was placing into the boiling pot. Making applesauce took time and patience. One had to be cautious around the hot water or get scalded. Trying to control her expression, she brushed some strands of hair from her sight. "What do you mean?"

"I mean I saw the way the two of you acted out in the orchard this morning, and again when he returned with the others to question me. You like him, and he likes you."

Was she spying on me?

Ashley heard Angelia move into the room. "She better not like that boy. We have more things to worry about than love."

Shocked, Ashley spun, facing her mother. They'd never talked about men or her future. She had the impression her mother never expected her to marry and move away. Or have a life of her own. "What do you mean, Mother? Francis and I are barely even friends. I hardly know him. But I have to say he was unbelievably kind to help me this morning with the harvesting."

She frowned. If not for him, they'd have so much more work to do. "A lot was accomplished in a short amount of time." She forced a small smile and lightened her tone. "I'd think you'd be thankful to him for lightening your load. He's taken some of the burden off our shoulders."

Her mother's expression softened. "I do appreciate his help. But plenty more needs to done in the next few days." She glanced at Blanche.

"I can't help. My ribs are still painful." She put a hand on one hip and slowly stretched her ribcage.

"We don't expect you to," her mother replied. "And I like the work. Hours in the air and sunshine keep me young."

Feeling the weight of the responsibility she'd carried for the past few years since her father's death, Ashley couldn't believe the course of the conversation. "I can't imagine what either of you have against Francis."

A sly smile stretched across Blanche's lips. "You can't? Could he be sweetening you up for a reason? Maybe getting you to trust him for some other aim besides just liking you?"

Ashley's hand stilled as she reached for the bowl of apples. Her gaze fell to the stack of long, jagged peels in the dry sink. "What on earth are you hinting at, Blanche? Why would he do something like that? That's awful to think, let alone say to me." Although she acted as if she didn't understand, a sick dawning spread throughout her body, bringing a crushing disappointment. *Is Francis using me to help free his boss? Is what Blanche is alluding to true? Everyone can see how much he thinks of Luke McCutcheon.*

Her mother shuffled forward, righted the stool Blanche had kicked across the room, and sat. "Blanche makes a very good point, although I can't imagine what he might think Ashley could know about Benson's murder or how she could help. You should be careful."

Blanche glanced into the pot of boiling apples. "Perhaps he doesn't think she knows anything at all. Perhaps he's just keeping her from giving me her full support. Those men could change the opinion of the town, one mind at a time. If that happens, public scrutiny may turn some other way. I think that's what they're doing. They aren't sitting around twiddling their thumbs while they wait for Joe and Pearl to return. You heard what good friends they are. Joe worked for McCutcheon's father for years." She stood very still. "You can bet once he's back in town he'll be working on Jack to set McCutcheon free."

"How could they do that, Blanche?" Ashley asked. "You're an eyewitness. You told the sheriff the truth. If truth is on your side, nothing else matters."

Her mouth thinned. "If?"

The way Blanche said the single word made Ashley's blood freeze. "I meant that metaphorically, because truth *is* on your side. Let them do and be whatever. Their efforts don't matter a bit." *Unless you're lying, and you* did *have something to do with Benson's death. At this moment, I'm really not sure what I believe anymore. And I don't like the way you're staring as if you'd like to kill me.*

Without one ounce of passion, Blanche began clapping her hands.

Ashley had heard stories about sicknesses of the mind. How a person could act like two different people at once without even realizing it. Was something like that wrong with her friend and mentor? Impossible to know, and very frightening to consider.

Angelia draped an arm over Blanche's shoulders. "You're worn out, Blanche. Go slip into your nightgown, and let me tuck you back into bed. You've been though a horrible experience."

Blanche looked deeply into her mother's eyes, bringing a smile to the older woman's lips.

"And this too shall pass," her mother whispered.

A phrase her mother used often in the years following the atrocity that had happened to her father, leaving him mangled for his daughter to find. Ashley tried to banish the horrible memory, but the action of peeling the apple made that difficult. Everything felt difficult today. Did a person's scalp come off as easily as this apple peel?

"Mother's right, Blanche. Go lie down, at least until suppertime." She glanced over her shoulder and forced a smile onto her lips. "Unless you'd like me to do something for you? Anything at all."

"Forgive me," Blanche replied, her tone back to normal. "I didn't sleep a wink last night, and then that man asking all those questions has me more than a bit rattled. Four days since we buried my love." She choked back a sob. "Thinking of Benson in that cold grave makes my blood turn to ice. I've never felt such a horrible sensation. I miss him. I can't imagine living the rest of my life without him." She sniffed loudly and held her handkerchief to the corner of her eye. "I just can't accept that fact." She looked between them. "I'm a widow. How will I make my way?"

Your eye looks as dry as a desert in July. Shamed for her wayward thought, Ashley cut her gaze back to her chore. Perhaps her friend was anxious from recounting the day of the murder. Or on the verge of a nervous breakdown. What she experienced would not have been easy for anyone—let alone someone who had suffered injuries, as well. Setting the apple down, Ashley turned and wrapped Blanche in her arms. "Nothing needs forgiving, Blanche. I'm the one who needs forgiving for not seeing your fatigue."

What Blanche and her mother said about Francis using her for his own purpose kept circling around in her mind. He had sought her gaze more than a few times when he'd come back with the other men. She felt a closeness to him that she shouldn't. She never got the impression he was leading her on, but maybe he was a good actor.

Blanche pulled away and patted her cheek. "I forgive you, then. You're a sweet thing. You'd never hurt a fly on purpose."

Her voice was gravelly, low, and her eyes at half-mast. Her skin was sallow and her head had a slight quiver. She was exhausted, that much was true.

Ashley nodded to her mother to help Blanche to her bedroom and then went back to her apples. Life wasn't so bad here with her mother. She should be thankful to have a roof over her head. When school started, life would be exciting again. Every day teaching the children involved something new.

But you'll miss Francis when he's gone. After the trial, whatever happens, he'll go back to Y Knot. That's a fact that can't be disputed. And a fact I better remember.

Chapter Thirty-Two

Still unarmed, and not liking the sensation one bit, the men rode the short distance back from Ashley Adair's home to the jailhouse in silence. That woman, Mrs. Van Gleek, gave Francis the shivers. She was creepy. She was nice-looking when she smiled, which wasn't nearly enough, but he didn't like the way her gaze kept searching him out. *Why me? Doesn't make any sense. I've never done one darn thing to her, and yet...*

Seemed she was thinking things she shouldn't. And that being the case, he didn't like her living at Ashley's. To his way of thinking, that woman was capable of anything, not just murdering her husband. Maybe someday she'd snap and hurt Ashley, or her mother. Why wasn't Jack Jones doing more to break this case?

Because he thinks he has everything all figured out.

Francis reached into his pocket and fingered the fancy money clip he'd found stuck in the cushions. Roady had told him to stay quiet until they knew more. That was easy. Who did he have to tell?

Ashley.

They reined up in front of the jail. Pedro was off doing what he did best. Watching the town without being seen. Tracking people. Staying out of sight.

Francis swung his leg over his saddle when he spotted Joe Brunn standing in front of the mercantile a few doors down. "Look who's back," he said, wrapping his reins around the hitching rail. "Joe. And he's headed this way."

Roady hitched his head. "Let's meet him halfway. More privacy." He cut his gaze toward the jailhouse. "I have no idea who's inside with an ear turned this way. And for now," he gave them all a stern look, "don't say anything about what we found at the cabin to anyone. That includes Joe. We'll know soon enough which way this trial is turning, but let me do the talking. That clear?"

Francis nodded, relieved Roady and the men had arrived to help when they had. He still didn't trust Nick Petty wholeheartedly, especially after this morning. The fella was either scheming or trying to get a laugh. Well, some of the tricks he pulled weren't funny at all. Someday one of the hands would get fed up and bounce him out of the bunkhouse onto his ear. And that just might be him. Still, Francis didn't like having irritated thoughts about one of the ranch hands, especially since he liked Shad so much.

Joe's face was unreadable as he approached.

Roady and Joe clasped hands as soon as they were close enough. "Good to see you, Joe. It's been too darn long."

Joe nodded to the rest of the group. He smiled at Francis.

Still thinks I'm a kid.

"How long has it been, Guthrie? Three years, maybe? I see you've taken on a couple of new faces."

"That's right. Shad and Nick Petty."

Small talk. Francis didn't like the feel of the conversation. Joe seemed nervous.

"Christine has just spent the past hour filling us in on everything that's happened. It's been a shock, I can tell you. And

Luke locked up for the crime? What the hell is going on around here, anyway?"

A whoosh of relief coursed through Francis. *Finally,* someone to take Luke's side. Someone with a good standing in the town. Someone the others would listen to. Joe could make a difference, if anyone could.

"Where's your wife?" Roady asked. "Still in the store?"

Roady probably wanted to get all the talking done before a woman filled with grief over her murdered brother was thrown into the fray. Francis wasn't looking forward to anything like that. Women were volatile. Mrs. Van Gleek looked about ready to explode behind a tight, angry smile when they said their goodbyes. He wondered how Ashley was making out.

"Still in the store with Christine. I helped her upstairs to Christine's bed so she could lie down." He glanced off down the street just looking for several seconds. "I'm having a hard time believing all this."

Roady jerked straight, as did Shad and himself. Nick looked angry, but Francis thought that was his normal expression when he was following a conversation.

"What d'ya mean, Joe?" Roady shot back. "What's hard to believe? Luke didn't kill anyone, and especially not Benson."

"Don't get your back up, Guthrie. I didn't mean that. Benson was murdered, and Blanche roughed up. You have to understand that Benson is—*was*—my brother-in-law. I've just spent a gut-wrenching hour witnessing Pearl's grief inside that mercantile and me unable to ease her sorrow." He jerked a thumb over his shoulder, his tone icy. "I'm sorry to say, but Christine believes Blanche. The woman's been living in Priest's Crossing for many years. They're friends. Blanche has been the schoolteacher and a model citizen for longer than I can remember. She's an eyewitness to the crime. She was there! What does that leave?"

Francis couldn't keep quiet a moment longer. "It leaves Blanche is lying!"

"Exactly my thought!" Roady blurted.

Reservation moved over Joe's face. "I know, I know. No way in hell will I ever believe Luke is guilty, but my wife—*my new wife*—does! Christine too! And just about every other person living here in Priest's Crossing. What're we doing about that? And since Luke didn't kill Benson, who did? That's what I'd like to know."

Roady and Joe were toe-to-toe. Their faces strained and bodies rigid. Francis would never believe a day like this could happen. He didn't want to see Joe and Roady fight.

They all turned at the sound of horse hooves clopping up the street. Pedro.

Francis also spotted Faith in the doorway of the jailhouse, watching their conversation. With the distance, he doubted she could hear their words, but their body language said enough.

Turning on her heel, she disappeared back inside.

Francis squeezed the money clip in his pocket, desperation growing inside. If the town took matters into their own hands without waiting for a judge, the men and him would have to take the matter back. That was all there was to it. He couldn't imagine that happening. People would get killed. Something had to be done and quickly.

From across the street, Daniel Clevenger watched them from the doorway of his eatery.

The icy stare he sent Francis was more than challenging.

"I'd like to take him on," Nick whispered close at his side. "Thinks he knows everything, but he don't."

Hmm, maybe Nick Petty wasn't all bad. "I know what you mean. And look down the street." The undertaker watched, as well as the livery man.

Nick nodded. "Tempers are short. I think the real killer must be getting nervous right about now. He's wondering what side Joe's gonna take. He's also wondering when a judge will show up, and what kind of evidence we've found." He nudged Francis's shoulder. "Something's always left behind at a murder scene. Some clue to point a finger. Someone hidden to whisper a name. We know what that is. But he don't. Maybe he's just now discovered he can't find his money clip and is sweating bullets." He gave a low chuckle. "He wants to see Luke swing. The sooner, the better." They exchanged a look. "Maybe he'll start something himself."

"Sounds like you're enjoying this, Petty. Like you think Luke's life is some game or something."

"Not true. I don't like seeing Luke locked up any more than you do. But I'm not gonna sit back and do nothin' to help. The killer is out there, watching, waiting. I can feel him like the air I breathe." He nudged Francis with his elbow. "I know I like to tease, but never doubt my loyalty."

Colton came out of the jailhouse and hurried over to the group. His eyes lit up when he saw Joe.

Faith hadn't passed on the news that he'd returned to Luke and Smokey. He wondered why. *Because she's scared half to death. And looks like she has more reason now than ever.*

Colton tugged on Francis's shirtsleeve. "Hey, Francis. My pa wants to talk with Roady as soon as he's available."

"I'll let him know."

"Did Roady find out anything talkin' with Mrs. Van Gleek today?" he asked. "Or anything out at the cabin?"

"Nothin' solid, Colton, just that the widow gives me, and the rest of the boys, the creeps." He hated holding back from Colton, but Roady had given a direct order about keeping his mouth shut.

Across the street, Daniel retreated inside his restaurant and now Jed Kasterlee, the hotel clerk, watched. What did they expect? For the ranch hands to sit around and do nothing? That wasn't going to happen. Luke's time was ticking. Making every second count was vital. They had no time to lose.

Chapter Thirty-Three

The café crowd was boisterous for a Monday morning, making it difficult to think. He glared at his cup of coffee. Ten days had passed since Benson surprised Blanche and him in the cabin. He didn't like to remember the moments that came after. His sudden decision. The look of surprise on Benson's face as he fell to the floor. He was usually a good, God-fearing man. Violence went against everything he was. His brother had pushed him beyond his senses. Blanche had tempted him beyond his resolve. *They* were to blame for his violent actions, not himself.

And on top of all that, he'd gone and lost his money clip and two whole dollars! That mystery bothered him more each day. Was it possible he'd had it with him at the cabin? He couldn't remember. If doing so wasn't so risky, he'd sneak out and search the place. But that would be foolish. If someone had found the clip at the crime scene, there's a chance he'd already be arrested.

Making a quick sweep of the room, he lifted his cup and took a drink. Nothing would happen. The judge would show up soon and put this whole thing to rest. Blanche was an eyewitness. McCutcheon couldn't get off. Still…

With a clatter, his cup settled back in his saucer, splashing a good amount of coffee on his hand, as well as the tablecloth.

People looked over.

"Oh, my, are you feeling unwell?" Mildred asked, her wrinkled brow crumpled. She scooted from her chair and came his way, leaving her table empty.

He took a deep breath and steadied his nerves. If he didn't watch out, he'd give himself away, first with almost getting hit by a wagon and now acting like a fool.

"Just fine, Mildred. I have a to-do list a mile long, and here I linger at the counter, sipping coffee like I have all the time in the world." He looked into the kitchen and then away. *Does she suspect me? Is a large M tattooed on my forehead?*

Mildred smiled. "I know how pesky responsibilities can weigh on a person," she replied in her shaky old voice. "Stop by tonight, say about six, and I'll prepare you a nice pot roast with all the fixings. A home-cooked meal is what you need."

Her come-hither smile almost made him recoil. Those eyes, those lips, those teeth. Who did she think she was? She was old enough to be his grandmother.

"You probably haven't had home cooking for some time. Am I right?"

He'd never get rid of her. He nodded. Still, the dark gravy she was known for did have his mouth watering. Mashed potatoes, caramelized onions, and her famous tender beef. Maybe he'd go. "You've hit the problem on the nail. I'm much obliged."

She tittered, patted her dry, gray hair, and tottered away.

He stared at his half-empty cup. He hadn't spoken to Blanche. He'd seen her from afar three times, one being the funeral. She'd looked old and rumpled. He'd heard Ashley Adair was seeing to her needs. A hot, angry bolt of hatred straightened his spine. If not for Blanche, he wouldn't be lying awake all night, looking over his shoulder, or hearing voices of people who weren't there.

And the boy. What did *he* know? Colton McCutcheon stared at him every chance he got. And his mother? He'd seen the way she watched him.

A snicker slipped out, and he quickly covered his mouth with his palm, glancing around to see if anyone noticed. Hadn't been all that long ago that her brother-in-law dragged her to Priest's Crossing in an old wagon that had seen better days. He remembered the boy too and the wails of the baby as Ward Brown pulled Faith off the wagon, dumping her in the dirt.

He'd witnessed the whole scene from the front of his establishment, his breath coming quick. So close, and yet he'd not step between a man and his woman, no sir, not him. He was actually sorry to hear that McCutcheon had rescued her on their getaway from Priest's Crossing. Him and that gang of ranch hands he'd unleashed on the town.

He'd not kid himself—they were a dangerous lot, even if they weren't armed. They'd hidden their guns somewhere so they wouldn't be confiscated, but he wasn't fool enough to think they wouldn't retrieve them. If they were uncovered, he'd laugh in their faces. Once that happened, no way in hell could anyone break out McCutcheon. Until then, so many facets existed to his predicament he could be found out at any moment. Good thing he had nerves of steel.

Blanche was his biggest risk. He really should do something about that. But what? Talk to her? Threaten her? Just being in the same proximity might shred her resolve. And then came the culpability. He could handle guilt. He had for years. But could Blanche? What if those cowboys offered her clemency in exchange for the truth? What if she snapped from the strain on her own accord?

Straightening, he looked to the door. Only one thing left to do.

Chapter Thirty-Four

At the livery, Francis went about seeing to the stock. Ever since last Saturday, when he'd helped Ashley pick apples, he couldn't keep her out of his thoughts. She was the first thing that popped into his mind each morning as soon as consciousness dawned, and today had been no exception.

Even before he'd opened his eyes, a vision of her vivid green eyes gazing into his made his heart skip a beat. In the still-dark room, he'd remained stretched out on his bed, listening to the others breathe as dawn settled over Priest's Crossing. The fact her searching gaze had taken precedence over Luke's predicament troubled him. No one was more important to him than Luke. How was his friend handling being locked behind bars for so long? Francis couldn't imagine.

The situation with Luke was at an impasse. Luke had told Roady about Fox Dancing and Painted Bear Stone, and in turn, Roady passed that information to the hands to keep under their hats. Nobody wanted to see anything happen to them. Francis remembered the skirmish he'd had with Painted Bear Stone when he'd discovered the Cheyenne brave hiding in the McCutcheon barn. They'd tumbled out in a test of strength, all the while Francis holding back the wicked-looking knife he wielded.

Francis shook off the memory, went outside, and dipped a bucket into the livery water trough. Inside, he filled each horse's water bucket. "Here you go," he said, rubbing Fiddlin' Dee's velvety muzzle. Continuing, he watered Redmond, War Bonnet, and the rest.

Trouble was in the air. The town was changing. People now spoke openly about the *half-breed* locked up for Benson's murder with a tone that made Francis want to take some of the salt out of their hides. They talked about the poor, suffering widow as she'd watched her husband's coffin be lowered into the ground. How would she get along now that her man was dead? How would she make ends meet? Life was hard enough already.

And to his shock, he hadn't seen much of Joe Brunn since Luke's friend returned to town, although Francis didn't believe Joe had abandoned them completely. He was walking a thin line between his friendship and his wife. Was biding his time. Francis just hoped he didn't wait too long to make a move. Francis had imagined, before Joe's arrival back into town, Luke's friend would be beating the drum of Luke's innocence as soon as he learned what had taken place. Talking up the citizens and gaining trust for Luke. Francis had expected more, a lot more. Just because his new wife was Benson's sister shouldn't make a difference. Luke was innocent, and nothing would change that. Would Joe act differently if Flood were here to take him on? A new wife might be a formidable opponent.

Surely the situation would ease on the arrival of a judge. Whoever he was, the lawman would no doubt know the McCutcheon family and most likely believe without a trial that Luke was innocent. Might even be a personal friend. But leaving Luke's life in the hands of someone else, a man who just might possibly be bought off, didn't sit well either. And what about the real murderer? Was he creating a case against Luke as they were collecting evidence of his innocence? They couldn't let this rest. Luke's side had to uncover the guilty party before he, or *she,* had time to poison the well. They had one article of evidence in the boot print. He needed to know if they had a second piece of evidence with the money clip.

Only one way to know existed.

The usual scents of hay, horseflesh, and sweet feed did little to soften Francis's growing unease. Finished with the chores, he gazed through the tall front doors of the livery and suddenly knew he couldn't wait another moment to do something constructive. The money clip he'd picked up at the scene of the crime was still in his pocket for safekeeping. He'd go see what he might find out.

The walk to Ashley's house took five minutes. He didn't trust speaking to anyone else, and besides, he couldn't go another minute without seeing her. A bevy of nerves raced down his back as he waited at the door. He sure hoped Blanche wouldn't be the one to answer. Her penetrating gaze was unnerving. He'd rather face a cloud of locusts than be alone with that woman. Something frightening lived in her eyes.

The door opened to the scent of lye soap.

A sour expression came over Ashley's mother's face, and her eyes went half-mast. He pushed away his disappointment and struggled to smile.

"May I help you?"

Francis had already removed his hat. "Yes, ma'am. I'm looking for Ashley. I'd like to speak with her for a moment, if I could."

"She's not here. You'll have to come back later."

Her tone let him know she was only too happy that she'd confounded his plans. "Is she out in the orchard, harvesting more apples? Because if she is, I can help again. For a few hours, anyway."

Blanche appeared in the background, still dressed in her bedclothes, her messy hair tumbling into her eyes.

The sooner Ashley was away from that woman, the better.

"No. She's away doing something else," her mother said.

The woman knew but wasn't saying. "Thank you. Will you please tell her I stopped by?"

"No," Blanche said from the hall. "Her seeing you can only come to no good. You may as well set your sights on someone else, cowboy. Ashley's not ruining her life by stepping out with the likes of you."

Seemed the woman had taken over the household. Francis didn't reply, just turned, securing his hat on his head. He wondered where Ashley might be. He'd been around town all morning and hadn't seen her. Where else would she go? Would she be in the schoolhouse? He'd heard that most Sundays the structure sat vacant since they didn't have their own preacher and relied on Reverend Crittlestick from Y Knot or another traveling minister. He'd gone right past the place on his way here. Still, he'd stop in on his way back and see if she was there.

At the church, he took the three steps and paused at the open door, propped wide by a large rock.

Ashley stood at the chalkboard hung on the side wall. She looked up. "Francis?"

He wiped his boots, removed his hat, and proceeded in, setting his Stetson on a bench. He halted in the middle of the room. Confidence warmed him through at seeing her. "Miss Ashley. I went by your house to see how you're holding up."

She glanced around the empty room and then at the doorway. "Mother told you I was here?" Ashley's innocent green eyes made him feel worldly, even though he'd never before been with a woman. The act of lovemaking was still a mystery. He and Fancy, the saloon girl in Y Knot, had a flirtatious relationship, but he liked her too much as a friend, *an older friend*. He couldn't imagine being with her in that way. Here next to Ashley, he felt like a knowledgeable king.

He chuckled. "Not on your life."

Ashley set down the chalk and dusted her hands.

A list of seven names occupied two columns, one for boys and one for girls. "You doing some schoolwork?"

She shrugged, her face turning a light shade of pink. "Just listing the names of the students I expect for the next school term. When the townsfolk come to church service, the names remind them about school. Some are still of the opinion children don't need much more than to know how to read and write. This keeps education in the forefront of their minds. Then my job in September won't be so difficult when time comes to round them up."

Not only pretty, but smart too. She was young to be a schoolteacher, but she was already preparing for the next term. She took her responsibilities seriously. "How long you been teachin'?"

She straightened and a smile appeared. "Just since last year when Blanche got married and quit, putting me in charge. I still have a lot to learn."

Everything about her brought his senses to life. The small lift to her lips, the dark lashes that rimmed her attractive eyes, and the way she made his chest fill up when she looked his way. Did he have any chance with a woman like her?

He came closer, now only a few feet away. She didn't smell like her mother at all, no lye or any other kind of soap, but he did detect a slight scent of honeysuckle, making him a mite light-headed. After closer inspection, he noticed a sprig pinned on the front of her bodice, camouflaged by the flowered pattern of her dress. "How've things been out at your place? How's Blanche? Feeling any better?"

She closed the small space between them as graceful as a flower petal on the wind, the deep concern in her eyes taking him by surprise. She'd always been so adamant that things were fine. As soon as she was close enough, he put out his hands, taking hers into his own, as natural as if they'd been holding hands for years. She was turning to him for help, and he wouldn't let her down.

"I fear she's getting worse. The past three nights she's thrashed around in her sleep so violently I've had to go in and wake her up." Her brow creased with worry. "I'm afraid she may be losing her mind." Her gaze searched his but her warm, soft hands cradled in his own held most of his attention. "Is that possible?" she asked quietly. "I've looked through a medical book I have for class, but haven't found anything. I know she'd be furious if she knew what I was thinking. I did ask her if she'd like to see a doctor. That I'd make the trip with her to Y Knot or Finleyville up north."

"Those are lengthy trips. You'd need others to go with you."

She nodded. "Never mind anyway, because she flatly refused. I don't know what else to do."

"You look tired," he replied, taking in the shadows beneath her eyes. "I don't like you staying in that house with her any longer. I know I'm just your friend, and a new one to boot, but I care about you. I think you should move into town proper. I think that woman might go off her rocker and harm you."

Ashley drew back, their hands fell away, and she stared at him with wide eyes.

He didn't know what had caused her surprised reaction, his saying that about Blanche or his saying he cared. Either way, if the reason got her out of that house, he'd be a happy man.

Her gaze skittered away. "Francis? I... I don't know what to say."

Well, she didn't slap me or tell me to scat. "What I said is true. I do care, Ashley. And I don't want to see you hurt. I won't lie; I don't like Blanche, and your mother doesn't like me. You seem different from them." He rubbed his palm across his face. Was he saying too much? "I think you would be much happier and safer away from those two."

The surprised, caring look fled from her face leaving annoyance. "How can you say such a thing? Who are you to judge *my mother*? You've barely just met her. She may be strict, but she's just looking out for my welfare."

He *was* saying too much, but he'd rather make her mad and keep her safe. Seemed the days were running together. Time was building toward a grand crescendo. He didn't want her involved when things finally let loose. "Maybe she is, but I've observed her enough that doesn't seem the case. I got my feel and I'm not changin'. The skill is like reading animals. With some you just know you have to watch your back. With those two, I'm keeping my eye on 'em at all times. I'm not stupid. I know when someone is out to get me."

Her back snapped straight. "I think you better go."

"Not until we talk about what I came here for."

"Your reason wasn't to denounce my mother and condemn my best friend?"

"If she's your best friend, you need a new one. If I didn't suspect you were in danger, I'd have the luxury of beating around the bush and hinting at my meaning. But I don't. I saw her this morning. That woman could snap any time. She's like a badger with rabies or a clock spring wound too tight. She's ready to blow. When she does, I don't want you anywhere near. And actually, why *is* she being so snappish? Has she always acted that way?"

Ashley's lips thinned, she drew back the tiniest bit. "No."

He longed to reach for her hand again but didn't. "I've seen people grieve before, Ashley," he said, thinking about everyone after Uncle Pete was mauled to death by wolves. "What she's doing ain't it. More is going on in her mind than you believe. And I think we'd both be frightened if we could read her thoughts." Ashley still looked a little put out about what he'd said about her mother and moving into town.

She turned and walked back to her chalkboard, putting a good ten feet between them.

"Y Knot's teacher has been sick on and off for months. The kids have been out of school more than they've been in."

She whirled to face him, something pleasing in her eyes.

Encouragement sprouted. "I heard Rachel McCutcheon talking with her mother-in-law, saying how the children are falling behind." What was he doing? Saying? He'd never felt so bold or certain about anything. He didn't want to lose Ashley after he left town, and he didn't want to leave her here either. Not with those women.

"I have no idea what you're rambling on about, Francis, but I think your doing so is totally inappropriate. Me, move to Y Knot?" She pulled back her shoulders. "That's preposterous. And besides, why would I? My home is here, in Priest's Crossing. My mother and friends. The orchard that we've tended for years…"

Their friendship was too new to tell her about his tender feelings and that she was all he thought about, even when he was supposed to be solving the mystery of who really murdered

Benson. She'd run far and fast. If she told her mother, he'd never get a chance to see her again or speak with her either. He had to play his cards carefully. Keep a few things close to his vest, so to speak, at least for now.

"Maybe I got a little ahead of myself," he replied softly. "But speaking with those two just starts my day off wrong. What I meant to say is: I believe Miss Langford, Y Knot's schoolteacher, is leaving. I heard she wants to be closer to her family. Mrs. McCutcheon was wondering if they should start looking for a replacement." He took a minute to let that sink in while he gathered his thoughts. He gazed around the small room, seeing mostly a country school but also parts of the church. A piano in one corner, a small altar. A cross on the wall. A row of hymnals in the bookshelf. The room had a nice atmosphere. Was this all Ashley's doing?

"I feel a smart young woman like yourself might find a larger town like Y Knot exciting," he went on cautiously. "A stage comes through almost every day. We have a hotel and several restaurants. And a slew of young women for you to be friends with. I haven't seen any here, just older wives or widows. I know Y Knot's not Saint Louis, but from town it's an easy day's ride to Waterloo. That town has a dress shop called the Red Door that all the ladies seem to like better than Christmas. Other shops too. And best, train access to Cheyenne and places beyond." He'd dug his grave. He might as well keep going all the way to China.

Her chin jutted out and she folded her arms across her chest. She couldn't see his vision... yet.

"Anything else, Francis, while you're sketching out my life? Why stop now?"

"Since you asked, yes, there is. I'd like the chance to get to know you better. If you were in Y Knot, I could do that. Take you to the Biscuit Barrel for pie or to listen to the Twilight Singers on a warm summer evening. You ever taste the huckleberry pie from the Biscuit Barrel?" He patted his belly. "If not, you're missing something special."

There. She'd almost smiled. Maybe the hole he was digging might not be his grave after all.

"I haven't had the pleasure," she replied, a bit softer this time. "But we have huckleberries here in Priest's Crossing, as well, and they're delicious. I've been to Y Knot a time or two. Been to the mercantile when I took a quick trip with Christine. Mr. Lichtenstein has a very nice selection of items—but the place is just a town." She gave a dismissive wave. "Just like many others scattered about."

"Oh, really? Ever been to the field of fossils?" This woman was educated. He'd need to pull out the big guns to get her attention. No way could she resist something so historical. He didn't miss the spark of interest in her eyes just at the mention. "I can see you there with a handful of schoolchildren, teaching 'em all about those prehistoric creatures—and then maybe having a picnic afterward under the tall cottonwoods with soft white cotton drifting all around. Everyone I know likes spending time there."

Her eyes had gone dreamy, but skepticism crept back into her face. "What do you know about fossils?"

He smiled, turning on all his charm. "Not much at all. But I've seen my share and would like to learn more." *Especially if you're doing the teaching.*

Chapter Thirty-Five

Y Knot? What was Francis thinking? Most teachers went through a two-year course at a normal school to receive a teaching certificate. They were proficient in their usage of the English language, could do their sums as well, and had a firm knowledge of the history of the Americas and Europe. What did she have to offer? Other than being the brightest student in the school, the oldest female, and an avid reader, devouring most books in a few days. Teaching here in Priest's Crossing was one thing, because everyone had known her for years. And not much money was provided for a salary, a pittance compared to most places. But going to a new town where she'd be expected to prove herself was quite another. Francis didn't know what he was talking about.

"Well," he said, searching her face. "Don't you have confidence in yourself? Would the children in Y Knot be any different than the children here in Priest's Crossing? I don't understand."

"Of course, you don't." That was all she had.

"Try me," he responded.

He was working to understand her. A tolerant look in his eyes warmed her through. They'd only known each other three days. How on earth could he have a grasp on any of his feelings? They'd never had a disagreement of any merit. She knew nothing about his family, and he knew very little about hers. What kind of a man was Francis, anyway? His having feelings for her was something he must have made up in his head.

Could that be true? I do feel something for him. Why, I was thinking of him a few minutes ago, before he walked through the door. I'm not being honest with him, or even myself. I've never believed in love at first sight, but now I'm not so sure. "I haven't had a formal education, Francis. Y Knot is so much larger than Priest's Crossing. I'm sure the school council will want to advertise in larger cities. Interview applicants who have a teaching credential. That's something I don't have."

The small smile pulling one side of his lips fell away. "That may be, but at least you should try. Be one of those applicants. Maybe your experience will outweigh their schooling. Maybe your living in the region will be a benefit. Did you have any experience helping the teacher before the year you took over?"

Excitement rippled through her. She hadn't thought about those tasks. "Yes, I do. For the past three years, I've assisted Blanche with all aspects of the day. Even helping some of the children who were older than me." Living here in Priest's Crossing and farming the apple orchard was so settled in her mind, she'd never considered she could do something else. Did Francis know what he was talking about? "And I was in total charge of the first and second graders. Only two students, mind you, but I was the one who taught them their letters and how to read. Simple math too." A small spurt of pride warmed her face. She'd done more than she realized. Perhaps Francis was right.

Francis glanced at the open door.

Did he have other obligations? "I'll consider your words. About Y Knot," she said.

Pride shone from his eyes. "That's all I ask."

She glanced at the chalkboard. She should finish here and get back home. Those apples wouldn't jump off the branches themselves. If she left them too long, the birds would pick the trees clean and the ants as well. When the harvesting rolled around, time really *was* of the essence. "Thank you for stopping by, but I really should get back to work."

"Actually, I have a question for you. One I'd like you to keep secret, for the time being."

Suspicion filtered through her. Was this the real reason for his visit? Something about Luke McCutcheon, she was sure. He'd certainly taken a roundabout way of buttering her up for the information he wanted. Angry at herself for falling for his duplicity, she once again crossed her arms across her chest. "This concerns Blanche, doesn't it? If your answer's yes, I'm not guaranteeing anything."

"In all honesty, I'm not sure who this concerns. Might be about her and maybe not. That's what I'd like to figure out." He gave her a long look. "But keeping quiet about what I show you could be a matter of life or death. After the trial, you can talk all you want."

How could she refuse such an earnest look? "Yes, I'll keep whatever we speak about between us. Go ahead, you can trust me."

Nodding, he reached into his pocket and then held out his hand. "Have you ever seen this before?"

She stared. Neil Huntsman's money clip rested in Francis's palm. The intensity of the way he watched her told her this matter was of great importance, that his friend's life depended on her answer.

"Ashley? Is this familiar?"

She didn't want to incriminate anyone. Especially Neil Huntsman. She loved Tilly, and Tilly set the stars by her husband. And she was expecting. How could she point an accusing finger his way?

"Ashley?"

Still… if Neil was involved, keeping back the truth was a crime. Luke McCutcheon shouldn't shoulder the blame. Had Neil been carrying on with Blanche and then killed Benson in his own cabin? That was difficult to believe. Neil and Tilly made such a beautiful couple. What would happen to Tilly, and the sweet, innocent babe, if Neil was taken away? Some other reason had to be why Francis was asking. Had she jumped to a crazy wrong conclusion?

"Your silence tells me everything. You know something."

She looked into his face. She couldn't tell a lie. "Yes. I believe Neil Huntsman is the proper owner."

"Neil?" The name gushed out of Francis on a breath. He cut his gaze away to stare at the ceiling. Seemed he didn't want to believe the fact either. "You sure?"

"Yes. I was in the store one day when he came in. Tilly was working. She mentioned she needed money for something she wanted to buy. He took that out of his pocket and peeled a dollar bill from the stack. I remember thinking he carried around a lot of money for a banker. You know, they're always telling people to deposit their cash in the bank."

He put the clip in her hand. "Could his have been something like this but different? We must be absolutely sure."

Agitation gripped her as the cold metal weighted her palm. "Mixing up this design would be difficult. I've never seen one to match. The gun is so intricate. What does this mean, Francis?

Do you think Neil killed Benson? That's the only reason you'd ask."

He arched a brow. "The fewer people who know, the better."

"You trusted me enough to ask. Now I'm asking you…"

"The clip was wedged between the cushions at the Van Gleek cabin. To your knowledge, were Tilly and Blanche friends? Would there be any reason that she and Neil may have gone out to the cabin on a visit? If yes, then Neil may have lost the money clip then."

"No, none at all. The two women hate each other. Blanche knows about Tilly's past. She's one of the only people in town that still holds her saloon girl days against her, and because of that treatment, Tilly detests Blanche. They aren't in a room together for long. One or the other always ends up leaving."

Francis frowned. "I was hoping for a different answer."

"That doesn't mean he's guilty," she insisted, still refusing to believe Neil and Blanche could have been involved in some way. "Maybe he went out to the cabin to talk with Benson. Maybe the two men had business. Maybe Benson was having money issues and had asked for a loan?"

"That's possible, I guess." Francis rubbed his hand over his chin. "Other than a loan, I can't imagine what a banker and a freighter have to talk about. This case just keeps getting stranger by the day."

He looked deep into her eyes causing a warm flutter in her tummy.

"I best be going," he said low, holding her gaze. "Thanks again for your help." He put the money clip back into his pocket and picked up his hat on his way out.

She watched him descend the steps and disappear out of sight. Concern for his safety pushed at her lungs. If

McCutcheon wasn't guilty, the real killer may be tracking Francis's every move. As he came ever closer to the truth, would he, *or she,* act again? The possibility was frightening. Was Francis watching out for her safety, when in all reality, she should be watching out for his?

Chapter Thirty-Six

"Good news, McCutcheon," Jack Jones said, sticking his head into the cell area of the sheriff's office. "Just got word by courier ol' Judge Wesley retired and is in the process of moving to Y Knot. Might even be there now. Denver circuit gave him dispensation to rule over cases when needed, *if* he wants. That's pretty handy, I'd say. I've sent word to Y Knot to send him this way. He could arrive any time."

Jack beamed as if that was the first right thing he'd ever done in his life. Probably *was*. Was Jack looking for approval? What a joke. He'd never get that from Luke... but Luke *would* play along. See what he could find out. At least Jack was trying. Clark, his deputy, was another story. He sat up. "By courier, huh?"

Jack nodded.

"About time we made some progress," Luke mumbled from his place on the cot. He ran a hand down the front of the rumpled shirt Faith brought him. After an early visit this morning, she'd yet to come back. Roady either, or any of the men. He wondered where everyone was and felt a mite put out. "Should we throw a party when he arrives?" he said, not hiding his cynicism.

Jack's hopeful expression hardened. He hooked one thumb in his waistband while he held a cup of coffee in the other. A heavy silver Colt rested in his holster, and a star was pinned to his chest.

Galling, to say the least.

"I thought you'd be pleased. But I can see that you're as disparaging as ever."

Luke scratched his scalp, thinking how greasy his hair felt. He hadn't shaved in days. "What was your *first* clue?"

"That ugly frown on your face."

Luke studied Jack from his sitting position. The days had blurred. He was damn ready to get out of his cell. Harrison Wesley was a good friend. How would the lawman deal with the fact Blanche would swear on a Bible Luke had murdered her husband right before her eyes? An eyewitness carried a lot of weight. Could the judge be swayed by her words? Could be too the judge might have good friends in Priest's Crossing like he did in Y Knot. Would that hold any merit? Nothing in this peculiar case would surprise him.

"Don't be so touchy, Luke," Jack said. "I'm doing my best. We're taking fine care of you. Making sure you have plenty of good food and coffee. Didn't I bring you a glass of whiskey the other night? What more could you want? The law's the law! I was obliged to lock you up."

Jack's stupidity was amazing. And his whiny voice made Luke want to holler. "What'll you do when Harrison sets me free, Jack? Scramble around and start your investigation then? The real killer will be long gone. Or maybe not. Could be he's right here in town under your nose, watching the show. You better hope no more innocent people get killed. That wouldn't look good on your record. You're not cut out to be a lawman,

Jack. You should have learned your lesson in Y Knot and tried your hand at something else."

Jack lifted his coffee cup to his lips, took a drink, and then studied him for several long minutes. "I don't know nothin' else, Luke. Being deputy for Brandon was my first full-time job. I did the best I could. I didn't hear anyone complainin'."

Luke grasped a bar in frustration. "That's hogwash! You weren't listening to the right people."

Deputy Clark stepped into the room. "Stop spilling your guts to the prisoner." He narrowed his eyes at Jones. "He's the one locked up, not you. Did I hear something about a judge being on his way here?"

Luke didn't miss his disrespectful tone and the way he glared at Jack.

"You heard right. Possibility we'll get Wesley. He's supposed to be in Y Knot."

That news seemed to go in one ear and out the other.

Clark smirked as he made a deliberate search around the room. "Your pretty wife getting tired of sitting in here day after day, holding your hand, half-breed? Can't say as I blame her any. She's way too good for you."

People might talk behind his back about his breeding, but this was the first time in years anyone besmirched him straight to his face and smiled in the process. Clark wouldn't dare if these bars weren't keeping him safe. Took some getting used to. He wondered what was being said out there on the street. He didn't like dragging the McCutcheon name through the mud, just like when he was a kid, but here he was, repeating history.

Jack glared at his deputy, which did little to wipe the smirk off his face. "Ain't no call to talk like that, Hoss. He's a prisoner and no need to rile him up."

"I got every right!" He pointed at Luke. "What kind of a man are you? Sometimes I wonder."

Jack looked like he was about to take the deputy on, but at the last minute, he didn't.

"Getting back to Mrs. McCutcheon," Clark said, "I like her. She's gonna need a new man once you hang. She's always smiling at me when you're not looking. I wonder if that means anything?"

Luke slowly lifted himself off his cot, wishing like hell he were free. "You better hope I never get out of this cell, Clark." The long, intense glare he gave the deputy made the man take a step back. "Because I don't forget. You'll regret you mentioned my wife. I can guarantee you that." His tone had gone deadly. Clark was strongly built, with powerful arms and legs. Jack would be powerless against him. But Clark didn't scare Luke. Not for a second.

Jack glanced back and forth between them.

Faith stepped through the door with Smokey and Colton. She stopped and scrutinized him and then turned to Jack and Clark. "What?"

Luke never took his narrowed gaze off Clark. Would the man dare touch his wife in any way? The thought made his fingertips tingle. Even worse, would he do something to harm her? Was he the killer? He needed to warn Smokey to be all the more alert. Could he find a way to get her home? "Nothin' important, sweetheart. Just jailhouse talk."

"Luke?"

Smokey looked tense himself. He'd worked for Luke long enough to know when to be concerned.

Jack's Adam's apple bobbed once. "I was just telling Luke he may be in luck. Got word about a judge. Harrison Wesley is on his way to Y Knot and might be there already."

Faith gasped. She turned back and smiled at Luke. "Harrison! Really? That's wonderful news, isn't it, Luke?"

Clark hadn't looked at Faith once, but his nostrils flared at her reaction. Luke wished she'd thought to keep their friendship to herself.

With his arms crossed over his chest, the deputy stared back.

Luke could just imagine what he was thinking.

Chapter Thirty-Seven

Roady held the door as Pedro and Shad entered his and Francis's small hotel room. "Take a seat," he said quietly. Pedro sat at the foot of Francis's bed, the covers thrown up haphazardly, while Shad took a chair by the window, the creaking of the old wood the only sound in the room.

Scents of dried grass, flowers in bloom, and the need for a long summer rain wafted inside. The blissful summer smells were in opposition with the seriousness of the meeting at hand. They'd eaten their breakfast across the street in the restaurant. Luke should be free by now. Out from behind bars and back in Y Knot. They were due some kind of break in the case.

Wary, Roady glanced at Shad and Pedro and mentally kicked himself for not bringing along more ranch hands.

After breakfast, Faith had insisted she take Colton for a walk out of town in the hills, somewhere where the boy could get his mind off his pa. The boy was brooding. Hadn't said more than a few words to any of them, believing this fiasco was his fault. And of course, where she and Colton went, Smokey went too.

Hopefully they wouldn't stay away from the jail too long. Luke was tense, and Roady couldn't blame him in the least. But Roady agreed the walk would be a good diversion. After they'd eaten, Francis went to check the stock. Roady didn't have a clue about Nick, and doubted Shad knew either. That kid was a livewire.

"I'm more than worried," Roady said. "We've only ruled out two men from Francis measuring boots he'd seen lying around. This case building is taking too long. By the time we find the real killer, we'll have one foot in the grave ourselves."

Pedro took out his cigarette papers and began to roll a smoke.

"Anyone have anything new to report? Any baffling sly looks, people who may have any unexplainable cuts or bruises? Things like that." He knew they didn't. If anyone came up with something, he reported right away. Roady was pulling at straws. "We gotta find out who made that bloodstained footprint in the cabin."

Shad leaned forward, resting his forearms on his thighs. "Has anyone done any checking on the money clip? That may be our best clue. Why wait?"

"Yeah, you're right. Ask Francis. As soon as he shows up, I'll get started with Joe's wife. Anyone see Fox Dancing or Painted Bear Stone last night? Luke says they're here, but I've not seen a trace."

"They stay hidden," Pedro whispered. "I see them, or should I say they let me see them. They make sure no one takes Luke from jail before trial." He inhaled, held the smoke for a moment, and then let a white trail drift up into his eyes.

For as much progress as they'd made, the lot of 'em could have just stayed home at the ranch. How was Sally faring? And Gillian? His brand-spanking-new daughter of only a few weeks. Did she miss her pa? He'd hated to leave them so soon after her birth, but with Brandon gone, he hadn't had a choice. He ached to hold her and Sally too.

Sally had done so well in labor, hardly making a sound even though the birth lasted over twenty-four hours. That night was the longest of his life. With each hour that passed, his fears had grown. Hayden did his best to keep him sane each time he heard a cry or whimper coming from down the hall, but delivery is a hell only an expectant father can know.

"Roady?"

The men looked at him, strange expressions on their faces.

"Where'd you go, man?" Shad asked.

"Slipped back to—"

At that moment, Nick came through the door. "Sorry I'm late," he said, making his way to the vacant bed to sit. "Heard some talk while I was at the barber." He motioned to his newly trimmed hair.

Shad's face turned stony. "You think you had time for a haircut and shave?"

Nick scowled back at his brother and ran fingers over his ears. "Sometimes the best place to hear natter is where you'd least expect, like under a barber's hot towel."

Pedro mumbled something, nodding.

"Anyway, if you'll let me finish, you just might be patting me on the back. Like I said, my face was hidden under a towel when I heard voices of men in the doorway. They asked how long until the barber would be free. Then one of them said Luke's name, and my ears perked up."

Shad leaned forward.

Roady held his breath. Nick better not be blowing smoke to get out of trouble for being late. "And?" he prompted. Sometimes Nick had a way of enhancing the story. "Did you see who was talking?"

Nick glanced around the room, looking each man in the eye. "They dropped their voices, but I heard the word rope and then lynch. That's when I pretended to sneeze and peeked out." He sternly raised a brow. "And I want you to know, I almost got my throat cut in the process too. Anyway, the men were Daniel Clevenger and Pink Kelly. They heard Judge Wesley might be on his way. Everyone knows the McCutcheons and Wesley are good friends. They were going on that he'll release Luke no matter what Mrs. Van Gleek says."

If Nick was worried, then they'd better up their game, get to work, *real work*, and also come up with an alternate plan in case Wesley didn't arrive in time. Roady squared his shoulders. "I won't let Luke be lynched."

The men watched him in silence.

"I'm in," Pedro whispered. "Smokey will be too. And no question about Francis."

"And me." Shad looked at his brother, who nodded.

Relief washed through Roady. These men were ranchers, not hired guns. He couldn't expect them to put their lives on the line if they didn't want to. "Then we need to come up with a plan in case anyone decides to do more than talk." The guns were still hidden in the ripped-up floorboards of an abandoned house on the outskirts of town. "Time to retrieve our weapons," he said. "To have on hand. Nick, when Francis gets back, the two of you take care of that. Split them up in these two rooms where we can get to them quickly but where they won't be found."

Nick sat up and glanced around. "Hey, where is Francis?"

"He'll be along."

Nick scoffed. "With Miss Adair, no doubt."

Nick's sour expression rankled Roady's nerves.

"He's more interested in her than springing Luke," Nick said.

"Hold up," Shad demanded before Roady could get out the words.

"Did you hear your orders, Nick?" Roady asked, reining in his temper. "I don't want you complaining you didn't understand." Nick was a flirt, where Francis was stalwart and a bit shy. Someday the two might come to blows.

"Sure I did. I can do the job myself if he don't show up soon. Probably easier," he finished, mumbling under his breath. "Just give the go-ahead, and I'll be happy to."

"Right now, I want the two of you to do the chore together. Won't be easy gettin' 'em moved without being seen. Clark knows they're stashed somewhere, and he's been watchin'."

Once they had some firepower, Roady would feel a hell of a lot better, even if hidden away close. Walking around town with the hostility aimed their way was no picnic. They were the good guys, not the bad guys. The sooner Harrison Wesley showed up, the better he'd sleep.

Chapter Thirty-Eight

Francis was daydreaming about Ashley when somebody screamed. For one instant, he thought Blanche had gone into the empty schoolhouse and somehow hurt Ashley, but then he realized the sound came from the opposite direction. The cry sounded like a female, but it wasn't Faith. He'd recognize her voice. He started to town with purpose.

Ashley appeared at his side, breathing hard. She gripped his arm. "I heard someone screaming?"

"I did too." He hitched his head. "I was just on my way back. Come with me." They turned onto a small connecting street. Several small row houses in need of serious repair leaned this way and that. Jack Jones and Deputy Clark had just arrived, evident by the way they gaped around. Daniel Clevenger stood on the porch of one house, the white apron still wrapped around his waist as he held an old woman's arm.

She sagged and looked about to faint.

"That's Mrs. Lee," Ashley said quietly by his side. "She's in her eighties and lives next door. This is Mildred Kane's house. Since Mr. Lee died, the women have been inseparable. I hope the worst hasn't happened."

They slowly drew closer as others ventured from the main part of town.

"I went inside when Mildred didn't answer the door." Mrs. Lee's voice wobbled with emotion. "We often looked out for each other. But I found her in the basement. Looks like she fell down the steps." Her words faded, and she began to cry. "What an awful way to die," she moaned between sobs. "Falling and hurting yourself all alone." An agonizing groan escaped her lips. "What will I do without her, Sheriff?" Turning her head, she looked up into Clevenger's face and then back at the sheriff. "I just don't know what I'll do."

Ashley and Francis exchanged a look.

"There's a dark cloud over this town," Francis whispered. "I'll be glad to return to Y Knot."

"I have to go to her." Ashley stepped forward.

"In a moment." Francis guided her around a handful of onlookers to the back of the house. They were alone. "I'm sure Jack won't let me go inside the house if I ask, so I'm not going to," he whispered.

"Why would you want to? What could you possibly want to see inside Mrs. Kane's home? I know you want to clear your boss, but what on earth would this tragedy have to do with that arrest? None of this makes a bit of sense."

He counted the few freckles across the bridge of her nose he'd just noticed in the sunshine. "You sure? Two deaths in thirteen days? We don't know what we don't know." He waited for her reaction.

"She was old, Francis! She missed a step and fell." Her lips pulled down, and she plunked fisted hands on her hips. "What could be strange about that? I think you've let this situation go to your head. You're running around town like a Pinkerton detective looking for clues—and I believe you're enjoying yourself."

"That's where you're wrong," he responded, fighting against anger at her words. "Things couldn't be more serious. Luke needs my help. I'll do anything I can to find the real killer so he can go free. The McCutcheons have been the only family I've ever known. I owe them *everything*. I'll not let them down, not if I can do something to help."

He hadn't meant to sound so gruff. Unable to stop himself, he touched the end of her nose. "I'm going in," he said softly. "Can you wait here?" Still quiet out back, most people, he was sure, had moved on, writing off Mildred's death to old age and an accident. A clothesline with a few towels drying wasn't far away and a barrel of water up against the house. Lattice on one side of the back porch was covered in flowering morning glories.

All seemed peaceful. Voices from the front floated on the air.

With his foot on the bottom step, she grabbed his arm. "Shouldn't I go with you?"

"No. If someone comes, keep them talking, and I'll try to sneak out a side window. Or hide behind a curtain." He couldn't stop a lopsided grin. "I'll think of something. The law in this town is already fed up with us McCutcheon men prying into their business. I don't want to add to our troubles."

When she nodded, a warm feeling pushed at his chest. Stepping away, he cringed when the door let out a loud screech. Moving even an inch was impossible without the floor squeaking, as well. Jack was already inside, as well as his deputy. Their voices carried easily from the front room. He looked around the kitchen as he listened.

"She misjudged her steps," Clark said matter-of-factly. "She was old as the hills. Everyone cashes in their chips eventually."

"I don't know," Jack replied. "I liked Mildred. She cooked me supper twice a month. Looked like maybe her neck broke."

Sunshine streaming through the kitchen window made the room bright. Francis glanced outside at Ashley wringing her hands as she kept watch. Was there anything to find? Any clues?

"We'll need another coffin." Clark's voice easily carried to the kitchen. "Business has been good for the undertaker this month." The sound of footsteps stopped. "Who's gonna pay for the pine box?"

"Geez, Hoss, you can be a real heel. I'll pay, if I have to. Just get over to the undertaker and report this."

More footsteps and then quiet. Francis hoped Jack had left too.

Had this been a murder or an accident like everyone thought? Clean dishes were stacked in a rack next to the sink as if they'd been washed, two of everything. On the counter was a half-eaten cake. Other than that, the place was as neat as a pin. Francis crept closer to the front rooms.

"Did you see anything?"

So Jack was still here.

"Why, Sheriff?" Mrs. Lee asked timidly. "Do you think foul play was involved?" A new round of tears sounded and then some shushing noises.

"No. My job entails asking. When was the last time you spoke with Mildred? Did you see her yesterday?"

"We always have morning tea. Then again in the afternoon. She came to borrow some eggs to bake a cake."

Francis looked over at the chocolate cake.

"Why was she baking?"

"Don't know. She often has company, but she didn't say anything."

Francis walked softly over to the cake, bent down, and gave a good sniff. His empty stomach growled in protest. Would eating a piece be unseemly? With his back against the wall, Francis slipped down the hall and darted into a bedroom. Just as neat as the rest of the house.

Who would want to hurt Mildred? What kind of a threat could she have posed? Had she seen something and finally decided to talk? Had she questioned the wrong person? Or had her fall been completely innocent and, like the deputy said, the grim reaper came to call? So many unanswered questions.

More determined than ever, Francis started back the way he'd come, anxious to see Ashley, when he spotted something on the kitchen floor. Squatting, he found several pieces of straw. He held them to his nose. *Manure.* Not unusual for a town like this. He glanced around. Not uncommon for a man's house, possibly, or someone who wore boots. But definitely unusual for Mildred's house. Besides the dishes stacked neatly, the place was clean—spotlessly so. No corrals were around her home either.

Did the straw come from my own boots? Unlikely. He'd walked a good stretch since leaving the livery. And he'd wiped them clean before entering the church. He should report right away to Roady, but first he'd speak with Neil Huntsman.

Chapter Thirty-Nine

Poor Mildred. What a horrible way to die. Sorrow gripped Ashley as she followed Francis up the street, moving quickly to keep up with his long stride. A few bystanders lingered on the boardwalk, glancing toward the old woman's house, which used to be a haven of hominess, in need of a little upkeep outside but cozy. Deputy Clark stood next to Jed Kasterlee, the hotel proprietor. She heard in passing the undertaker was on his way to collect Mildred's body.

"Francis, you never said if you found anything inside her house. You were gone more than a few minutes. Can you share?"

"Not here. And not until Roady hears what I have to say. The boys were having a meeting this morning, and I went and forgot."

"That's because you were speaking with me in the schoolhouse." She responded to his warm smile with one of her own. "Where are you going now, back to the hotel?"

His jaw clenched and released several times, capturing her attention. He was a good foot and a half taller than she was, and with his wide shoulders, strong, chiseled chin, stately nose and oh-so-expressive eyes and eyebrows, she thought he was just about the most handsome man she'd ever seen. And he seemed so wise for his age. She liked that about him. Most men's gazes went to one place fast. She'd never noticed him once trying to ogle her in that way.

"Not quite yet," he replied. "This money clip is burning a hole in my pocket. The sooner I find out about Huntsman, the better. If the piece is not his, my work is not done." He stopped his strides and looked down into her eyes. "Do you have to be somewhere? Or do you want to come along? My work could turn into your work too." He smiled.

I need to be harvesting my apples, but I really want to spend time with Francis. What will a few more minutes matter? "Yes, now that you've involved me in your detective work, I'm curious as well. I hope and pray Tilly's husband's not involved."

"In what?"

They both skidded to a halt, and she exchanged a wide-eyed glance with Francis when she realized Jed Kasterlee had caught what she'd said as they passed by his door. She'd had to put the man in his place a time or two over the years, but now he treated her with respect.

"In letting the secret out about a gathering I'm planning for the coming baby," Ashley blurted, feeling horrible about being the one who may have blown Francis's cover. "I'm having a small surprise for the ladies." She waggled a finger in his direction. "Now, don't you go and say anything to her or anyone else."

He smiled and ambled out of his doorway where he'd been standing in the shadows. "I don't much speak with Tilly anymore. Neil makes sure of that. Your secret is safe with me."

"Thank you, Mr. Kasterlee." She chanced a glance up at Francis, who regarded her with a skeptical half smile. "Sorry," she said quietly as they walked off. "That was close. I'll have to learn to keep my mouth shut if I'm to help you."

His brows rose but he didn't stop walking. "Does this mean you're on our side?"

The small sardonic smile was back, making little flutters warm her insides. "Partially. And if I learn information that will corroborate Blanche's story, I'll share that as well. I'm keeping an open mind."

"That's all I ask." Francis opened the door to the small bank next to the mercantile, allowing Ashley to enter before him.

Neil was in the back of the room, doing something next to a large standing safe. When he turned, a friendly smile lit his face. "Miss Adair. What brings you into the bank today?" He glanced at Francis and nodded.

She was at a loss and glanced at Francis.

"Hello, Mr. Huntsman. I don't know if you remember me. I'm Francis, and I work for the Heart of the Mountains ranch in Y Knot. I'm the one needing your help. Miss Adair was just showing me the town."

The corners of Neil's lips pulled up into a small smile. He gave her a secretive wink.

Word would be around town that she was stepping out with Francis. The thought pleased her until she thought of her mother and Blanche. Neither one would welcome the news.

"What can I help you with, Francis? Did you want to open an account?"

"Uh, no. We'll all be gone as soon as Luke's released from jail, and we expect that to happen soon."

Neil's brows rose. "I hope you're right. Then what do you need?"

"Can I get a wire transfer from the bank in Y Knot? We're running low on funds."

Was that true? Everyone knew the McCutcheons were wealthy. Hadn't Luke's wife arrived in town a few days ago?

Surely she'd have brought enough money to last the extent of their stay.

"Not until Priest's Crossing gets another telegraph," Neil replied.

"Any plans for that to happen?"

"Nope. I'm sorry. Not much call for wire transfers, although that doesn't help you. If you'd like, I can talk to my boss about giving Mrs. McCutcheon a loan for the time you're here, but under the circumstances, that might be a problem as well. But I won't know for sure until I speak with him."

Francis leaned his elbow on the counter between them and rubbed his chin.

Ashley didn't like fooling Mr. Huntsman, even for a good cause.

"I'll tell Mrs. McCutcheon." He straightened and crooked his elbow. "Ready, Miss Adair? I guess we'll…" He quickly turned back. "Oh, by the way, I overheard talk in the café that you have a special money clip that looks like a gun. Thing is, I have a memory of something like that from before I was taken in by the McCutcheons. Way back when I was a child."

Neil's smile faded. "Who was talking about me? Do you remember when it was?"

Francis shrugged. "The days are all runnin' together like molasses in a can. Even if I could recall, I hardly know anyone. Just wondered if I might have a look, for old time's sake." He held up a hand. "But only if you don't mind." He glanced at Neil's pocket.

Neil gave a small laugh and headed to the back of the room. "I keep that piece locked up. Give me a moment."

Francis seemed intent on looking at the teller's feet.

"What on earth are you doing?" she whispered close to his ear.

Francis hadn't stopped looking at Neil's boots since the teller turned away. "I'm killing two birds with one stone." He smiled into her eyes, making breathing difficult. "Would you say he and I wear the same size boot?"

Shocked, she pulled back. "What?"

Neil worked the combination to the safe.

"His boots?" He held up his for her to see.

She glanced to the door and windows. "You're crazy."

"Maybe. But check out his feet before he comes back to the counter." He glanced at the safe and then back at her. "Well?"

"Uh…" Francis was much taller than Neil. "His are smaller," she whispered.

"You're doing fine," Francis softly said. "I like working with you. I think we make a darn good team."

Heat rushed to her face, which only made his smile widen.

Mr. Huntsman was on his way back with something in his hand.

"Well, I'll be," Francis said, his eyes going wide. "It's just how I remembered. Would you mind if I…?" He held out his hand.

"Course not." Neil placed the clip in his palm.

"Where'd you get it?" Francis asked, never taking his attention off the clip. "I'd swear the design is exactly like the one I recall. But that's all I remember. Not where I was or who I was with."

"A peddler came through town about a year ago. Had a bunch of stuff in his wagon, but only two of these."

A clue! Francis really was good at this.

"Two, you say. Do you know who purchased the other one? I'd sure like to see that too."

Neil lifted a shoulder. "Nope, I don't. When I bought mine, the other was still there."

Francis handed back the money clip.

She almost laughed at his dreamy look of nostalgia. He was a good actor, as well as a good detective. An aspect of him she should remember.

"Thank you, Mr. Huntsman. I appreciate your time."

Back out on the boardwalk, she grasped his arm and hauled him to a stop when he started toward the hotel. "I'll ask again… what on earth? What was all that business about boot size? I've never heard the like."

"Just doin' a day's work."

Feeling a bubble of annoyance she stepped back and raised her chin. "You're not the kind of man who does senseless things to impress others or get a laugh, I hope. I didn't take you for that, Francis, and I'm disappointed if you are."

He let out a loud chortle. "No. I'm just a regular ranch hand, nothing more, nothing less. Matter of fact, most times I let others run the show. But not now. Luke's life is too important. And I like Tilly too much to hornswoggle her husband. Mrs. McCutcheon isn't really looking for a loan, but at the time I needed an answer that made sense. And I can tell you I'm greatly relieved I can mark Neil Huntsman off my list of suspects. I never want to see anything bad happen to Tilly now that she's found happiness."

That was a sweet sentiment, she thought, moving slowly by his side. Francis was clearly enjoying himself. His eyes fairly danced with humor.

"I guess I better get back to my work, and then I have more harvesting to do."

She dreaded going home. Surely her mother would ask where she'd been for so long. She'd only meant to stay at the school for a few minutes. To get out of the house and stretch her legs. Now she'd have to do some explaining.

But why should I have to? I'm an adult. I have a job and am making my own way, albeit with my mother, but I'm supporting her as well. Do I ever get to have a life of my own?

An unbidden thought of Y Knot slipped into her mind. What would life be like there? Living on her own? Working hard but enjoying every moment? With Francis to keep her company and other friends to make? Did the town really have young women with whom she could socialize? The thought was more enticing than she'd like to believe.

Francis never looked as handsome as he did today, and the fact he had her grandfather's manly name made him all the more attractive. Was she just a summertime fling to him? Did he sweet talk all the girls? Did he have young women all around the countryside sighing at his every word? Surely someone as handsome as Francis must have admirers falling at his feet. As soon as the trial was over, would he pack up and leave, move on to another adventure and another woman? She needed to be smart. She didn't want to end up with a broken heart.

"I'm sorry to part ways, Ashley, but I have to go find Roady and see what I missed at the meeting. He won't be happy that I skipped. Thanks for your help—and company. Remember what I asked you."

He warmed her with another heart-stopping smile. "I'll not say a word," she replied. "You already have my promise, but if you want to double-pinky promise, I'm willing."

He chuckled. "Double-pinky what?" He cocked an eyebrow. "What's that? And do I really want to know?"

She quickly glanced around and then pulled him into an alley by his shirtsleeve. Satisfied they weren't the object of anyone's attention, she explained, "It's a practice that comes from Japan, of all places. Go like this." She held up her baby finger and waited until he did the same. Going slowly, she wrapped her finger around his, all the while smiling like a fool. The contact of his rough skin on hers caused a cocoon of euphoria. She thought she might faint. The only thing that kept her on her feet was the fact he was grinning like a fool as well. They stared into each other's eyes, the feelings holding her spellbound.

He gave a gentle tug.

She came closer. So close the front of her blouse touched his shirt. With the brevity of a sparrow's wing, he brushed her lips with his. She felt her heart melt, and she opened her eyes to find him smiling still. "You're not acting now, are you, Francis?" she whispered, her lips touching his.

"I can assure you I'm not, Miss Adair. And if you give me permission, I'd like nothin' better than to kiss you again. A proper kiss, not that little peck. I'm hoping you'll say yes."

Giddy happiness bubbled inside as Ashley nodded and waited for another trip to heaven she knew was about to happen in Francis's arms.

Chapter Forty

Colton hunkered down by the front door of the sheriff's office, his chin resting in his palm as he gazed into the street. He was forbidden to leave this spot. His pa had asked him to keep an eye out for clues, but Colton knew that was just his way of making him feel better.

Everyone thought him a kid. Even Pa. *Especially Pa.* If Colton hadn't snuck off the morning of the wedding, none of this would have happened. A deep, hurting hole opened up inside.

How Luke must rue the day he set eyes on me. Because of Colton, Luke might actually be hanged for murder.

Nobody, not even Francis, had shared with him about the bloody boot print the men found in the cabin six days ago. He'd heard bits and pieces from the hands by eavesdropping.

Sullenly, he kicked out and sent a dirt clod into the street. His mother was in the jail now, with Smokey and his pa. What would happen? Each day that passed, Colton's fear grew. All sorts of horrible outcomes tortured his mind. How he wished his grandfather were here. Flood would take care of the misunderstanding straightaway. Or either of his uncles. Jack Jones, or, more to the point, Hoss Clark, his toad-faced deputy, had the men at a standoff.

Francis secretly, but slowly, ruled out suspects, but the process took too long. Reverberation of the wooden boardwalk made him look around.

Tilly and the woman from the mercantile were headed his way. Feeling conspicuous, he glanced in the other direction as they advanced, his face heating, cheeks stinging with shame. His pa had taught him a man didn't ignore anyone. To do so was rude. Everyone deserved at least to be acknowledged, even with a dip of a chin or a touch to his hat brim, but he just couldn't today. He'd been the recipient of countless angry, speculative looks.

"Colton?"

Too bad. She was using proper manners and not giving him an easy out by walking by without a word. Heat stung the backs of his eyes. He turned up his face and then slowly stood. Tilly's boss, Joe Brunn's sister, looked none too pleased to be speaking with the enemy.

"I thought that was you," Tilly said with a caring smile. She wore a starched white apron over a pink dress. A creamy-white cameo was pinned just below the soft-looking lace around her neck.

He knew the story of how she used to be a saloon girl in Y Knot and how she'd set her cap on marrying a McCutcheon—especially Luke. Colton didn't remember much, being he was younger when he'd first come to town with his ma. But Tilly had been there then, behind the scenes, vying for his pa's attention. At least, that's what Billy told him. None of that mattered now. Her worry-filled eyes were almost too much for him to endure. He glanced up for one second, smiled, and then looked away. "Yes, ma'am."

"What are you doing out here?"

Embarrassed to tell her the truth, that he was forbidden to take a step away from the sheriff's office door without his protector, Smokey, he shrugged. "Just passing some time is all." He chanced another look at Mrs. Meeks.

The woman checked her watch and then stared at the mercantile.

Colton wished they would do the kindly thing and move on.

"If you have time, why don't you come to the store? I have a plateful of fresh oatmeal cookies on the counter I just took from the oven not fifteen minutes ago. They're for our customers." She winked. "A way to draw them in. There's plenty, and I'd enjoy getting to know you better. I've seen you around but haven't had a chance to talk."

Her words strengthened him. Not everyone considered him a dung beetle. "I can't, ma'am, but thank you all the same. I'm keeping watch out here." *Sort of the truth.*

Mrs. Meeks snorted. "I need to get back to the store, Tilly," she said. "I don't want to leave Joe for long. He's only so good with the customers."

Colton hadn't missed her disdainful expression. As she walked away, he heaved a sigh of relief.

"I admire your pa, Colton," Tilly said, placing one hand on his shoulder and the other on her growing stomach. "All the McCutcheons, really. Back in the old days, when I was a saloon girl, they never looked down their nose at me. Not a one of them. And that was rare. Good things happen to good people. Don't you worry about your pa. Somehow, this whole mess will be cleared up, and the nightmare will be over." She tipped his chin up with a gentle finger and then leaned close to whisper, "I believe your pa is innocent. He'd never murder anyone. I don't know why Blanche is saying the things she is, but I've never liked that woman. Something dishonest about her."

All the attention from the ex–saloon girl had his face aflame and heart pounding. But hearing her proclamation roused his courage.

"Unfortunately," she continued softly, for his ears only, "because of my past, not many hold my opinion in any esteem at all. Still, I'm on the lookout too. You have a friend and ally in me. If you need anything, don't hesitate to seek me out. Do you know where I live, with my husband, Neil?"

Gratitude for her heartfelt words washed through him. "No, ma'am."

The restaurant man was watching their conversation with interest, but he couldn't hear their words.

"Down that way, at the end of the street, are some small houses. Mine is in the middle of two others. I have yellow curtains in the window. Come by any time you'd like to talk. And until then, I'll be keeping your pa in my prayers."

Colton took a deep breath and couldn't believe that a smile popped out. "Thank you, ma'am. I'll keep that in mind." He'd heard his ma say those words more times than he could count. Perhaps Tilly was right, and this nightmare would work itself out. Then again, wishes didn't always come true.

She didn't ruffle his hair like every other adult in town who thought him a child but put out her hand, and they shook, sealing their friendship.

The man across the street tossed his cigarette into the dirt and stalked back into his restaurant.

"Mr. Clevenger's not real happy to see us talking."

She glanced over her shoulder at the now-empty boardwalk. "He doesn't frighten me, Colton. I've faced many a worse adversary. I've come to know that only things we fear can hurt us. Neil has taught me not to worry about what others think. Their opinions are none of my business." She smiled and tipped her head. "Remember what I said about the cookies. The invitation is extended to your mother and Mr. Smokey as well."

He watched her walk away. He liked Tilly a whole bunch. Maybe things weren't as bad as he thought.

Two men riding up the street all but stared him down.

Then again, maybe they were.

Chapter Forty-One

"Luke McCutcheon, you're talking nonsense!" Faith marched to the connecting doorway, collected her thoughts, and marched back.

Smokey, hanging against the back wall, stuck his nose in a flyer he'd pulled out of his pocket when their argument had started. He glanced up sheepishly and she shot him a defiant frown.

Luke could be so pigheaded. He was the embodiment of a domineering boar. If the tables were turned, she knew exactly what he'd be doing. But she was a woman—fragile and to be protected. After six days of seeing her love locked behind bars, she'd had enough. The time to take action had arrived.

"Just calm down, sweetheart," Luke commanded. He held out a placating hand. "You're exhausted and vexed. You know as well as I do you returning to Y Knot with Colton is best. He's taken this to heart. Thinks he's at fault. Don't you see the strain on his face, his slumped shoulders, and the worry behind his eyes?"

"Don't you dare pin this on Colton." She pointed at Luke's face. "You want me out of town. You can talk until the birds fly south, Luke McCutcheon, but I'm not going. You'd *never* leave me. Never! Why on earth do you think you have the right to send me away?"

"Faith, whatever you say won't change my mind…"

Something inside her snapped and anger boiled over. "Do you know what being married to you is like?" She pierced him with a cold stare. "Do you? No, you haven't any idea. You're demanding, opinionated, and headstrong. You expect so much of yourself—and everyone else as well."

"Aren't I usually right about things?"

So what if he is! "Don't change the subject. I've lived under your iron rule, bailed you out of scrapes when you let your temper run afoul, eased tensions when one of your brothers steps on your sensitive toes. Without me, you'd be a mess."

He nodded. "You're right on all counts."

Blood pounded in her ears. She clenched her hands. "Don't you dare agree with me, Luke, not today. I won't be bullied—or sweet-talked. We both realize this is much more serious than we first thought. The whole town is building a case against you. Everyone in Priest's Crossing has lost their minds. Something's wrong with this town. Any other sheriff wouldn't have locked you up in the first place, let alone say he believes lying Blanche Van Gleek. And look at you!"

She hated to bring up his appearance, but he'd gone behind her back and arranged for Smokey, along with Nick riding guard, to head back to Y Knot with her and Colton this afternoon, leaving the group short of men. Well, by God, she'd not go. And he couldn't make her.

"What about me?" Luke gritted out, pacing his cell, all the while never taking his gaze from hers.

"Your hair," she sputtered, realizing her bringing this up was childish, but she couldn't switch horses in the middle of the stream now. Luke would pounce on her weakness and have her agreeing to go home.

"What about my hair?"

"It's…" She waved her hand around her face, not wanting to hurt his feelings. "I've done my best to keep you cleaned up, with laundered clothes and such, but Jack won't let you have a proper bath. He's terrified you'll escape." She'd found the sheriff at his desk, fearfully muttering in his sleep about being scalped. He'd better watch out, or she just might scalp him herself. "If you look like this now, can you imagine if I weren't here? If nothing else, I see you get clean water and soap."

Halting his pacing, Luke frowned, anger simmering on his face. "Think of Holly. She's still tiny. What if something happened to her ma? And Dawn? You think either girl would ever get over losing you?"

At the mention of her daughters, she blinked back tears. Every night sleep eluded her as she imagined all of them together in the big bed, snuggled together. She missed them with all her heart. "Lay all the guilt you want, Luke, but I'm not going!" She grasped the bars to make a point. "And since you're locked up, you can't make me."

His nostrils flared. "Smokey," he said low.

The man jerked straight. "Yeah, Boss?"

"Why don't you go out and join Colton? See what he's doing. I'm sure your ears are scorched red by now. Go make sure he's still close where I told him to remain."

"Sure thing."

She was relieved both the sheriff and deputy were nowhere about. This angry exchange was the first for their marriage, and she felt off-kilter. Of course, they'd had their fair share of disagreements throughout the years, but they'd been civil and always ended with a kiss… and maybe more. Today was different. She'd made a stand, but to do so she had to make her point. She wouldn't back down. And she wouldn't care. He'd do the same for her in a heartbeat.

"I can see your mind is set, wife," Luke said. "Without a thought to your boy out there or your girls at home. Never mind that you're their only ma. You'll keep yourself in danger, no matter what I say. Did you hear about elderly Mildred Kane? She died last night, right here in town." His eyes glittered with irritation.

"Yes, I did. She fell and broke her neck."

"You sure about that?"

Inwardly Faith shuddered. What a horrible way to die. She nodded.

"Francis feels different. He had a look around. She'd made a cake that had a couple of slices cut out. From the stack of dishes in the dry rack, looks like she'd entertained. Everything was clean and in place except for some straw on her floor that smelled like manure. Unlikely for her state in life."

A chill crept up Faith's back. Could a man actually kill a defenseless old woman?

"Will you reconsider?"

Everything in her hated to go against him, but there was no help for that now. "I'm not sure about anything. That's what I aim to change." He seemed ready to explode. Did she dare provoke him more? "My mind is made up. One other small fact: I'm not being followed around by Smokey any longer. I can do and learn things, but not with him announcing my arrival more flagrantly than if I carried a tall McCutcheon family flag."

He slammed his palm against a bar. "You've lost your mind, woman! I don't want anyone to get hurt. And they will if a gunfight over me erupts. My men won't let things go too far before they step in. You or Colton could be hit, God forbid, or one of the men. I don't want that to happen."

Strain showed on his face and in his eyes. She swallowed, regretting such a scene. He'd never looked so lost. Beaten. They needed each other. But feelings would have to wait. "Maybe I have, but at least I'm finally voicing my mind. And taking a stand. I won't put myself in any undue danger. But sometimes a woman can find out things a man can't."

In a swift move, he grasped the bars. "Don't you do it, Faith! Leave this to the boys. They're making headway. Neil Huntsman has been ruled out. Francis told me so about an hour ago. Just be patient a little longer."

A wave of warm longing washed over Faith. Everything about Luke was special. She loved him more than the air she breathed. These last few days had drawn her back to the time he'd been helping her escape Ward. Begging her to tell him the truth. She should have then. She'd not make the same mistake now by burying her head in the sand and hoping the danger would go away. She was a McCutcheon! She'd go after this head-on. Just changing her thinking felt right. Still, she needed to console him. She went to the bars and reached though, caressing the side of his stress-lined face. Drawing her fingers through his whiskers. Were those tears in his eyes?

"I love you so much, Luke, I won't let you take the fall for some monster. You're the most decent man I've ever known. Nobody can fill your boots. Please, trust me. I won't be foolish." She felt the depth of his emotion down to her soul. "Just give me your blessing. All I want is a little freedom to do my own investigating. That's all."

When he leaned his cheek more firmly into her palm, her heart thwacked painfully against her ribs. He took her hand and stroked the back. "Faith, if things don't go as planned… I mean, if Harrison Wesley doesn't show up soon and the town gets impatient, you'll tell Holly and Dawn about their pa?"

She jerked back. "What on earth are you saying? Stop this inane talk. Nothing will happen."

His lips pinched tight. "I just want your word."

She leaned in, getting closer. "Your children will know all there is to know about what a wonderful man you are, but the telling won't be from me. They'll learn from watching you and loving you. You'll be the one raising them; I have no doubts at all."

"I don't want to lose you," he whispered.

He wouldn't say the words, but she could see the stark fear deep in his eyes. "You won't lose me. And I'm not losing you." She waited until his gaze connected with hers. "I promise."

His cheek in her palm and forehead resting on the cold steel were enough to freeze her insides. He didn't believe that they'd beat this travesty. He thought he would hang.

Chapter Forty-Two

Smokey put out his arm, blocking Francis's entrance. "I wouldn't go in there if I were you."

Confused, Francis darted a glance at his companions, Shad and Nick, and then back to Smokey and Colton. He turned his ear toward the building. Several moments passed in silence. "Jones and Clark?" he asked, not hearing anything.

"No. Luke and Faith."

Francis snapped straight. He couldn't remember ever witnessing an argument between the two, except when they'd been on the cattle drive when Luke first brought Faith back to the camp site, her old dilapidated wagon squeaking along. Luke had been mighty put out with her presence, even though she'd just had a baby. But the ranch hands were delighted. Luke worried her being there would be a disruption to his men. Someone might get hurt. The distracted person had turned out to be Luke.

"That's too bad," Shad said. "Darn sad to hear that news." His brow pulled down as he leaned his shoulder against the building. "I thought Smokey taking Colton and Faith back to Y Knot was a good idea. Then none of us would have to worry about 'em. You know, with the possibility of a gunfight…"

Colton stood straighter. "I'm not going anywhere. I'm glad my ma is laying down the law."

Francis playfully punched the boy's shoulder. "You best be careful what you're saying. Your pa wears the pants in the family, and you shouldn't buck his wishes. If he asked me to..." Francis let his words trail away. He realized that if Luke asked him to leave now, he wouldn't go either.

"Miss Adair has a ring in your nose already, Francis," Nick said and then smirked. "You wouldn't leave Priest's Crossing because of her, not Luke."

Francis had heard enough from Nick for a lifetime. He stepped forward, chest to chest. "That so?"

Shad grasped Nick's shoulder. "I told you to lay off Francis. I'm not tellin' you again, brother. Rein in your mouth!"

"I can speak for myself, Shad," Francis shot back, his body still tensed. "You don't have to ride herd over Nick. He doesn't scare me."

"Aren't you boys supposed to be doing something about the you-know-whats?" Smokey asked.

"Roady changed his mind. Town's too busy today," Francis said. "We're goin' out tonight."

Faith stepped out of the doorway, color high and eyes glistening with unshed tears.

"You ready to go back to the hotel, Faith?" Smokey asked, keeping his gaze directed across the street.

"Not quite yet. I think I'll take a turn around town while the sun is still out."

Smokey hitched up his pants, a smile spreading. "Anything you want."

"Alone."

The men gaped.

"You no longer have to escort my every move. Everyone has to step up their efforts, and that includes me. I can't be efficient with a ranch hand by my side day and night." She smiled warmly at the bowlegged cowboy. "As much as I've enjoyed your company, Smokey, you're released from your assignment. I expect you men to dig deeper as well. Leave no stone unturned."

"Yes, ma'am!" they said.

"I want Luke out of that cell!"

"Yes, ma'am!"

"Colton, you're to stay with Smokey, just like before. Do I make myself clear?"

Her smile wasn't fooling any of them. She was scared to death.

"Yes, ma'am. Can Smokey and me go to the mercantile?"

"Why would you want to?"

"Tilly invited me. She has fresh cookies, but I knew I had to wait to ask."

She connected with Smokey's gaze for a moment then shrugged. "I don't see why not."

Across the street at the undertaker's, the sounds of hammering rang out into the stillness.

"That's pretty creepy how old Mildred Kane died last night," Nick said. "I spoke to her a time or two, in the café or on the street. She was friendly." He looked at Francis and then the others. "Just goes to show, you can't know the mind of a killer."

Faith tugged at the collar of her blouse. "She fell. Died from an accident. Or perhaps she died first, and that's what made her fall. Don't get spooked." She looked around the group. "Where's Roady? I haven't seen him since leaving the hotel early today."

"That's a good question," Francis said. "I spoke with him a little while ago. May have gone looking for Pedro. He hasn't checked in since the meeting, and he may have something to tell him."

"For those of you who haven't heard, Jack got word Judge Harrison Wesley is on his way to Y Knot and may even be there now. If that's the case, and he got the news about Luke, perhaps he's on his way to Priest's Crossing. I won't breathe easy until I see his face."

"Judge Harrison?" Smokey's face split into a wide grin. "That's good news."

Francis nodded. "I'm sure everyone is glad to hear that. I can't say how many games of checkers he's beat me at, but I'll let bygones be bygones if he gets Luke out of that cell." As good as saying those words made him feel, Francis agreed with Faith. He wouldn't let down his guard until the judge arrived.

Chapter Forty-Three

Standing from the small eatery table he shared with Roady in the hotel lobby, Francis stretched and glanced out the window. Darkness had replaced twilight. Shad sat with Nick. Pedro was out somewhere, hidden on the street, keeping an eye on the jail. He'd be relieved by Shad sometime after midnight. Smokey had retired upstairs with Faith and Colton.

Jed Kasterlee sat half a room away at his counter, reading a paper and drinking the same rotgut coffee they had in their cups.

Most places in town closed up tight after eight o'clock. The plan was when he and Nick left, Roady would keep Jed talking so he didn't venture out and see where Nick and Francis went. Earlier, Shad and Pedro had quietly pried some loose boards free in each room of the old hotel and made space for the weapons. They didn't need much if the guns were stacked.

Nick stood and reached for his hat on the rack.

Francis did the same and, making sure his voice carried across the room, said, "We're gonna take a walk round around town. Stretch our legs. Can't remember ever feeling this useless."

Mr. Kasterlee looked up.

"You be sure to stay out of trouble," Roady replied sternly. "We've got enough on our plate. Don't stay out long."

"Just going to the saloon for a quick beer."

Shad chuckled. "We're turning in shortly. To be young again…"

Francis almost rolled his eyes. As if Shad were old? "We won't get into trouble. I don't think any could be found in this place. Makes Y Knot feel like a metropolis."

"Metropolis, Francis?" Shad laughed, a silly grin on his face. "That's a mouthful to use."

Francis tossed him a cranky stare. "Coming from you, Petty, that's rich."

When Roady's eyebrow tweaked, Francis ambled over to Jed.

The hotel owner glanced up from the newspaper. "What?"

Francis positioned his foot as close as he could to the man's without seeming suspicious.

Kasterlee frowned and leaned back.

He must not like me in his space. "Just wondering what you're plannin' to serve in the mornin'? I'm sort of tired of the breakfast Clevenger dishes out."

Everyone agreed the cold oatmeal the hotel served was a last resort and took their meal in the restaurant.

A pleasant smile replaced Kasterlee's frown. "I think I'll make flapjacks, if you're interested."

Miracles do happen. Francis gave a hearty nod and rubbed his hard belly. "Good. Count me in." With a glance at Roady, he followed Nick, who'd been waiting at the door, out into the night. "Well?" he asked.

"Too close to call in the dim light."

They paused, letting their eyes adjust to the darkness.

"And even if his boot did fit the print," Nick said. "Doesn't make him guilty."

Francis drilled him with a look. "I know that. I'm narrowing the field."

"Just wanted to be sure you were aware there's some play in this reasoning."

"I've thought of everything." Francis scanned the street, sure Nick was doing the same. All seemed quiet. Across from the hotel was the jail. Behind the backdrop of darkness, two lanterns burned inside, illuminating Jack behind the desk, writing away at something.

"Wonder where Clark is?" Nick whispered at his side.

The abandoned house where the guns were stashed was around the corner from the livery, which was all the way down at the end of the street past the mercantile and bank. Around the corner in the opposite direction from the livery was the pitiful establishment the residents called a saloon, set out by itself on the edge of town.

Nick hitched his head across the street. "Should we stop in and check on Luke?"

Walking slowly side-by-side, Francis looked around. "Not yet. Maybe after we get the job done. Then we'll have something to report. Besides, if he's restin', I don't want to bother him."

They paused at the eatery window. Tilly was having supper with Neil, but Daniel Clevenger was nowhere to be seen. When Nick went to move on, Francis touched his arm. "Wait. I want to see if Clevenger comes out of the back room."

After about ten minutes, Francis felt certain the man wasn't around. "Give me one second." He left Nick on the boardwalk and stepped inside, removing his hat. Going to Tilly's table, he smiled. "Evenin', Tilly, Neil."

Tilly smiled back. "Evening, Francis."

Neil set down his fork and nodded, wiping his mouth.

"Was wonderin', is Clevenger anywhere about? I have a message for him from Roady."

Tilly glanced toward the stove and then back at him. "I haven't seen him. Has his assistant cooking tonight. Is the message important? Something I might pass on if he does come in?"

"Nope. Just a request for the mornin'. We eat here pretty much every day. But thanks."

Back outside, the sounds of a horse coming up the street drew their attention. They waited as a stranger rode past on a tall bay without so much as a nod. They continued on. Across from them, the mercantile was buttoned up tight, and a light shone in the upstairs window. Christine Meeks and her children hadn't yet turned in.

Between the empty building and the undertaker's, Francis paused, and Nick followed suit.

Nick unbuttoned the top button of his shirt. "What d'ya think?" he asked, the words barely audible. "Feels deader than a doornail. Should we go straight to the shack and get to work?"

They shouldn't be hasty. If they messed this up and Jones and Clark confiscated their weapons, they'd be defenseless if a sudden move happened on Luke. They couldn't chance the risk. "No, we stick to the plan. Head to the saloon, spend some time over a drink, and then we'll decide. One chance at this is all we get."

With a nod from Nick, they started off.

Leather shop was dark. They rounded the corner and came face-to-face with Deputy Clark. He reeked of whiskey, not that Francis was anyone to judge.

Clark pulled up and sneered. "What're you boys doing out after dark?"

"On our way to the saloon," Nick said. "Where you've come from, if I had to guess from your smell."

Having been shot down by nearly everyone today, Nick was sporting a chip. Francis nudged his arm.

"Thought I told Guthrie I didn't want you men out at night." He glanced around, his jaw slack. "It's long past sundown."

"You didn't say anything about sundown, Deputy," Francis replied in a calm tone. "Just midnight. We plan to be tucked in tight by then. All we want is a quick beer."

Clearly drunk, Clark drew his revolver. The barrel waved unsteadily between Francis and Nick. Angry, Francis glanced at Nick. They needed a plan to disarm Clark, and they needed it fast.

"Can we buy you a drink?" Nick quickly asked. "No need for you to be rushing back to the office, is there? A minute ago, we noticed Jack Jones at the desk. I'm sure he's watching the prisoner with a sharp eye."

"A drink?" The man's demeanor changed completely. He blinked several times followed by a halfhearted shrug.

Francis smiled. "Have time?"

"Don't see why not."

From across the table, Francis and Nick sent a silent message with their gaze.

Deputy Clark was on his fourth whiskey.

Nick and Francis on their second. At this rate, they'd never complete their task tonight.

"Good one, boys," Clark slurred. He pointed at their half-full glasses as he slumped in his chair. He wobbled precariously to one side.

"And what's that fella's name over there?" Nick asked, pointing at a drawing on the wall. "He looks important."

When the man turned his head, Francis snuck his glass under the table, dumped the remainder on the floor, and covered it with his boot.

"You boys don't know nothin'," Hoss chortled happily, slapping a palm on the scarred tabletop. "You're stupid. That's Duffalo Dill Cody," he slurred. "Any fool would recognize him..."

"I sure didn't." Francis made a show of draining the last bit of whiskey from his glass. They couldn't go off and leave Hoss here in case he stumbled out later, catching them as they worked. He'd shoot to kill. They'd need to make sure he was on his way back to the jail before they attempted anything. "Nick, you about ready? Roady'll be plenty mad we stayed out so long."

Clark chuckled, his face scarlet from all the whiskey. "Tell him you was with me." He picked up his half-full shot glass and looked at Nick's.

"On the count of three?" Nick asked.

Clark nodded.

"One." Nick lifted his glass. "Two..."

Clark swilled down his drink, but Nick tossed his over his shoulder, no one the wiser since they were in the back of the room.

Francis and Nick stood easily, but the deputy had to struggle to get to his feet. They linked his elbows with theirs.

"This is might nice of you boys," he said, slobber leaking from the corner of his lips. "Frankly, I'm surprised."

Outside and rounding the corner, Francis hitched his head to the undertaker's, the nearest building to the saloon. The deputy stumbled between them, totally unaware of anything. The moment they set him down, he'd be asleep. After checking the street, they scooted around back where two open caskets sat on the back porch of the establishment.

"I sure hated wasting all that good whiskey," Nick said as they shimmied the deputy's large frame into the too-small pine box. "Should we nail him in?" He pointed to the hammer and nails on a workbench. "He'll have a real scare when he wakes up."

Francis pressed his lips together. "No. He's so drunk he won't remember how he got here. He'll think he stumbled and fell in. I'll bet we don't hear a word about this." He gave a low humorous whistle. "At least we don't have to worry about him walking the streets tonight." He hitched his head. "One last thing before we leave." He went to the end of the coffin, where Clark's feet rested on the rim and held up his boot to the deputy's, measuring the size. "Look at that," Francis exclaimed. "Small feet for such a large man." He lowered his foot. "Let's go."

By the time they hit the alley, the deputy was snoring like a bear.

Across the street, a lantern hung from a tree branch outside the livery's front doors, illuminating the area, and behind that, the abandoned house. "Let's cut through, see if Pink Kelly's anywhere around. If anyone were to discover us, the sharp-eyed liveryman would be the one. He watches me every time I go to check on the horses. Pretends he's working, but I'm never out of his sight."

"I've noticed that too," Nick whispered back. "Let's get this done. The longer we stay out, the longer someone is bound to back-shoot us and ask for forgiveness after the fact."

Francis nodded, feeling twenty years older than his years. "My thoughts, exactly."

Chapter Forty-Four

Tossing beneath her blanket, Blanche struggled to get comfortable. Nothing she did gave her rest. Her ribs ached mercilessly from the vicious beating she'd taken, and the bruise on her face, although almost completely faded now, was still tender to the touch. Feeling prickly heat on her leg, she reached down and scratched the hives tormenting her. Her skin felt alive. Her nerves shot. She was a mess—the reason only too evident. Did anyone else notice? Were they becoming suspicious?

Frustrated, she let out a disgruntled sigh. She hadn't slept well since Benson's last job. He'd wanted to cancel, rearrange the dates so he wouldn't miss his sister's wedding, but Blanche had thrown a fit. Work was scarce. The printer in the next town would contract with someone else to move his books, and Benson would lose the agreement completely. The freight business was dying, but Benson needed to milk each client for all they were worth before all his opportunities evaporated into thin air, leaving them paupers.

That wasn't the first contract she'd pushed him into. There were the dry goods that needed shipping to a tiny village in the Rockies, the barrels packed with china to go up to Canada, and the seed he'd gone all the way to Cheyenne to pick up and take to Soda Springs. And other opportunities too. Her job had been to spur him on. To look for better-paying contracts. She regretted nothing.

A month after she'd been foolish enough to fall for Benson's handsome smile and marry him, she'd been shocked to learn the pittance he earned each time he actually moved freight. The trips hardly made a profit. As a bachelor, he'd been financially stable in his two-room cabin, or so she'd thought. Everything had appeared so romantic, especially the secret encounters they'd shared in the quiet of his woodland home. As a wife-to-be, she couldn't wait to turn her teaching position over to Ashley and be rid of those brats tugging on her skirt, asking unanswerable questions and sneezing in her face. But without her salary, they'd scrimped. Gone without. She'd hated poverty and pushed Benson into taking on more and more. Leaving for this last trip, which made him miss Pearl's wedding, he'd been furious.

Her ambition didn't make her a horrible person, did it? A wife needed a few nice things. Setting up a suitable home was important. As was presenting a proper picture for others to see. A dress now and then or a fine pair of Italian-made shoes wasn't asking for the moon. Certainly each season necessitated a new hat. Was that asking so much?

Benson had complied, the best he could, until only a few coins were left from the payments he brought home. Staples became slim, and they relied more and more on his hunting and her baking. How she hated the gamey taste of venison.

Sitting up, she punched her pillow angrily and then settled on her other side, but her head was still tender from falling and striking the floor.

So what if I wasn't the best wife in the world? Nothing I can do about that now. I wasn't the one who came home early. He only wanted to be at the wedding to give Pearl away. *I wasn't the one who panicked and hit him in the head with the fire iron. I'm not to blame. I shouldn't dwell on what-ifs and whys.*

Wide awake now, she had no other option than to get up. She'd not sleep tonight. She flipped back her covers and swung her legs over the side of the bed. Agitated, she needed a cigarette. That was the only thing that would calm her ragged nerves. If she didn't make the effort, she'd lie awake all night.

Padding silently across the room, she opened her wardrobe with a shaky hand. She wondered how long Angelia and Ashley would allow her to live there. She'd like to stay forever. Never go back to that wretched cabin in the woods. That would suit her just fine. Angelia cooked meals, and Ashley kept the house nice. What more could she want?

Quivering, she lifted the folded shawl that hid her pouch of tobacco and small rolling papers and went back to her bed. She lit her candle. If she did stay here, she'd make clear she had no intention of hiding her habit any longer. No doubt they already knew. The smell of the smoke only too evident. And Ashley catching her at the window the other night.

Rolling the paper and twisting the end, she was just about to light it when a soft tap sounded on the window behind her. With a violent jerk, she stifled a frightened scream. Had a twig fallen against the glass? Or perhaps a squirrel, out at night, had dropped something from the tree. Her curtains were drawn, but with her lighted candle, if a person was outside, he or she saw her walk across the room.

She swallowed her fear. What should she do? Blow out her candle and cower under her covers? Was the hard-faced ranch foreman back to ask more questions? Or Jack Jones? No, the sheriff wouldn't sneak up in the night and scare ten years off her life. Was Benson's ghost so close? She was a believer. Had her loving husband come back to haunt her or to exact revenge?

The tapping sounded again. Louder. More persistent.

Blanche forced herself to lean over and cup the candle with one hand. With a ragged breath, she blew out the flame and then sat motionless in the dark room.

He's here. Outside.

She'd locked her window every night, worried this might happen. Why would he chance this? If he was seen, they could never explain that away. But was he in a sane mind? Mildred was dead, she reminded herself with a foreboding shiver. Dead! How on earth had that happened? And why?

"Blanche."

She'd know that deep-throated whisper in her sleep. The stupid fool! What did he want? How dare he put them in such jeopardy! Gooseflesh rose up on her arms. Her scalp prickled. She remembered his expression as he'd landed blow after blow, as if he'd been enjoying himself. She'd not go outside. She'd pretend she hadn't heard, even if he kept knocking all night. He was deranged to come here.

He tapped again.

They didn't need to talk. Their blatantly stupid story had worked so far, even if the circumstances were so far-fetched Jack Jones was the only one gullible enough to lock up a McCutcheon. She scoffed at herself. Why hadn't she recognized McCutcheon? Even under whiskers and rumpled garments.

"Blanche," he whispered in a raspy voice. "I saw the light. You don't fool me. I've come to tell you to stay calm. If you think to go to the sheriff and blame me, you'll end up like Mildred. That woman couldn't stop asking questions. I'll be watching you."

Petrified, Blanche eased down to the mattress and rolled into a ball, praying he'd go away. After they hanged McCutcheon and everything calmed down, she'd have to sneak away. Go somewhere where he couldn't find her. She'd not stay in Priest's Crossing with him watching her every move. Maybe intending to kill off the only person that could have him hanged later down the road.

He was still out there. She could feel his presence. Her ears hurt from straining. Her heart beat against her sore ribs. The desire for the cigarette all but gone.

What should she do? She wished Ashley's house was in town, where she could scream for help, but not out here in the sticks. If he got frustrated, this dark, lonely stretch at night could easily hide many sins. Many indeed.

Chapter Forty-Five

Ashley blinked and opened her eyes. What had disturbed her sleep? She held her breath, listening intently. She'd been dreaming about Francis and the kiss they'd shared. After a moment, her eyelids once again drooped. He'd surprised her, so bold in the daylight. The thought tickled her fancy. Her lighthearted peace was chased away by the weight of her responsibility. She must consider her mother, the orchard, and of course the school children too. She couldn't be led astray by a handsome face.

Francis was an interesting mixture. A tease and a sharp-eyed protector of his boss. She admired his conviction. And his playfulness. He'd been nothing but straightforward with her.

What did her future hold?

There! Again. The noise. Was a mouse burrowing a hole somewhere in the house?

An uneasy feeling slid down her spine. She wished she hadn't awakened. Wished she could go back to dreaming of things to come. And yet that didn't sound like a mouse. Or her mother. Gathering all her courage, Ashley scooted to the wall side of her bed and very carefully lifted the corner of her curtains, looking as far down the back side of the house as she could manage.

Nothing. Her heart slowed, and she actually smiled at her runaway imagination.

Turning her head, she jerked back so sharply she bit her bottom lip, the metallic taste of blood slicking the inside of her mouth, the pain keeping her from crying out in surprise.

Somebody in the darkness of the orchard trees stood not five feet away at Blanche's window. Ashley struggled to see. Identify the person. She couldn't. As she lowered the fabric, moving slower than cold honey, she thought of Francis.

The man tapped again on the window glass.

She strained to hear.

"Blanche," he whispered in a raspy voice. "I saw the light. You don't fool me. I've come to tell you to stay calm. If you think to go to the sheriff and blame me, you'll end up like Mildred. That woman couldn't stop asking questions. I'll be watching you."

The murderer!

Francis was right! Fear froze Ashley's limbs. Blanche and this unknown man had murdered Benson and intended to pin the crime on Luke McCutcheon. And poor Mildred! Ashley grabbed her sheet pulling it up to her chin. The monster had killed her too.

Something had to be done, but what? This might be the only chance to clear Francis's boss. She had to see who the night visitor was. Moving as if in a dream, she slipped silently out of bed, went to her wardrobe, and swung a black cape over her nightdress, tying the cords under her chin. Finished, she pulled on socks and then her boots, the darkness making it difficult to get them laced.

Only two or three minutes had passed. If she could sneak out the kitchen door and then run down to the road and hide in the bushes, she could identify the man when he went back to town. She felt certain he wouldn't break in. If that had been his intention, he would have done so already. Probably just wanted to threaten Blanche. As long as her mother stayed asleep, she'd be in no danger.

With her heart wedged in her throat, Ashley pushed quickly out the side kitchen door, pulled it tight behind her, and slipped away into the trees, all the while expecting a hand to reach out and grasp her shoulder.

Before exiting her room, she'd peeked out one more time, confirming his still immobile presence. Her heart thundered, and her hands shook so much she could barely hold together the edges of her cape. Once behind a thick buffalo berry bush, she stopped and listened. Had he come on foot or ridden a horse? All she had to do was get down the slight hill, cross the road, and then wait. But she needed to hurry.

A quarter moon hung in the sky, giving little light. She didn't dare use the footpath that most everyone in Priest's Crossing used. He'd most likely come that way himself. She needed to pick her way through the brush, staying low and keeping quiet. Almost to the bottom, she breathed a shaky sigh of relief. Now she'd just need to dart across the road and hide on the other side.

Crouching low, she edged closer to the road and was about to examine both ways in the dim moonlight when a twig snapped. She jerked back into cover. To be able to see his face, she'd need to be across the road so he came toward her and not just beside.

The man emerged from the hillside, doing as she'd done, staying off the well-known path. He was dressed in black and was on foot. He was tall with wide shoulders, just like most men in town. He had a cloak or something over his head. He paused, searched his surroundings, crossed the road, and disappeared on the far side, walking in the direction of town.

She'd been so close! She couldn't let him get away. This was the answer they all were searching for. Once he was gone, if she stayed on the road and ran, at least for some of the way, she might beat him. Going overland, he'd have to move slowly in the dark.

Fear had her mouth dry as parched earth after a drought. She counted, huddling behind her bush. How much time had passed? So much rode on her efforts. She couldn't worry about getting hurt. That poor family. Luke McCutcheon. She had to make her feet work.

Enough hiding. Seeing the man leave her property was a blessing. She didn't have to worry over her sleeping mother's safety. Descending the small rise to the road, Ashley gathered the length of her long nightgown and set off. She'd run this way before, when she'd been late for school or on an errand. The distance to town was only about a quarter mile. She wasn't afraid of the night—just the killer she knew was out there.

"Strap on the gun belts," Francis instructed Nick. The weight of the guns felt good on his hips. "We'll divide up the rifles." Each man had brought along his Remington as well as his sidearm and bullets. Two saddlebags were heavy with boxes of ammunition.

Nick handed him two rifles and cradled three in his arms. "We'll need to take the long way around and come in behind the back of the hotel."

Francis nodded.

Nick had followed orders and thought quickly on his feet. Maybe the two had more common ground than Francis had previously thought. "I'm counting on Roady having that back door unlocked. I'm ready to go. How about you?"

Nick nodded. The creaky floor was unnerving, but they'd cleared the area. No one was around to hear. Pink hadn't been anywhere near the livery, and the windows of his small shack out back were dark. No telling if he was in or out.

They emerged from the rickety building, keeping to the tree line. Hunched over with their load, they snuck along the side of the road and then ducked behind some underbrush. They were about to start picking their way toward the hotel when Francis pulled up short.

Someone whispered.

He put a finger to his lips then placed his feet carefully so as not to snap any twigs. They went farther into the brush, curious to see who was out there. Ike! Jonathan Burg! Other men from the ranch. Francis straightened and walked forward to a barrage of guns drawn from their holsters. "Hold your fire."

"That you, Francis?"

Relief surged through him. "Sure, it's me! And Nick. Am I ever glad to see you. How could you leave the ranch?" Bob and Tanner were there as well... *and* Leonard Browning, attorney in Y Knot, and the ever straight-standing Judge Harrison Wesley. Francis hadn't seen the judge since last May when he'd come through Y Knot to take care of the Sangers. "I can't believe my eyes!"

"With no new reports reaching our ears and no one returning, we got worried," Jonathan said, his beat-up, sweat-stained hat still pulled low over his eyes, even in the darkness. "We got word back from Flood. They're set to reach Y Knot tomorrow, so they sent us on ahead. Didn't want to risk somethin' happenin' to Luke." He glanced around at the others, who nodded. "Justin's still in town as well as Hayden Klinkner, Morgan Stanford, and others. This was important."

Ike's face was drawn. "We wanted to come sooner. But we couldn't until we got an order. Browning returned from Waterloo on the same day the judge here meandered into Y Knot with his family and two loaded wagons." His crooked smile appeared in the scant moonlight. "We were just about to ride into Priest's Crossing and find you men, but the hour's late. We didn't want to startle Jack, knowing his history. We don't want a war."

Jonathan edged in closer. "Felt prudent to wait until morning to see who was friend and who wasn't." He eyed all the weapons Francis and Nick held awkwardly in their arms and gun belts buckled around their hips.

At the moment, Francis felt a little amused himself.

"And what in sake's name are you two doin'? Raiding the town of their guns?"

"No, but that's not a half-bad idea," Nick said.

Francis pulled back his shoulders. "We're gettin' ready for trouble. Jack confiscated my firearm when I arrived and will take yours as well or anyone else associated with Luke. Before he could take these, I told Roady and the others to hide 'em. Today Nick heard talk of a lynching. They don't like the fact Harrison and Luke are friends. Think the judge will be partial. We don't want to be unprepared if they decide to act on their words."

"A lynching will not take place," Harrison barked out. "After all the years judges serve riding up and down the territory, we end up knowing everyone. The outlaws, the law keepers, and everyone between. Jack Jones and the rest of Priest's Crossing can go suck eggs for all I care. Familiarity can't be helped with so few judges serving the territories."

Nick tipped his head. "They might not be quite so understanding."

"Don't bother me in the least," Harrison replied.

Francis was close enough to see the fire in the judge's eyes.

"How's Luke holding up?" Leonard Browning asked. "His confinement's going on two weeks. That would be difficult for anyone."

Francis and Nick exchanged another brief glance. The men would be shocked when they saw Luke. "Not good," Francis said. "Townsfolk blame his Cheyenne blood. Rumors have run rampant. In their heads, he's been tried and convicted. Luke's confinement is hard on Faith and Colton as well. Sooner this is wrapped up and we're on the way back to the ranch, the better. Oh, another interesting fact. An old woman died last night. They say she fell and broke her neck. But to me, looked like she'd been doing some entertaining. The killer may have struck again."

"That'd be a bold move. Killing twice in the same town," Ike mumbled.

Francis shrugged. "Maybe he's gettin' jittery. Maybe she knew something…"

The horses looked worn out. They stood quietly as Bob held their reins. A modicum of pride stirred in Francis's chest. He realized, without being asked, he was almost running the show. A fleeting thought of Ashley went through his mind, and he was grateful she was home in her bed, safe from murderers feeling the heavy burden of their guilt.

"What do you think about staying out here for a while longer?" Francis asked the men. "Let Browning and the judge ride in together alone tomorrow morning?" He glanced at Nick.

"Just keeping some cards close to the vest feels righter than wrong. Things have been strange around here. No one's talking sense. They believe the widow's far-fetched claim of Luke killing her husband for money and then beating her too. To tell you the truth, I don't know what the heck will happen."

"I can't be plotting a breakout or sneaking around," Harrison said.

"Me either," Browning joined in. "We'll follow the law."

Francis nodded. "Good. That's what Luke wants. You tell the town that and see if they listen."

Jonathan gripped Francis by his shoulder.

In all actuality, seeing these friendly faces was nice.

"You can count on me, Bob, Tanner, and Ike, to remain here. Is this the best place to camp to stay out of sight? Sure wish we still had Uncle Pete with us."

Pain at their fallen comrade's memory sliced at Francis. "I know. I miss him too." He glanced around. "This is as good a place as any. Now, Tanner, being new to the ranch, I have a different job for you. No one knows you around these parts or even much in Y Knot, so you're gonna do some undercover work. Come into town but steer clear of us. Pretend you're a stranger. You might learn something we can't." Fighting to get under the three gun belts buckled around his hips, he fished in his pocket and pulled out the money clip. "Flash this around and see what happens. Someone's bound to know something."

The men gathered around to see what Francis was talking about.

"That we know of, only two of 'em were in town. Neil Huntsman, Tilly's husband and the clerk at the bank, owns one and he's been cleared. I found this one at Benson's cabin wedged in the cushions of a chair. Might belong to the killer. Find out what you can."

Tanner, the youngest of the Petty boys, flashed his easygoing smile. "Will do, Francis."

"Good man." Francis glanced to the judge and attorney to see if they would object.

"That's not breaking any laws that I know of," Browning said. He shrugged and looked at Judge Wesley for confirmation.

"None. Just don't ask me any questions, and I won't have to lie."

"Good enough, then," Francis replied, feeling a whole lot better about the situation. He and Nick still had to get the guns back to the hotel unseen, and the hours were slipping away. "Luke will be damn happy to see you, Harrison. You too, Browning." He grinned at the ranch hands. "And you know how he feels about all you. Thank you for coming. We never thought this arrest would go on so long." Francis hefted the two rifles back into his arms. He looked to Nick. "You ready?"

"As much as I'll ever be. That's a good idea with Tanner, I'll give you that."

Francis smiled, knowing how much that compliment must cost his rival. "Wish us luck, boys," he said, looking at the group. "We'll see some of you in the morning, God willing."

Chapter Forty-Six

Like a trembling rabbit, Ashley crouched behind a thick brambleberry bush, her breath hissing between her teeth. As she'd made her way to town along the road, she'd gotten the distinct feeling she was being followed. At first, she'd shaken off the wariness, believing the sensation was just her fears running wild. She could walk to town in the middle of the night if she wanted without being questioned for doing something crazy.

Fortifying her mind, she'd briskly walk on. But then she'd thought, or imagined, she'd heard something behind her. The sound fueled her imagination. Was Blanche trailing her? Had her friend gotten up, rattled by her accomplice chancing the midnight visit, and observed Ashley leave from the kitchen side of the house? The memory of Blanche's eyes filled with insanity sent a chill up her spine. Did her friend believe Ashley was turning her in? If yes, surely the woman would want to prevent her reaching town. Maybe she'd even take some deadly action. If Ashley had her way, come morning, her former teacher would be in the jail cell that held Luke McCutcheon now, and he'd be free.

With her heart rate back to normal, the dizziness in her head gone, and the intention of continuing onward, Ashley straightened. In her fright, she'd veered off the side of the road to hide in the brushy landscape. Now she needed to press onward. Town was close. She'd arrive in less than five minutes and find a place where she could watch for the midnight caller. Identify him. Perhaps she could climb onto the roof of some building. Afterward, somehow, she'd find Francis and report what she knew. She'd not trust Jack Jones or Deputy Clark. For all she knew, the man outside Blanche's window could be either of them.

Just as Ashley took her first step, she glanced over her shoulder one last time. Some distance away, the cloak-covered man stood very close to a large oak, as if trying to hide. He was wrapped in darkness, and she still couldn't make out who it was.

He's waiting for me to make the next move. Stupid! I've been so stupid to come off the road. Down here, no one will find me.

She didn't have a second to spare. Benson's murderer—Mildred's too—was planning to make her his next victim. With every ounce of strength she had, she pushed off with her back leg and darted in the opposite direction than he'd expect her to go, taking her away from town, but toward a deer trail that would bring her back in and around. The undergrowth here was dense and unforgiving. Her every move was hampered.

She heard a curse. Then he came after her, the crashing of his feet loud. He didn't care who heard. A desperate man was dangerous. Her life could end in the blink of an eye. Gasping for breath, she dug deep for energy and pushed off. She had to get away.

Ashley stumbled. Searing heat sliced across her cheek. Ignoring the pain, she sprinted on, pushing at branches and jumping the difficult-to-see rocks and logs that threatened to trip her stride. She had no choice but to outrun him. How far away was the trail? She should have reached it by now. The going was difficult. By the sound, she thought he'd reach her any moment. Her cloak caught, and she almost fell again but jerked the fabric away to freedom. Hot tears scalded her cheeks. She had to tell someone the truth. She had to free Luke McCutcheon. She was his only chance. And what about Francis? Her heart surged at the thought of him. Her legs faltered, and her lungs screamed for air, for rest, for life.

Unable to sleep and sick with worry, Faith sat at the hotel window, staring out on the quiet town, the darkness reminding her of evenings back on the ranch. Would their lives ever be the same? What was in store for Luke? Surely the townsfolk of Priest's Crossing would come to their senses. Today, after she'd left Colton with Smokey, she'd sought out Joe and Pearl Brunn. Finally getting a chance to talk face-to-face, they were more able to speak freely since she was alone. She saw the guilt in Joe's face. He was trying to help—talking to people and countering suspicions and lies when he heard them.

It was Pearl who worried Faith. The new bride held firm to her conviction Blanche would never lie, especially not about her beloved brother's death. When Joe said something positive, one would only have to look at Pearl's face to make no progress at all. As Faith spelled out the impossibility of Luke being guilty, she did her best to hold her temper. The woman's steadfast demeanor was infuriating.

Tomorrow she'd walk out to the Adair house and speak with Blanche herself. That chore was long overdue. If the woman wouldn't come into town, Faith would search her out. Roady had questioned her, but Faith wouldn't get another wink of sleep until she took care of that task herself.

Movement on the street below caught Faith's eye. In the darkness below, someone was creeping along, staying close to the ground. A cloak covered most of him—no, the person might be a woman. Was Blanche up to no good? Moving slowly, carefully. Now in front of the eatery, the person paused, but then moved forward again. Did whoever was out there have a gun? Were they set on shooting Luke before he could prove his innocence?

Faith pulled on her boots and gave Smokey's shoulder a shake. "Someone's outside. Sneaking toward the jail."

Smokey sat up instantly. "Wait. Shad's out there standing watch, but..."

Faith was already out the door.

By the time Faith ran down the hotel stairs and into the lantern light of the boardwalk, the cloaked figure had spotted her and was coming her way. Did Blanche want to speak with her as much as she wanted to question the woman responsible for jailing Luke? Or did malicious intent move her forward?

The cloak fell away just as the person reached Faith.

"Mrs. McCutcheon! Thank God I've found you," Ashley gasped and then crumpled into her arms. A bleeding scratch marred her left cheek, and the fabric of her dressing gown was torn at the hem and one sleeve.

Had the young woman Francis was rumored to be taken with just run to town without dressing?

Ashley gripped at Faith's arms as she looked over her shoulder her body shaking. "We have to hide. He's coming!"

"Who?" Faith asked. "What's wrong? What're you frightened of?" They stole close to the side of the building as Smokey and Roady appeared.

"Catch your breath," Smokey said. "You're safe now. We won't let nothin' hurt ya."

"But… but my mother could be in danger. I need to get back to my house before something terrible happens. Blanche might turn on her."

"What's going on?" Roady asked.

Ashley took a deep breath, clutching her cape at the neckline. "Please, I need to speak with Francis."

"He's not here," Roady said. "He'll be back soon."

She glanced back the way she'd come. "We need to get out of sight. The person chasing me was on his way back to town. I ran cross-country to get to Priest's Crossing first so I could identify him. He's the one who killed Benson! Along with Blanche. He was tapping at her window…"

Roady drilled her with a stare.

Excitement roared through Faith. *Finally* someone who could, and would, clear her husband's name. "What do you—"

"We can't stay out here," she whispered. "Jed Kasterlee might see us. Or he might be the one. I don't know." Ashley stepped inside the open hotel door and the others followed. Her frightened gaze searched Faith's. "The man probably already knows we're here."

Fear skittered around Faith's chest. She searched the darkness outside, feeling like they were being watched. "We need to take care of that deep scratch on your cheek."

Ashley pressed a handkerchief to her face that Smokey had given her.

Roady touched her arm. "Do you think your mother's in danger?"

She told them everything she'd witnessed that night.

"How frightening!" Faith said. "And brave." She glanced at Roady. "Should we tell Luke? What if Jack is guilty, or his deputy, Hoss Clark? No wonder they'd want to keep him locked up and tried for their crime."

"We won't tell Luke—yet," Roady said, keeping watch at the street. "We'll wait until Francis and Nick get back with the weapons." He scanned the alley. "I need to return to the back door of the hotel. That's where Francis is bringing the guns. Faith, take Miss Adair upstairs to your room and tend to her wounds."

Faith arched her eyebrow. "Don't you think Mr. Kasterlee would have heard us by now and come to see what was happening, if he were here? Maybe he's the one chasing Miss Adair."

Roady nodded. "Could very well be, but we have to keep an open mind. Since the old lady died, this town's a powder keg. People are scared. Even though Jones and Clark are passing the death off as an accident, some of the townspeople are changing their minds about Luke. The killer must be anxious to hang him before that happens. We need to be careful."

Ashley fisted her hands. "But my mother!"

"Smokey, saddle up and ride out," Roady barked. "As soon as Francis and Nick return, which should be any moment, I'll send Nick to your house as well. You'll have to tell Jack tomorrow what you know. Think you can do that?"

Ashley nodded. "I'll tell everything, Mr. Guthrie." She looked at Faith. "Your husband won't take the blame for Blanche's crime, even though she was once my friend."

Overwhelmed with gratitude, Faith reached out and stroked her arm. "Thank you." Her throat tightened and she had to look away.

"You might suffer at the hands of the others who think she's innocent," Roady said.

Ashley shrugged. "That can't be helped."

"Good. Faith, take her upstairs and be sure to lock the door. The killer thinks you know the truth about him. Pedro is in the next room. I'll be in to check on you just as soon as Francis and Nick arrive."

Faith placed a guiding hand on Ashley's back in a surge of thankfulness. Miss Adair had put her life on the line to get the truth back to town. Faith owed her so much. Perhaps by tomorrow noon Luke would be free. That was a thought too good to be true.

Chapter Forty-Seven

Drenched in sweat, Luke sat up on his cot, the stillness and stuffy, hot air pushing at his lungs. His clothes, the fresh ones Faith had brought him, were stiff from a couple of nights' sleep. Feeling movement on his neck, he slapped away the insect, uncaring. Remnant fleas from the blanket Faith had replaced still shared the cell with him, making his life miserable. He needed a real bath in the worst way.

When would this ordeal be over? By now, Flood and his brothers must be on their way, not that Jack would be persuaded by anyone at this point. Brandon might talk some sense into him since he'd been his boss for several years, but that was no guarantee. This murder charge would go all the way to trial, and he couldn't do a thing to change that.

Luke looked out of his bars into the darkness as someone stepped into the room.

"Luke," Joe Brunn said, coming closer.

Surprised to see his old friend, Luke pushed away his disappointment. Five days had passed since Joe's return and not much had changed. "Joe. What're you doing out this late? It must be past one o'clock."

"Couldn't sleep. I hope I didn't wake you."

The scant moonlight coming in the window high above his cot made seeing his friend possible. "Nope. Fleas keep me scratching."

"I was surprised to find the office empty," Joe said, looking around. "Where're Jack and Deputy Clark?"

"Don't know."

They gazed at each other in the darkness.

Joe's shoulders sagged and he heaved a deep sigh. "Beyond what you might think of me, Luke, I *am* trying, but no one is listening. I've decided to ride out tomorrow. Head for Y Knot where I can send some telegrams myself. See what I can do for you. Maybe round up that lawyer Flood uses."

"What about Pearl? Won't she mind?"

Light enough to see Joe, but too dark to read his eyes, his friend's lack of a response gave Luke his answer. "You don't have to do that, Joe. I don't want to put you in a bad spot with your new wife. I'm sure Flood and Brandon are on their way. The last time I heard, the law says I'm innocent until proven guilty. I've got nothin' to worry about since I didn't kill Benson. They've got no proof."

Joe scuffed his boot. "I hope that's the case, Luke. I feel like I don't know these people anymore. But since Mildred's death last night, people have been more apt to listen. That's something. A handful think she was murdered by the same person who killed Benson."

A crack in the wall. Hope squeezed his chest. "That could be true. What do you think?"

Joe sputtered. "How can you question me? You know I'm on your side. I don't know what to think about Mildred, if she was murdered or not, but someone out there killed Pearl's brother. Whether he's still around, I aim to clear your name. No

McCutcheon would kill in cold blood for any reason. That's a fact I can stake my life on."

Luke forced a smile and tried to dredge up some of the old feeling he'd once had for Joe. "That's good to hear."

Joe stepped close to the bars.

His face was tortured. Too bad Luke didn't have any words of comfort. He had his own problems to worry about.

"Come on, Luke," Joe said. "You can't think that little of me. I've never doubted you or your innocence."

Luke steeled against the retort he felt like slinging. "I don't think anything about anybody, except Jack Jones. That man is difficult to figure out. And I've had plenty of time here to do my fair share of thinkin'. Either he's guilty or he's covering for someone else. He can't be so dumb as to take that woman at her word."

"I never have liked Blanche. I was surprised last year when she and Benson began courting. He was in way over his head. She never seemed like she liked him much, let alone loved him. She henpecked him nonstop. Made his life a living hell…"

Luke grasped the steel bar, appreciating the coolness on his warm palm. Here was a topic he was interested in. "That right? She have anyone else around town she seemed to like more than Benson?"

In the darkness, Joe straightened. Grasped one of the bars himself. "You mean like a gentleman friend?"

Joe's tone said he'd never given that a thought. "I wouldn't call him that, if you catch my meaning. More like a scoundrel. From what I hear, Benson was often gone. Maybe she got lonely. Didn't like all the solitude out at the cabin. Those woods a quarter mile out of town are the perfect place for a clandestine meeting."

Joe frowned. "Pearl wouldn't like you talking like that. She's fond of Blanche."

"Good thing Pearl's not here. You ever see Blanche frequenting a business or house more often than others?" Luke lifted his pant leg and rubbed off some crawly creature. "Joe?"

"I'm thinkin'." His father's good friend shifted his weight from one leg to the next. "She'd walk into town often enough, most times without Benson. I've seen her in the restaurant frequently chatting with Daniel Clevenger or passing the time with Jed Kasterlee outside the hotel, since the hotelier thinks all married women are fair game. Passed him a little while ago on my way over, as a matter of fact." Joe made a humming sound in his throat. "Now that I'm thinking on the subject, I can see where you're going. Deputy Clark used to follow her around like a sick puppy up until the day this happened. I've noticed her in discussion with Pink Kelly at his livery. Laughing with him, more than a married woman ought. Now that you brought this line of thinking to the forefront of my mind seems all the men liked her. She even used to look in my direction before I made my feelings for Pearl known."

"But which one did *she* like, Joe? That's what we have to figure out." Luke wished he could trust Joe enough to tell him about the bloody boot print the men found in the cabin, but he didn't dare. Before Joe married Pearl, Luke wouldn't have hesitated. "What about Jack Jones? Did Blanche ever have any doin's with him?" Him being guilty would explain Jack's eagerness to lock up Luke.

"Jack? Heck no. She belittles him constantly."

Hmm, the deputy, the liveryman, the innkeeper, the restaurateur. Four single men who could easily have taken up with the ex-schoolteacher behind Benson's back. But he needed to keep an open mind. Not limit the possibilities. Priest's Crossing had plenty of men, and any could be the murderer.

He thought about Fox Dancing and Painted Bear Stone. Were they still around town somewhere? They hadn't made their presence known to anyone else since her first visit. The last thing he wanted was for his little sister to be hurt trying to help him.

"How's Faith holding up? And Colton? For a time on that ride I gave 'em into Priest's Crossing years ago, before they met up with Ward Brown, I thought I might have a chance to win Faith's heart for myself." He chuckled, but the sound didn't hold much mirth. "That feels like thirty years ago, my friend. I was mighty glad to hear you rescued her and took her back to the Heart of the Mountains. Everyone knew you two were meant for each other. She doing all right?"

"The best she can under the circumstances."

Joe took a deep breath. "I best get back before Pearl misses me. Is there anything I can get you before I leave? Or tomorrow?"

Luke couldn't stop a quick glance around the dark enclosure. Was he actually getting used to being locked up? Tomorrow would be two weeks! Thirteen days longer than he could stand. "Only my freedom, and you can't deliver that. Roady stopped in around eleven, and Shad is out there somewhere standing guard." *And Fox Dancing and Painted Bear Stone.* For an imprisoned fella, he did have a lot of people looking out for his hide. That alone should make him feel better.

"All right then, I'm gone."

"If you remember anything else about Blanche, get the information to Roady or Francis if you can't to me." His grip tightened on the bar. "Don't tell Jack. I appreciate what you shared tonight."

"You know I will. G'night."

A foreboding sensation swirled inside Luke as he watched his friend exit. Was he kiddin' himself? Would Jack and Deputy Clark act on the trumped-up charges? As the days passed, Luke was less sure of anything. That he'd ever get out, see the ranch again, or hold his daughters. What he wouldn't give for a deep lungful of clean mountain air.

Chapter Forty-Eight

Francis crept along the back of the buildings, getting closer to the hotel, the recovered gun belts strapped on his hips and rifles balanced in his arms. Nick followed behind so quietly Francis had to look behind to be sure he was still there. Knowing Judge Wesley had shown up and would appear in town tomorrow was a relief. This whole mess could be wrapped up soon and without a single shot fired.

"Over here."

Glancing up, he spotted Roady holding the door of the hotel. "Hustle. Strange happenings going on tonight."

Francis and Nick hurried forward.

Scooting inside, Roady closed the door without even a click of the lock and took a couple of rifles himself. They stealthily crept toward the stairs.

"You don't know the half of it," Francis whispered. "Judge Wesley and a bunch more of the ranch hands are camped just outside town as we speak. Ike, Jonathan, Bob, Tanner, and Leonard Browning, attorney at law. We're sitting good."

Nick's smile stretched across his face. "I was never so glad to see those men."

"And you don't know the other half," Roady replied smugly. "Your sweetheart saw the real killer talking to Blanche through her bedroom window but can't identify him."

Fumbling forward, Francis grasped Roady's arm and pulled him to a halt. "Is she all right? Was she hurt?" The kiss today was fresh in his mind. He'd had to work to keep his thoughts on task. She meant the world to him.

"She's fine but scared. She snuck into town to tell you and was chased by the killer. We have a lot to discuss once the weapons are hidden. The murderer may make a move soon, even tonight, since his game is almost up."

Alarm raced through Francis amid the cigar smoke permeating from the rooms and parlor. "Where is she?"

"Upstairs with Faith. Has a few scratches, but overall, she's okay. Let's get these guns taken care of. Nick, as soon as we do, go get your horse and ride out to Miss Adair's house. Smokey is already there keeping watch. Miss Adair is worried about her mother being alone with Blanche. In the morning, we'll present the new evidence to Jones and Clark and get Luke out."

Faith had just finished dressing Ashley's wounds when a soft tap sounded on the door.

Ashley bolted to her feet. Had whoever chased her found where she was hiding?

Faith padded softly to the door and put her ear next to the wood.

Colton, who'd woken up when Ashley arrived, followed his mother.

"Who's there?" Faith whispered.

"Francis."

Relief stormed through Ashley. Did he have news of her mother? She couldn't get the sight of the murderer by Blanche's window out of her mind. She'd have to tell Jack Jones everything. What if he didn't believe her? What if he called her a liar and the whole town turned against her? Several people had noticed her attraction to Francis. Her mother might even think she'd made up the story to please the young cowboy.

Without giving a response, Mrs. McCutcheon opened the door, being careful not to make a sound.

Instantly Francis's gaze found hers. A feeling so strong almost made her cry. When had he become so important?

He closed the distance between them in three strides and wrapped her in his arms.

"I heard what happened," he whispered against her hair, rocking her from side to side.

They fit together perfectly, and nothing had ever felt so right. He didn't seem concerned in the least that Mrs. McCutcheon watched.

He pulled back far enough to see her face. "Are you okay?" His eyes softened at the sight of the now-cleaned wound, which felt hot and angry. "Does it hurt?"

"Only when I smile." And she did. Unable to keep the sentiment away now that Francis was here and she was in his arms. "But I'm concerned about my mother, if she's safe. Blanche *is* involved, just like you thought. I don't understand much of anything at the moment, and that makes me emotional." She glanced at Colton, who watched them with interest.

Faith had crossed the room, most likely to give them some privacy. Ashley had liked the woman's warm concern when they'd met on the street. She could understand why Francis was so loyal to his employers. She'd only met Luke briefly, and at the time she'd thought him Benson's murderer, but now she knew the truth. "Tomorrow, we'll set things right," she said softly. "Mr. McCutcheon will be free."

Francis stepped back and unbuckled first one gun belt, laying it on the bed next to the rifle, and then the second. Bending, he shimmied loose the wall board behind the bed and began placing the guns inside. "The man responsible will want you dead, Ashley," he said softly as he replaced the board back in its slot, hiding the guns. "So you can't tell what you know. Do you understand? We have to keep you safe."

She did, but here in the room with Francis, she felt completely safe. He'd not let anything happen to her. "I do. And I'll be careful. Mr. Guthrie said I was to stay in this room with Mrs. McCutcheon. The cowboys next door will keep watch all night."

"That's right, they will. And I'd trust any of them with my life. But I'll not leave you alone." He gazed into her eyes. "With Smokey out at your place, you, Faith, and Colton need a guard inside. That person is me."

She followed his gaze to the bed and the one gun he'd put on the bedside table, feeling a mixture of nerves and relief.

"Don't be afraid." Francis stretched out on the bed, leaned back against the headboard, and opened his arms.

Feeling a mite self-conscious, Ashley eased her way into his embrace, careful of her wounded cheek. "He found me in the woods on the shortcut to town," she whispered close to Francis's ear. "He chased me through the trees. I fell. I thought I was dead. Somehow, I escaped." To her horror, hot tears pooled in her eyes, and a moment later, they spilled out. She had no way to express her relief at being here with Francis's arm tight around her. As bad as her words would sound, she *was* worried about what others would think when she told the sheriff what she'd seen and heard tonight. But only because they would be her words against Blanche's.

With a gentle touch, he brushed a few strands of hair from her face and then dried her tears with a handkerchief Mrs. McCutcheon handed him. "You've nothin' to worry about now. You're safe. We have men and we have guns. When you tell Jack tomorrow what you know, he'll have to lock up Blanche where she can't hurt anyone else." He looked at her and then over to Faith. "And there's more good news, Faith. Colton. We have reinforcements camping close by. As well as a well-known judge."

Even in the dim lamplight, Ashley saw Faith's expression brighten.

"Really?" Faith said. "Harrison Wesley?"

Francis nodded. "He'll be in the sheriff's office at sunup. We thought better than him riding in tonight with everyone's nerves on edge. Men're jumpy. The town's walkin' on eggshells. As long as things stay quiet, we just have a few hours to wait."

Ashley's stomach squeezed. "But my mother? I need to do something."

"Smokey won't let any harm come to her."

Trusting Francis, she laid her head on his chest, liking the sound of his beating heart. She was drawn to him like no other person in her life. Did they have a future together? His idea about moving to Y Knot was never far from her mind. Would someone actually kill her to keep her silent? That threat was difficult to believe.

"You're still trembling, darlin'," Francis whispered, taking her into his arms. "You've nothin' to fear. Roady'll set up the meeting tomorrow so you'll only have to tell your story once. Rest now. You'll need your strength in the mornin'. Close your eyes and sleep. I'll stay awake."

Ashley snuggled onto Francis's warm chest feeling as if she'd been there her whole life. She *was* safe. Francis wouldn't allow anyone or anything to hurt her. Faith had lain down on the other bed in the room and pulled her son close. Danger was just outside that door. Too bad they didn't know whom they had to fear.

Chapter Forty-Nine

Jack Jones and Deputy Clark were having coffee at the sheriff's desk when Francis walked in before sunup with Roady and Judge Wesley on one side and Ashley on the other. Ike, Jonathan, and Bob had stayed in the woods. Following behind were Faith, Leonard Browning, Pedro, Shad, and Colton. All the men, except him, had their sidearms. He would remedy that soon enough. An hour ago, Francis spotted Tanner outside the eatery, waiting for the place to open. The two made brief eye contact, but that was all. No one had heard from Smokey and Nick.

When their group crowded into the small office, Jack shot to his feet, overturning his cup onto his messy desk. Coffee went everywhere.

The deputy stood, a menacing scowl pulling his face.

"What the hell?" Jack barked out. He shook the scalding liquid off his hand, splattering Clark in the face.

The deputy gave an angry growl and wiped away the moisture.

"That's exactly what I'd like to know," Harrison responded.

The judge was an imposing figure when angry—and he was angry. Had been since he'd heard the news about Luke being locked up. The glower on his face exceeded that of the deputy and would scare the toughest criminal.

Shock and then relief crossed Jack's face when he recognized Harrison. "Judge! You've arrived. Thank you for coming. Tensions here are running high. I don't like keeping a man locked up longer than necessary. He needs his day in court. Now that you're here, should we plan on tomorrow? Will that—"

"Be quiet, Jack," Harrison commanded stepping forward.

Jack stumbled back.

"I'm not trying Luke McCutcheon on some trumped-up murder charge. You have no evidence except the uncorroborated word of Blanche Van Gleek."

"I… I do have other evidence," Jack sputtered.

"What's going on out there?" Luke called from his cell. "Is that you, Wesley? Damn good to hear your voice!"

Faith broke away and hurried in to where Luke was confined, followed by Y Knot's attorney-at-law, Leonard Browning.

Others must have witnessed their group enter the sheriff's office, because people began to pile inside as well, lining the walls on either side. Jed Kasterlee from the hotel, a few early morning diners from the café, as well as Daniel Clevenger, Joe Brunn, Neil, and some cowboys Francis didn't know.

"What other evidence do you have?" the judge asked.

Jack straightened and held his head high. "Horse tracks to the Van Gleek cabin that come south from Y Knot and then continue into town."

"Luke admitted he rode into her yard and went up to her door to ask if she'd seen Colton. From there, did they go straight into town?"

Jack's gaze roamed the group. "No."

"No? 'Course not," Wesley went on. "After Luke spoke with Van Gleek, he went back to his campsite where Colton eventually returned. Then they went into town, got cleaned up, and went to Joe's wedding that afternoon. Those tracks mean nothing."

Jack's face flamed scarlet. "You haven't even spoken with him."

The judge looked at Jack intently. "I don't have to. You got anything else?"

Jack shook his head.

"Release McCutcheon," Judge Wesley said. "Everyone in this room knows he'd never kill a man for money. He's rich. Besides, who commits murder and then goes to a wedding, for God's sake? The whole bloody situation is preposterous!" The last word he all but barked out.

Deputy Clark rose to his full height, his face enflamed and forehead slicked with sweat.

Seemed he knew his authority was about to be usurped.

"You don't have the jurisdiction to march in and—"

Harrison's eyes flashed. "I have *every* authority, Deputy! With or without new evidence. Just so happens new circumstances *have* come to light that will absolve the prisoner."

Francis was grateful he wasn't on the receiving end of the judge's anger.

Grumbling from the townsfolk went around the room.

"We knew this would happen…"

"They're friends, what did you expect…"

"McCutcheon won't pay for his crime—not like the rest of us would have to…"

"Quiet!" Joe Brunn said. "It ain't right to keep an innocent man locked up for something he didn't do."

Harrison stuck out his hand palm up while nailing Jack to the back wall with a heated glare. "The key."

Feet defiantly spread wide, Jack bit out, "First let's hear the new evidence."

Judge Wesley's face became so red Francis feared the man would suffer a stroke.

Harrison turned to the townsfolk. "You'll need to clear out so we can settle this matter now. I don't want any disgruntled bystander pulling his gun to even any scores."

Everyone filed out the door and crowded around the windows looking in. When the room was empty of bystanders, Roady closed the door and started for Luke's cell.

Luke stood at the bars, a wide smile splitting his face. "Harrison, seeing you is about the best gift I could get today!"

Judge Wesley gave Luke a stern look. "Now you hush up, Luke, and let Browning do the talking for you."

Browning nodded. "We want to explain what we now know about Mrs. Van Gleek and what happened last night."

Luke glanced at Jack, his expression turning dark. "You gonna let me out of here or not?" Faith placed her hand over Luke's.

Jack slid his hand into his pocket and felt around. His gaze skimmed over to Clark and then to the floor. "You got the key?" he whispered to Clark, but everyone in the room heard the question.

The deputy's nostrils flared. "You brought him his breakfast." Clark looked like he wanted to storm out.

"So I did," Jack mumbled. "I'll find it soon enough."

Luke pushed his fingers through his hair. "Soon enough is *not* soon enough!"

"Never mind," Judge Wesley said. "Let's hear this new evidence."

"What's this about last night?" Jack asked, looking at Clark, who shrugged.

"Tell 'em, Miss Adair," Colton called out. "Tell what you saw and heard."

Francis encouraged Ashley forward until she was in front of Judge Wesley, who stood next to the cell bars.

Behind Luke's head, faces peered in through the small window above Luke's cot. Francis wondered briefly how they'd managed to get themselves up that high. Must be standing on a wagon. "Just say what you told me, Ashley. Everyone here, besides Jones and Clark, have already heard the tellin', so you don't have to be frightened."

"Now, miss, you ready to swear on this Bible that you'll tell the truth?" Judge Wesley asked.

Ashley swallowed and stretched out her shaky hand.

Francis knew she'd stay strong. Her voice soft but steady, she pledged to tell the truth. Her good word would be measured against the lying Blanche Van Gleek. Ashley had a lot to lose. He hoped she knew she also had much more to gain.

"Speak up, Miss Adair, with your important information," Jack snapped. "Why didn't you come to us straightaway?"

The judge weaved his fingers together and leaned back against the cell bars. "Let her tell her story, man."

"Last night, a sound outside awakened me after I'd gone to sleep."

Francis didn't miss all the men in the room, as well as Faith and Colton, intently watching the sheriff and deputy to discern their reaction to the news about Blanche's nighttime activities. Pride for Ashley's strength pushed at his chest. She recounted the story with barely a waver in her voice.

"The moment I saw the figure of a man, Francis's speculations flashed into my mind," Ashley continued, and looked straight at Jack. "He'd been right all along."

Jack's gaze widened as he digested her words. "W-What? I can hardly—" His gaze cut around the group. "Who *was* it?"

"A cloak covered his identity."

Clark puffed out his chest. "That's the most outrageous invention of a falsehood I've ever heard." He glowered at the judge. "This hick has seduced Miss Adair, and now she'll say anything, do anything, even lie to all of us to set McCutcheon free." He frowned at Ashley and pointed a finger in her face. "Did he ask you to marry him, darlin'?"

Without warning, Francis lunged forward and shoved the deputy against the cell.

An outburst went up from the group.

The man outweighed Francis by at least twenty pounds, but he didn't care. Satisfaction registered in his gut when Clark's head snapped back and hit the bars. How dare he imply that about Ashley? "Is that cut on her face a lie?" he gritted out as he pressed the man back, Clark's stale whiskey breath hot in his face. "And the one on her arm?"

"Order! Order!" Judge Wesley shouted. "Cease and desist immediately, or I'll throw you both out of here."

"Francis!" Luke said. "Ease up."

Clark, no longer taken by surprise, shoved Francis.

He stumbled backward, both their gazes full of anger.

"Go on, Miss Adair," Judge Wesley said. "What else did the unidentified visitor say?"

"For Blanche not to get jittery. To stick to their story. That the law didn't have any other evidence but her word against Mr. McCutcheon." She glanced over her shoulder at Luke. "And if

Blanche did get any ideas about turning him in, she'd end up like Mildred."

Jones and Clark took in the new information without twitching an eye.

"We'll have to worry about the key to Luke's cell later," Judge Wesley turned to Jack. "Your next move is to go out to that house immediately. Arrest Blanche Van Gleek before she has a chance to run off."

Jack nodded.

Clark glowered but remained silent.

Judge Wesley turned and in a loud voice addressed the faces in the window. "If any of you people dare to interfere with your sheriff in the execution of his duty, I'll be pleased to hang you as accomplices after the fact to murder. So don't you all go running off telling tales and encouraging people to flee the law."

The faces drew back, their mouths open and gazes wide.

Then the judge leaned in toward Jack and Clark. "Roady has two men out at the house now, standing watch to make sure Mrs. Adair isn't hurt. Be sure not to confuse them with the murderer. I don't want any Heart of the Mountains men getting shot. Is that clear?"

Jack inhaled, his hand falling to his sidearm. "Perfectly."

"Well, what are you waiting for? Get moving!"

"Roady, Shad," Luke called. "Go with 'em. Let's keep everything on the up-and-up." He looked at Judge Wesley. "But what about the key? And me getting out?"

"We'll start the search while Jack and Clark go dispense justice. The key must be around here somewhere."

Jack gave a dirty look around the room and then pushed through the men and out the door, followed by his deputy, Roady, and Shad.

Chapter Fifty

What was happening? This morning, Blanche finally got up after lying awake through the night, elusive sleep playing with her mind.

Angelia made her toast and told her Ashley must have risen early and gone into town—for what, she didn't know.

Blanche thought she might. Was it possible the girl overheard any of the conversation last night? Had she gone to the sheriff? Not knowing was almost worse than being in jail. She was in a prison of her own making.

How long can I continue? Feels like I'm losing my mind… Either I'll have to confess or sneak away in the night. I'd better make a decision before my options are gone.

A loud knock sounded on the front door.

Blanche's cup clattered into its saucer. She glanced at the clock, and a sick feeling welled up inside. "Who could that be, Angelia? It's barely past six."

Angelia set the dish she'd been drying into the cupboard, fear flashing across her face. "Another mystery? I pray nothing has happened to Ashley. Now her absence is scaring me. Could she have eloped last night with that young cowboy? She's been acting very strange of late. I've never seen her so taken with anyone."

Blanche made a movement to stand.

"You stay put," Angelia commanded. "I'll see who's at the door."

Francis and Ashley were together again yesterday? My situation is more precarious than I thought.

Blanche glanced to the hallway with an overwhelming desire to flee.

The door opened. She heard men's voices and then footsteps. Her stomach painfully clenched. Sheriff Jones and the deputy, as well as men from McCutcheon ranch.

Jack Jones's gaze flitted to the side and then back at her. His chin dipped low. "Blanche, you're under arrest. Stand and come peacefully."

Words she'd thought she'd never hear. Every ounce of energy drained away. Jail. *Will being locked up keep me safe, or will I be more vulnerable for Mr. Romantic to kill me?* "W-Why? What for?"

Mr. Guthrie's eyes twinkled. He and two other ranch hands tried to hide their wobbly smiles, but their delight was clear as water at the turn of events.

"Killing Benson," Jack said. "But then, I'm sure you already knew that."

Her muscles tensed and she glanced at the kitchen door. Was a getaway possible? There were five of them and one of her.

"What's this?" Angelia demanded. "That's preposterous. What evidence do you have? Blanche was an eyewitness to his murder."

"You're correct, Mrs. Adair," Roady said. "But not by Luke's hand."

Angelia's narrowed gaze slid over to Blanche, and she slowly backed away. "Where's Ashley?" she whispered. "She wasn't here this morning." She searched one face and then the next. "Do you know? Has Blanche hurt her too?"

"She's safe in town, ma'am," the cowhand named Shad Petty said. "Has been since last night. No need to worry about her."

Blanche sat there, stunned, moisture slicking her palms. What did they know? "On what grounds do you arrest me?" she found herself asking. She didn't recognize the deep, calm voice that came out of her mouth.

"We'll go over that when we get you into town," Jack said. "If you don't want us taking you in in your nightclothes, I'd advise you get dressed."

"Nick's standing guard outside, so don't think you can climb out your window," Mr. Guthrie said, his tone hard.

She stood, went to her room, and dressed. Soon they were on the way to town, her hands shackled behind her back as she walked ahead of the horsemen. Cool air kissed her cheeks. How had her life gotten so out of control? One bad decision had led to another, and another, until she lived each day in a web of lies. A breeze swayed the green treetops, and she raised her face to the sun. This might be her final walk on this road. Regret gripped her stomach, making her want to be sick. She did her best to take in the view, the frilly birch trees, the hawk floating in the wispy clouds, the tiny lacy flowers growing beneath the small buttercup leaves. Nothing was worth losing all this…

The handcuffs pinched and she straightened. What had Ashley heard? If only she knew, perhaps she'd have a chance to lie her way free. Maybe Jack and the others were bluffing, waiting for her to confess or say something they needed to know but didn't. For now, she'd stick to the story, like she'd been told. Maybe a miracle would happen.

Leaning against the saloon's bar top, Tanner took a sip of warm beer, letting the brew ease his midmorning hunger. He'd needed to wet his whistle, even though the saloon was around the corner and off the main street where he'd been flashing the money clip Francis had given him last night. So far, only a couple of people commented that Neil Huntsman had one like it. He'd had to wait until they asked about the unusual thingamajig and then he'd casually pick up the conversation. People had been interested, some only because they'd never seen the likes before. Still, he shouldn't get discouraged. He'd only just started. Hopefully somebody soon would give him a lead. At the moment, the piece, holding the original two dollars, sat beside his glass of beer.

Being the only one standing at the bar, Tanner rested on his elbows and lifted his almost-empty mug to his lips, scanning the room.

A man sat in the back of the room by himself. His hat rested crown down on the tabletop next to a bottle of whiskey. Even this early in the day, he was sunburned and his clothes sweat-stained.

The bartender came through the side door, three bottles in his hands, and proceeded around the bar, setting the whiskey on the back wall shelf. "You want another, friend?" he asked, looking at Tanner's empty glass.

"No, thanks. Best be on my way." He made a show of peeling off a dollar bill and then waited for change which he dropped into his pocket.

"I like that clip," the bartender said. "Seems I've seen one like it." He looked up at Tanner. "But you're new, aren't ya? You with the ranch from Y Knot?"

"Nope. Looking for some odd jobs before moving on. You say you've seen a clip like this before? I thought mine was one of a kind." He bounced the clip in his palm.

"Sure. A man don't forget something like that."

Tanner winked. "I've never been in Priest's Crossing until today. Who has one like it?"

The bartender scratched his chin. "Darned if I can remember."

The man in the back stood and ran his hand through his thick hair. He glanced around and then tossed a coin onto the tabletop, starting their way.

"Who's that?" Tanner whispered to the bartender. "Maybe I'll ask if he needs help. From the looks of his clothes, he's been working."

"Livery man, Pink Kelly. He just might give you a go, at that." The barkeep's face brightened. "I know! Neil Huntsman, teller at the bank, has one exactly the same." A narrowed gaze slid Tanner's way. "That ain't his, I hope."

"Said the clip's mine," he said defensively, guilt pricking his conscience. *For the time, that is.*

The livery man looked over Tanner's shoulder as he passed. His feet stopped as he stared.

Tanner tried to read his eyes. "The piece gets me a lot of attention."

"I can sure see why." Kelly pushed on his hat and took a step.

The bartender reached out and stopped him. "This young fella is looking for work, Pink. Can you hire him on? You're usually running a couple of weeks behind. He might give you some relief."

The man swung around.

The dark gaze taking in his countenance sent a chill down Tanner's spine.

Chapter Fifty-One

Luke stared into the next chamber that held the woman who'd accused him of murder. This was his first look since she'd pointed a finger into his face, proclaiming to the world he was a killer. Without the bruises and cut lip, she looked different. Younger. Smaller, as she huddled on her cot pushed into the corner. Her limbs trembled, and she hadn't glanced in his direction once since Jones and Clark had escorted her inside and locked the door. Too bad the key that had opened her door didn't work for both cells.

Sounds from the other room attested to the fact Jack and Clark were still searching. Lunchtime had come and gone, with Daniel Clevenger handing him a sandwich through the bars since they couldn't open his door for a tray. Luke and the others had insisted Faith, Colton, and Ashley return to the hotel and lie down after getting a bite at the café.

Seemed he wasn't the only one who hadn't slept last night. Unbeknownst to the women, Shad, Smokey, and Pedro were keeping watch on their room, one in the next room over, one at the back door, and another at the front. The rest of the hands, as well as the judge and lawyer, were taking their noontime meal in the eatery across the street, after which they intended to take up the search.

Luke rubbed a hand across his face. He'd have to call for a blanket for privacy if they didn't find that blasted key. "The sentence'll go better for you if you cut your losses now and confess."

Unless she turned totally away and faced the wall, he could see her profile. Right now, she stared open-eyed at nothing, her cheeks wet with tears. He shouldn't feel pity for such a woman, but locking up a female in a jail cell next to a man went against his conscience. "Your accomplice is still free. He can make a run for it, day or night, and leave you holding the bag. You want that to happen?"

She was like a figure carved out of stone. She didn't even wipe her tears.

"I may be half-Cheyenne, but my pa raised me and my brothers with an honorable backbone. We were taught to take responsibility for our actions, no matter what they were. As bad as the circumstances can get, they can't be as heavy as a guilty conscience. At least, not to my way of thinkin'."

Faith had wanted to stay to speak with Blanche, but Harrison thankfully dissuaded her. There was no help for what Mrs. Van Gleek had done. At least Faith now had Miss Adair to talk to. The strain on his wife's face these past few days had grown worse. Seeing a loved one suffer was never easy. The end of his ordeal was in sight, just as soon as the key was located. For Blanche Van Gleek, who knew what would happen?

"I didn't kill Benson."

Startled out of his woolgathering, Luke looked up in the dim room to find her watching him. Her gaze was suspicious and hard. The things Joe said about her henpecking Benson came back to him in a heartbeat. And her flirtatious nature.

With what Ashley witnessed last night, the lawmen had enough evidence to try her for murder, and her alone without an accomplice. A person didn't have to pull the trigger to be guilty. They had more than Ashley's testimony. They had the bloody boot print and, hopefully, the money clip. "That right? Who did, then?"

"You."

She was still playing this game. He took a deep breath to keep his voice calm.

"You know that's not true. And just as soon as Jack finds the key he lost, I'll be out of this hole, but you won't. And your friend, your accomplice, whoever he is, may be laying the groundwork to convict you good and tight. You'll hang, and he'll be free. The longer you wait, the worse off you'll be. Tell us who he is before somebody else gets hurt. Remember the old woman two nights ago? His next victim could be anyone." He'd like to say her friend, Ashley's mother, but he didn't bully women, not even one who'd tried to ruin his life.

"You're trying to frighten me. But you won't win, Mr McCutcheon. I'm very calm. And I'll remain very calm until they have more evidence against you."

She didn't look calm. Her repeated deep breaths said different. And the way she rolled the hem of her blouse with her fingers. He'd say she was on the verge of a breakdown. "Then why are you shaking?"

"Because I'm locked in the same room with the man who killed my husband and beat me within one inch of my life. Being in the cell next to yours makes my blood run cold."

She's good. I'll have to give her credit for that.

Jack stepped into the room. His shirt was stained in sweat, his face shiny.

Luke stood. If Jack irritated him before, the anger the sight of him created in his gut now didn't feel natural. The fool didn't even have to speak for Luke to know he hadn't found the key. The expression on his face said everything.

"Think, Jack!" he growled. "I've been unjustly locked up in here for more days than I like to remember and now you can't find the key? Retrace your steps!" He grasped a bar and gave a good shake. "Where've you been? Call the smithy. He can break the lock."

"Just calm down, Luke," he responded. "I've already thought of that. Been down to the smithy several times but can't find Pink. What's a few more hours? Lie back and relax. I've retraced my steps a couple of times over. The key will turn up. If not, as soon as Pink's back from wherever he is, he'll bust you out."

How badly would he be crying if the tables were turned? That easygoing tone he used when he knew he was guilty of some stupid mistake grated on Luke's nerves. The sound was seared in Luke's memory from Jack's days in Y Knot. "How come the blasted thing was off the key ring where it belonged? I've seen you use that several times."

"I figured they're too easy to spot and steal in a clump."

"Or lose?" Luke tipped his head. He recalled the large ring with three keys, one for each cell. "Whose idea was it to separate them?"

Jack took a big swallow, making his Adam's apple bob up and down.

Anger hissed through him. "Jack?"

"Clark's. Two days ago. Was worried one of your men would steal the keys and break you out. Sounded like a good move at the time, but now I wish I'd said no. I hate tearing apart the jail or breaking the lock just to release you."

Is the deputy preparing to make a move? Why would he suggest such a thing if he weren't? And just when I'd begun to breathe easier.

"I'm headed over to speak with Daniel at the eatery. Have another look around there. Can I pick you up something? You know, since you should be released by now."

The dolt. "No! Just don't stop looking until you find that key! I want out." *Before your deputy, or someone else, gets desperate and acts.* Jack didn't know that when Luke was cleared, Roady had slipped him a weapon he'd stashed under his cot. He had six shots, and if the time came, he'd make each and every one count.

Still, he felt an urgency. Something was in the air, and the foul stench of the jail wasn't it. A plan was underway, and he didn't like not knowing what that was. Or the fact that a killer, one who had almost been identified last night, was still on the loose. He had to get out of there to protect Faith and Colton. Time wasn't waiting on some key. No sir, not at all.

"Before you leave, bring me another blanket, a hammer, and some nails so I can have a little privacy." Blanche Van Gleek hadn't moved a muscle since Jack arrived.

"That'd be considered a weapon."

"I'm a free man!"

"Oh, that's right," Jack said, a smile appearing. "Sure thing, Luke. I'll be right back."

Chapter Fifty-Two

With a burning cough, Luke sat upright on his cot. He blinked, the searing air bringing him quickly to his senses.

They hadn't found the key.

It was the middle of the night.

He was still in his cell.

Rolling to his side, he stood, only to drop to his hands and knees, gasping for air. Black, acrid smoke roiled around the room and an amber glow radiated through the doorway to the front office. The place was on fire!

"Wake up!" he shouted to Blanche. "Get on the floor!" With blood pounding in his ears, he jerked down the blanket he'd nailed to the ceiling to give her a modicum of privacy and plunged the covering in the bucket of water, which he and Jack had filled only halfway by passing glasses of water through the bars the day before. Soaking up as much moisture as was available, he pushed the dripping wool through the bars to Blanche. "Stay down and cover yourself with this until help arrives!"

"We're going to die! Burn to death!" Her eyes, rounded in fear, cut from corner to corner of her enclosure. "Benson has exacted his revenge straight from hell!"

You won't die, but I might. Luke quickly stripped off his grimy shirt, soaked up the remainder of water left in his bucket, then held the garment to his mouth. Climbing onto his cot, he grasped the bars with one hand and pulled his face close, trying to find fresh air while scanning the area as he looked for help.

"Fire!" he shouted. Had anyone seen the flames? All seemed quiet. "Fire! Fire!"

Suddenly a cry went up. He didn't recognize the voice.

Coughing, he looked around. Flames snapped around the edges of the door. It creeped inside. If they were going to rescue Blanche, they'd have to move soon. After the doorway was blocked, no one could enter. "Fire!"

"Fire, fire, help me, please!" Blanche shrieked, her volume loud even over the crackling flames. "It's hot! The heat's unbearable! Help me, please!"

The town bell clanged.

Luke sensed movement all around. Roady yelled from outside his window. Stepping up on his cot, he saw Faith and Colton. "If you don't get in here quick," he yelled. "Blanche will die! The way is still clear. But not for long!"

"Luke! Luke!" Faith screamed, her face contorted in horror. Her head twisted back and forth as she searched for something to do, some way to save him. She reached up. "My love, my love!"

Colton was at the side of the building, jumping toward the window. "Pa! Pa!"

Fear, an emotion he wasn't used to feeling, speared through him with exacting pain. Reaching out, he touched the tips of Faith's fingers one time and then glared at Roady. "Get them out of here! Now!"

One last touch. One last look for eternity. How had this travesty come to pass?

From behind, Shad grasped Faith around the middle and hoisted her up, kicking and screaming. Nick did the same with Colton. Ike had arrived as well as Jonathan and the rest. In the blink of an eye, Faith and Colton were gone.

"Get on the floor and wait!" Roady shouted. "I'll be right back with horses and ropes. We'll bust out the bars."

"That'll take too long. Blanche will be dead by then. She can't last much longer in this smoke." He looked over his shoulder, first at her and then at the spreading fire. "It's risky, but I think someone can still get through the flames to her cell. Hurry! Jones has that key!"

All Luke saw was a blur of movement. With his head turned and face pushed at the bars, he gasped for breath then stepped off his cot and swabbed the empty bucket with his shirt, hoping for a few more drops of water. Through the smoke, he saw Blanche's form huddled under the wet blanket on the floor. She wasn't screaming anymore, and he wondered if she was dead.

Suddenly Shad was inside, darting around the flames. He jammed a key into Blanche's lock and swung the door wide. He barely gave Luke a moment's glance before scooping her up, blanket and all, then dashed from the room amid racking coughs. A moment later, the blanket, freshly drenched in water, was pushed through the bars of his window.

The wet cloth fell on his back, giving an instant of relief from the sweltering heat. He tried to stand but collapsed to one knee, pulling the blanket to his face. Who would have thought that this wretched, flea-filled blanket would feel like a blessing? Next to him the flames ate up the side of Blanche's cell. They'd be overhead soon.

A moment of clarity filled Luke's mind. Everyone he loved was here in the cell with him. His parents, brothers, Charity, and of course Faith, and all his children. His heart filled so tight pain crushed his chest. A male Indian face became clear. *My father. His blood flows through my veins.* A Cheyenne death song he'd never heard before came through Luke's lips, surprising him. The chant was so weak he was sure he was the only person to hear.

Peace descended over his mind, and he crumpled to the floor.

Francis tore down the street toward the livery, the heavy weight of his Colt back on his hip. Halfway there, Fox Dancing and Painted Bear Stone met him, each leading three saddled horses. Not a word was said as Francis swung aboard his, noting the ropes on the saddles, and grasped the reins of the others. With feet still out of the stirrups, he hauled his horse around and galloped back to the orange inferno, lashing the end of his reins over and under to demand more speed, dragging the other horses behind.

Who set the fire? Bob, the newly arrived ranch hand who Roady had recruited to keep watch over the jail, had been hit over the head and was just now coming around. This blaze was deliberate. The killer wanted Blanche dead so she couldn't talk. Wanted Luke dead, as well, probably thinking the case would be put to rest if somebody paid.

Rage ripped inside. Not at the killer, but himself. He should've done more! Dug deeper! Moved faster! Because he hadn't, Luke might die.

As diligent as the water brigade of townspeople worked, their buckets of water weren't doing much.

He circled to the back. Roady, Shad, Smokey, and all the hands didn't need orders. Within seconds, six ropes wrapped around the window bars, strung back to the horses, and wrapped around the saddle horns. The men mounted up.

"This won't be enough!" Jonathan yelled, his face contorted with anguish. "We need tools!"

Amazingly, Harrison Wesley and Leonard Browning appeared around the building with two hefty splitting mauls and an ax from the blacksmith shop. Nick, Tanner, and Pedro grabbed the gear, ran forward, and began chopping away at the window frame.

Sixty seconds felt like sixty years. The men worked as if the devil was spurring them on with a flaming-hot pitchfork, and in some ways, that was true. Redmond, fearful of the fiery sparks, snorted and pawed the ground. With an aching clenched jaw, he glanced over to the others mounted beside him. Roady, Smokey, Shad, Ike, Jonathan. They waited for the signal like contenders in a horse race. Francis felt their pain. The sight was the only thing that kept him from breaking down. He couldn't lose Luke. *They* couldn't lose Luke. This was a nightmare that wouldn't end.

Turning, Pedro shouted, "Go, go!" He waved them away as the others stepped clear from the window and ropes.

The riders swung their horses around and spurred with a vengeance. Francis goaded with every ounce of strength he had and galloped forward, bracing himself for the jolt to come.

God, we're all counting on you! Let's get this done…

The horses hit hard. Redmond went down on his knees and almost rolled to his side. Clinging to the saddle, Francis stayed aboard as the gelding scrambled to his feet. Smokey hadn't been as lucky. Through the thick, cinder-filled air, Francis couldn't see if they'd been successful. Sparks rained down, singeing Redmond's ears and crest, making him snort and jerk to the side. Francis felt a drag on the rope. Not heavy, but something anchored to the end.

Hope leaped up. He forced Redmond forward, unwinding the rope from the saddle horn and flicking it out of the way of his horse's prancing hooves. When he was closer, he saw the men hefting Nick up on their shoulders. Petty disappeared into the window. Would he be strong enough to lift Luke out if he were unconscious? Dead weight was a curse.

Whoever tried to kill Luke will pay! Francis swung out of his saddle, not minding when Redmond galloped off. He pushed his way through the crowd until he found Tanner. The boot print had only excluded Neil Huntsman. Clark and Kasterlee could go either way. Whenever Francis was in the restaurant, Clevenger never stopped long enough for him to get a fix.

"Tanner," he shouted above the ruckus, his eyes glued on the jail window. "Give me the money clip." Having the piece once again in his possession, Francis, determined, strode to the front of the building. He shoved the clip in everyone's face as they worked. "Seen this before?" All he got were head shakes and shrugs until finally, a man he didn't know said the piece belonged to Neil Huntsman.

Frustrated, he saw a man and the local bartender standing at the mouth of the alley with their hands on their sides as if they needed to catch their breath. Francis ran forward. "You ever see this before?"

"Sure," both said at the same time.

Don't say Neil Huntsman. "Where? Who's the proper owner? I found it in the dirt."

"Pink Kelly, the livery man," the stranger said.

"That ain't so," the bartender countered. "Belongs to some young man new to town. He showed me today, in the saloon," the barkeep said, looking smug. "Pink was there too. Asked about the clip, being the shape is unusual and all. If the thing belonged to him, he would've said so then and there."

Oh, no, he wouldn't! He knew the money clip was an albatross that could drop a noose around his neck.

Without a word, Francis turned and scanned the melee of men through the smoke. Pink had been missing when they'd needed him to break the lock on the cell. He'd been staying out of sight until he could set the fire. That piece of dung was here somewhere, and Francis aimed to find him before he got away. He ran to the back. Counted the men. Who was with the women? Had anyone stayed back to make sure they were safe?

Chapter Fifty-Three

His time was up. Blanche hadn't died. He should have used more lanterns. She would spill her guts any time, and they'd come put him in handcuffs. He had to get out of town, but with all those men he'd be tracked in an instant. What were his options? He couldn't think of one.

"Hey! Get over here and help. We need every man," Jack called, spotting him standing in the shadows of the hotel across the street. The sheriff filled a bucket from the horse trough and ran toward the burning building.

Earlier, he'd seen two of the McCutcheon hands carrying a fighting Mrs. McCutcheon and her son up the stairs. Was Ashley there too? The thought of her made his fists itch to exact some revenge. She was Blanche's friend and had turned tail the first chance she'd had. If only he'd caught her last night, none of this would be happening.

He'd been a fool to stay in town so long. He'd had days to ride out, get lost in the mountains. Head for Mexico. But that would have meant leaving everything he'd slaved over a hot forge to accomplish for countless years. Huntsman would have wondered why he was withdrawing his savings. He wouldn't have any good answers to the questions the teller might ask. He felt like a rat in a trap with no place to run or hide.

That may be so, but he'd not go down alone. Turning, he made for the back door of the hotel. He had no intention of helping put out what he'd started. He'd try his chances across country, but he'd take along a little insurance. Using the back stairs, he rapped on the door to the room Jed told him the woman and boy occupied.

The door handle violently rattled. "Open the door! Let us out!"

That must be Mrs. McCutcheon, because her voice didn't sound like Ashley.

"Open the door!" the boy called. "Please!"

He lowered his tone. "Where's the key?"

"We don't know. Look around."

That was Ashley. Her tear-filled voice sounded frightened, just like the other two. He'd take all three along if he could, if he was prepared. That would teach everyone a lesson they wouldn't soon forget. For now, sneaking off would be difficult enough without two screaming females. He spotted the key on a table at the end of the hall. Without saying a word, he unlocked the door swiftly and stepped inside.

Ashley jerked back, her eyes large.

In a swift move, he grabbed the kid by the arm and yanked him into the hallway, slamming the door behind. Smaller, the kid would fit behind him on the saddle and act as a shield for anyone thinking to shoot him in the back.

"Knock off the shenanigans," he yelled as the boy kicked him hard in the shin. "Calm down if you don't want to lose a mouthful of teeth!" He smacked him up against the wall. "You'll learn fast enough I ain't kiddin'!"

"Take me instead!" Ashley begged through the door as he locked the women inside. "I'll go calmly. I won't make a sound. I'll do anything you want, just please, leave the boy here."

"I'll go," McCutcheon's wife pleaded. "Leave Colton, please, leave Colton."

The two women pounded madly on the door. They'd soon attract every man out there with their loud, ear-piercing cries. He needed to move and fast.

The boy, frenzied like a wild bear cub, fought him every step of the way. Twice, Colton bit his wrist, and he had to jerk his flesh from the boy's teeth. He didn't have time now to straighten him out, but he would later, oh yes, and enjoy the process.

Dragging the boy along behind him, he doubled back the way he'd come. At the door, he peered out to be sure the way was clear before he ran out into the night. Once out, he'd toss the kid over his shoulder and make for the mountains, stealing a horse along the way. His livery was no longer safe.

People were still frantically tossing buckets of water on the glowing red sheriff's office, making his getaway quite simple. He hadn't taken more than ten steps when, somehow, the boy smacked him on the side of the head with a rake he'd snatched along the way. His hand must have slackened from the blow because the boy kicked him and then jerked his arm free, spinning on his heel.

"Colton, run!"

The young ranch hand! The one who'd first shown up. But this time he was armed, and his face shone with burning resolve.

Resignation filled him. "Go for your gun, and I'll shoot the boy instead of you. I'm gonna die, anyway. Either here or at the end of a rope. I'll take the kid with me."

Colton stood only a few yards away, staring wide-eyed.

Once the kid heard his intent, he'd lost his chance to dash out of range. He'd kill the boy. Make a mark on the high-handed McCutcheon family they'd never get over.

A standoff.

His body stiffened, and he went for his gun.

So did the cowboy.

BAM BAM

Kelly's eyes jerked open as he took in the kid's astonished face and then looked down at the arrow sticking out of his chest, the white feathers of the fletching catching his eye. His own gun still rested in his holster. What happened? He didn't know. He tumbled forward, not feeling a thing.

"Somebody get Faith!" Roady shouted.

Francis and Colton arrived at the jail just as the men were pulling Nick back through the small window. Heat engulfed everything. The blaze crackled loudly as it consumed the whole building.

Luke lay stretched out in the dirt. Francis hadn't taken the time to check Kelly's body, but with his two shots and the arrow, the man was clearly dead. With a sorrow as large as the Bighorn Canyon, Francis dropped to his knees at Luke's side and lifted his limp hand. He couldn't bear to ask the question.

"He's alive," Roady said, his face covered in black ash and soot. "But just barely."

Some of the town transferred their attention across the street. Embers had rained down in front of the eatery, and flames licked slowly along the boardwalk toward the building. Heart of the Mountain men stood around in a half circle around Luke, their stricken faces a mirror of what Francis felt inside.

Roady's gaze was dead, beaten. "He hasn't moved since we stretched him out," he whispered.

Francis stared at Luke's face—which actually looked peaceful, like he was taking a Sunday afternoon nap. Lunging forward, he placed both his hands on Luke's chest and pressed up and down with all his strength, remembering how Matt had saved Mark's life after he'd almost drowned in the river on the cattle drive about four years ago. The oldest McCutcheon brother had driven his knee into Mark's back with no restraint, giving little thought to how his actions might injure. Feeling crazy, Francis grasped Luke's shoulder and hefted.

Roady helped, the glint in his eyes saying he remembered now too that incident along the rushing river bank.

With single-minded seriousness, Francis drove his knee into Luke's back.

A moment later, Faith, running full tilt, collapsed at Luke's side. An anguished sob tore from her throat.

Luke gasped.

Amid a stir in the men behind them, Francis thought something else must be happening. Still, all he could think through a rush of happiness and relief was that Luke inhaled. Where there was a gasp, there was life. Luke would live.

They rolled Luke back, and Faith enfolded him into her arms, holding his face next to her neck. Her grief-stricken eyes, drenched with tears, met Francis's. "That madman took Colton," she whispered. "I told the men, and they're trailing him, but I'm scared."

"No, here I am, Ma," Colton said, coming closer. "Will Pa be all right?"

Roady nodded. "He's weak, but he's breathing. He should come around anytime."

That was when Francis saw Ashley standing a few feet away. Their gazes locked. Francis stood and strode to her side, taking her in his arms. "You all right?" he asked, relieved things hadn't turned out differently. Something about him on this trip had changed. He felt older, wiser. Ready for uncharted waters. Now that he'd found Ashley Adair, he wasn't letting her go.

Glowering from the confines of his hotel bed, Luke was antsy to get up and get moving, but his men, and wife, weren't listening. He was fine. Better than fine. Right now, he and Faith were alone, with her asleep in the chair next to him, never having left his side since he'd been pulled from the fire last night.

He would never take the sight of his home for granted, even for a second. He wished Fox Dancing and Painted Bear Stone had stayed around, at least so he could thank them for all they'd done. But that was not to be. Any more time spent saddling the horses, and he would have died—and, of course, their help with saving Colton. Hopefully another year wouldn't pass before they returned.

Last night, after the arrow had been pulled from Pink Kelly's chest, Deputy Clark divulged the livery owner was the person to suggest to him about separating the cell keys, and he passed the idea to Jones. The implement still hadn't been found, not that it was needed since the jail was gone, and everyone felt certain Kelly was the reason. They'd never know for certain because the man was dead, and good riddance too.

A knock sounded on the door.

"Come in," he said, as quietly as his smoke-tortured voice allowed.

Harrison Wesley, as well as his attorney, Roady, Smokey, Ike, Pedro, Jonathan, Colton, and a dog-faced Bob all filed into the small room.

"How ya feeling?" Roady asked.

All the men were as anxious as he was to hit the trail.

Faith stirred, and then her eyes opened. After a split second, she smiled, lighting up his
heart.

"Like I told you last night," he said to Roady, "I'm fine. I'm well enough to ride. I say we pack up today and head out." He sat straighter and then grinned at Roady. "Sally'll be happy to finally have her husband home, and I'm sure you're longing to hold your daughter in your arms."

"That's no lie."

Shad, Nick, and Tanner looked through the open door from the hallway.

"Come on in, boys, everyone else is in here." He looked around. "Except Francis. I owe him a lot, from what Faith says. Anyone seen him around?"

"Find Miss Adair and you'll find him," Nick said with a lift of his shoulder. "Last I heard, he was heading to her house and wasn't taking no for an answer."

"Oh?" Faith straightened. "What's this about? They've only known each other barely two weeks." She glanced at the window.

Luke barked out a laugh. "If my memory serves me correctly, falling for you and your charms didn't take me *tha*' long. We had a little over a week on the trail after I discovered you in that dilapidated wagon."

"You were still aggravated with me then. Afraid I'd distract your men."

Her smile warmed him and made him remember exactly why he'd fallen for her, his love. "And I was right, wasn't I? You *were* a distraction. Then we had maybe another week at the ranch? I was a goner." He glanced around at all the smiling faces. The men were nodding, their eyes full of the memory. "Practically every one of you were smitten too."

She laughed and covered her mouth with a shaky hand as the men's faces colored up and avoided her gaze.

Colton was eyeing her like a stranger.

Her cheeks pinked, and she looked more beautiful than she ever had. Luke lifted a brow. "Leave Francis alone. He's no longer the boy he was four years ago. He knows what's best for him."

Jed Kasterlee tapped on the doorjamb. "You have plans for heading out?"

"Today," Luke said. "Just as soon as I get a bath and shave. Still haven't done those yet. I'll be down soon to settle up. What about the Van Gleek woman? What's happening with her?"

"She confessed to everything," Harrison said, jumping in on the conversation. "With the jail out of use for now, she's locked in a room a few doors down. Clark will take her to the women's penitentiary as soon as she's able. She said she didn't know Kelly would kill her husband. I have no way of knowing if that's true or not. She was an accessory, lied about Luke, and would have seen him hanged for their crime, so I sentenced her to twenty years."

Smokey let out a low whistle. "I'm glad I don't have to make that decision."

Luke nodded. That woman had twenty years coming. After what he'd been through, he didn't like to consider that. "And Jones? I haven't seen him since last night."

"He turned in his star before dawn and rode out. No one knows where he's headed."

Roady reached into his pocket. "Any chance you want this?" he asked, handing the money clip to Luke. "Francis gave it back to me last night."

Jed came closer. "What d'ya have there?"

Luke held out the interesting piece in his palm.

"I'll be," Jed said. "Neil has a money clip just like that. And so did Pink Kelly."

Luke noted the hotel owner's deep color, probably for the bad treatment he'd given the family these past days "You're a little late, Kasterlee," Luke said. "Could've used that information six days ago. This one *was* Kelly's. My men found the thing out at Benson's cabin, stuffed between two cushions Too bad your sheriff and deputy hadn't shown an interest in justice. Maybe they'd have figured the truth out sooner. Before the sheriff's office was burned to the ground." Luke cracked a smile and picked up Faith's hand, holding the softness to his lips. "And before I was almost roasted alive." He gazed around at the group, feeling a deep, abiding joy in his heart. "One important fact Kelly didn't count on, and should have, before he tried what he did. I'm not an easy man to kill."

Chapter Fifty-Four

Covered in black, smudgy ash, Francis stood at Ashley's front door. Some four hours prior in the wee hours of the morning, he, along with Harrison Wesley and a few of the other men, had escorted her home with orders for her to get some rest.

A gnawing anxiety tormented his gut. He'd killed a man. A man had died because of his action. When he'd gone after Kelly, he hadn't given much thought as to what would happen when he found him. If Colton's life hadn't been on the line, Francis wasn't sure he'd have had the nerve to shoot.

Killing an animal was one thing; killing a human being, something totally different. Francis was different inside because of it. Changed. He wasn't the same man who'd pulled on his boots yesterday. One thing he did know, he'd do it again for Colton or any of the McCutcheons. Ashley too, of course. Any of the people he loved.

And what about Ashley? When they'd said good night, she'd kept her gaze trained far from his. Granted, he'd been flanked by the judge and others, but still, he'd thought they had something special between them.

The scent of cooking apples wafted to where he stood at her front door. Perhaps he should have taken time to wash and change, but Luke and the men were making ready to set out for home. Taking a calming breath, he removed his hat, then lifted his hand and knocked. He heard footsteps. Prayed they belonged to the girl he loved.

Her mother opened the door.

When she recognized who was calling, her gaze softened, and a smile resembling Ashley's appeared on her face.

"I'd like to apologize for being so hard on you, young man," she said first. "I was wrong about a lot of things."

"Nothin' to apologize for," he said in a clear, strong voice. "You were only lookin' after your daughter. I've come to speak with her, if I could."

"She's resting."

The time was nearing eleven. Her room would be filled with the eastern sun, making sleep impossible. Surely she'd want to speak with him before he left Priest's Crossing. How far should he press her mother? He'd only just crossed over from her bad side, and he was not anxious to return.

"I figured as much. My boss is almost ready to pull out of town. Do you think I might have one minute to say goodbye?"

Mrs. Adair ran a trembling hand down her apron and glanced at the hallway.

She'd forgiven him for seeing to her daughter, but she still didn't seem keen on him as a suitor.

"I guess checking wouldn't hurt." She nodded for him to step inside and then quietly closed the door. Hurrying away, she returned in less than a minute. "Actually, she's not in her bedroom as I'd thought. I'm sure you will find her out with her trees."

Relief flooded his body. They'd get to speak in private. "Thank you." He offered a friendly smile.

She nodded.

Not seeing Ashley close to the house, Francis walked down one row of trees, the scent of the fruit strong. Much work remained to be done. More, he thought, than the two women could accomplish before the critters ruined much of the fruit. He went deeper. Didn't see her anywhere. Glanced about. Went to the patch of saplings, and still no Ashley. Without telling her mother, had she walked into town to see him? Was she as worried as he was about their parting? They were young and had just met, but that didn't change the way he felt. A man knew when the right girl crossed his path.

Climbing the rise, he spotted her sitting on a rock by the stream. His heart swelled and happiness filled his soul. She must have caught sight of him, because she stood and waited. For the first time ever, her hair was loose, flowing around her shoulders. Strands glimmered in the sunshine and danced in the breeze. Her unreadable expression caused more trouble with the butterflies in his stomach. Red rimmed her beautiful green eyes. She'd been crying.

He reached for her hands taking them in his own. "Ashley." That word was all he had. Unless he poured out his heart. He was sure that wasn't the right thing to do. The men in the bunkhouse always said the fastest way to lose a woman was to proclaim your undying love too soon.

The warmth of her hands felt so right in his own. The connection the most magnificent feeling Francis had ever experienced, even over the kiss they'd shared. This moment could define his future. Never had he experienced a more significant instant in his life, except, maybe the day he'd been born. He didn't want to lose her, and yet, in her eyes, he knew he already had. "I've come to say goodbye." *And beg you to come with me.*

She nodded. Her lips twitched as she struggled to smile. "I thought as much." She lifted her hand and cupped his cheek. "You look tired. Did you get any rest at all?"

"Naw. Still too much happenin' in town."

"And you're leaving? Soon?"

"I'd say within the hour. The men are anxious to get home. I can't blame 'em in the least."

Her shoulders slumped. She dropped his hands to gaze at the water. So many things rushed through his mind. What would she say? Was this the end?

"I'm glad Mr. McCutcheon is feeling strong enough after what he went through." She turned back, wiped away a tear. "I'm so thankful he survived and no one else was hurt."

Pink Kelly is dead. A Cheyenne arrow lodged deep in his chest, next to my two bullets. But he knew what she meant. He was thankful, as well.

"Ashley, I'd like to stand here and make small talk all day, but my time's run out. If I don't speak now, I may never get another chance. This moment will pass, and be lost. We'll separate and grow into different people. I don't want to have a regret like that hangin' on my heart. I want to tell you how I feel and what I'm thinkin'. I hope you'll hear me out with an open mind."

Her lips twisted and her brow drew down. A trembling came over her limbs.

He'd never seen such devastated sadness on her face. *Stop now, before all is lost. Give her some time. Ride back next month. Absence makes the heart grow fonder, and all that…*

Stifling his feelings would be the prudent thing to do, but he couldn't. He *had* to know how she felt.

"I love you, Ashley. I want to marry you."

In one blink, her eyes filled with tears and overflowed in a mighty gush. She brushed them away and kept staring at his face.

Not the reaction he'd hoped for, but she was still listening. "I plan to always work for the McCutcheons, but I promise that will provide a good life. You won't be sorry. My goal every day will be to make you happy."

She placed her fingers on his lips. "Please, Francis, I can't. Even if I wanted to with all my heart. I can't leave my home. My mother. She has no one else." She brushed away more large, glistening tears and then looked off at the orchard. "And I can't leave my trees. This truth will be difficult for you to understand, but they're everything to me. I've been tending them with love for nine long years. So many things tether me to Priest's Crossing. And what about my teaching position? I can't forget about the children who depend on me either. I love what I do. My hands are tied well and good. Even if I wanted to marry you, Francis, I just can't."

Two large crows landed in the tree on the top of the bank and cawed out a mocking taunt. The fruit was in danger. And so was his heart. She couldn't give up her life for him, but in all honesty, if she asked him to move here to Priest's Crossing, would he give up the McCutcheons and the ranch for her? That was a scary thought.

"Twice you've said, 'even if I wanted to.' Do you want to, Ashley? Do you *want* to marry me? I know we're only eighteen, but that's not so young. I know plenty of couples who have done just fine starting out young. If you could, would you? If all those other factors weren't issues?"

"That doesn't matter. They *are* issues. And my heart is breaking because of them."

Crushing defeat almost cut his knees out from under him. This exchange was really the end. He'd been dreaming for days, and especially since the kiss, that somehow, like in a fairy tale, everything would work out. She'd return with him to Y Knot, they'd marry, and everyone would live happily ever after. That just wasn't happening.

When he returned, the men would give him sad looks and pat him on his back. They'd say he'd get over her in time, that he and Ashley were young, didn't know their minds. That he'd thank God when he met the *real* woman that was meant for him, but Francis didn't think so. All he knew was the love of his life was turning him down. In the next hour, he'd ride out of her life, and the break would be final. He never figured this result to be the end of his dreams.

I can't make you love me.

Stepping closer, he wrapped her in his arms, pulled her close, and found her lips. He'd probably regret this move, but he couldn't stop himself. His heart, as large as he'd believed it could grow, ached, and then pushed out farther, throbbing with love, with want, growing in his chest even as sorrow pushed in behind. He didn't know if he could look her in the eye when the time came to walk away.

Her hands pulled him closer, running up and down his chest to finally loop around his neck in the most perfect fit. The kiss turned from sweet to urgent. She understood as well as he did this embrace was the end.

Chapter Fifty-Five

Standing at the side of his saddled horse at the hotel hitching rail, Luke noticed Francis slowly walking Redmond up the road in his direction. Actually, Luke had been waiting for him. He was worried about Francis. Hearts were breaking at this moment, he was sure.

His young friend reined up three horses over and looked around. "Where's everyone else?"

"Finishing up their noon meal in the eatery."

Francis chuckled. "Gettin' fortified for the ride home."

"That's right." Francis wasn't giving anything away. He'd have to dig if he wanted answers. "Where you been?"

Hunkered in his saddle, Francis leaned onto his saddle horn, looking like he'd been on the trail for a month. He hadn't yet cleaned up, and now he'd have to ride out dirty. Luke was sure that was the least of his problems at the moment.

Luke grasped his Stetson hooked on his own saddle horn, and pushed the hat on, shading out the glaring sun he hadn't seen for quite some time. "Want to talk?"

Pain sliced across Francis's face. He glanced away and blinked several times. "She said no."

Whoa. That was fast. Even in comparison to his and Faith's short courtship. He hadn't realized Francis was quite there. But still, when he knew what he felt about Faith, nothing would have changed his mind. "You asked her to marry you?"

Francis nodded.

"And she turned you down?"

Again, the nod as he gazed off into the distance.

"You're eighteen, Francis. Young to settle down. I was twenty-six when I met Faith. Had done a lot of living." *And suffering. How much better has my life been since we married? Do I wish I'd met her sooner? Hell, yes!*

"I don't think age has much to do with anything," Francis answered. "And she didn't actually say no. Just that she couldn't leave the things she loved here in Priest's Crossing. Her mother, her teaching, and mostly, the apple orchard she's been tending for nine years. Thing is, I can sort of understand what she means."

That was good news. Not all was lost! "You know, we've always considered you family, Francis, and that when you do marry, you'll have some acreage of your own, part of the ranch, to build a home on, just like the rest of us." He nodded. His parents, Flood and Claire, had taken Francis in as an orphan. "You're family. You'll have the McCutcheon name, as well, if that's what you want."

Wonder crossed Francis's face first and then a storm of emotion. He looked away and rubbed an unsteady hand across his mouth. "I… I couldn't."

Suddenly Luke grinned like a fool. *I like the sound of another little brother.* "You could… and you *should*. You have as much McCutcheon blood in your veins as I do. You know Flood's not my real pa. I was sired by a Cheyenne brave. Same goes for Colton and Dawn, since I'm their step-pa. You're one of us, and you have been for a long time. Feelings are what makes a family, not blood. Think on it, Francis, before you turn it down."

Luke chuckled to lighten the mood. Francis was still stewing over losing the women he loved. "You mentioned a while back Miss Adair has been growing some saplings, to increase her orchard. How would she feel about diggin' 'em up and bringin' 'em to Y Knot?"

Francis's expression relaxed. His chest lifted as if he'd been holding his breath since Luke had spoken of taking the family name. Being a McCutcheon meant a lot, as Luke knew it would. "I don't know much about growing fruit, Francis, but somewhere I remember hearing that maybe they'd produce in three to four years. She'd know better than me."

Francis straightened in his saddle.

His lost little puppy look vanished, and he drilled Luke with an intense gaze. Luke shrugged. "It's worth a shot. Might not take much to get her thinkin' along those lines. The sooner they're planted, the sooner they'll grow—in Y Knot. Her mother can come along if she wants, and I do believe the school might have an opening soon. Doesn't sound like a lost cause to me." He glanced at the eatery. "With all the hands, diggin' those saplings won't be a problem at all, and we might convince the new Sheriff Clark to lend us Benson's mules and wagon. Seems the least he can do for keeping me locked up so long on trumped-up charges."

Francis lifted his hat and ran his dirt-smudged arm along his forehead as a wide smile appeared on his face. The temperature was climbing.

Smokey ambled out of the eatery, rubbing his belly. He smiled and started their way.

"Or, if she wants to wait on moving the saplings till a better time of the year, we can spare a day or two and help her get what's there now harvested. While I'm feeling generous, having just cheated death, tell her we'll all stay back. Get her orchard cleared."

Francis's mouth opened and closed.

Luke shrugged. "Well, what're you waitin' for?" He pulled out his pocket watch and flipped open the lid. "You're on the clock. Go win your woman's hand. You're a McCutcheon. We don't take no for an answer."

Chapter Fifty-Six

The Heart of the Mountains Ranch

"**S**uch a beautiful spot," Ashley whispered, snuggled in Francis's arms, his hands locked together in front of her. Her back was to his chest as they gazed over the patch of land that would, after today, be their orchard, and where their house would someday be built.

"I don't think a dream could be prettier," she said. "The stream, the mountains, and the hill where the wildflowers will grow in the spring. I'm beside myself with happiness." She turned in his arms and his lips claimed hers, shushing all the talk.

The warm sunshine on his shoulders felt nice. He'd been impatient for a few kisses but had learned over the two months since she'd moved to Y Knot that giving her time to express her feelings was always a good thing.

She pulled back but kept her hands up around his neck. "Are you as happy as I am?"

The feeling of his heart expanding had become a regular occurrence these past few months. "Happier. The *happiest* I've ever been. And I'll be even happier come spring, when you become my wife. The baby green grass just sprouted, wildflowers blooming everywhere, hundreds of calves bawlin' for their mamas…" He glanced up at the clouds filled with wonder. "That's a heady thought. You, my wife. Me, your husband. This whole thing has been quite the surprise."

Smiling, she nuzzled his neck. "I hope you like surprises. I've always been fond of giving them. I'll fill your days with surprises and your nights with love."

A flush broke out on his face. When they were alone, she wasn't shy in the least. He loved that about her but was still getting used to being one half of a couple.

"The Klinkners were kind to invite you to live with them until the wedding. Lots of exciting events planned for next year. We'll start on the house. Then, after the wedding, you'll keep teaching for as long as you can…"

Dreaminess filled her eyes and she smiled. "You mean until we're blessed with a babe?"

He nodded. "Well, yeah, that usually…"

"You'll be a fine father, Francis." She went up on tiptoe and kissed his chin. "You're so patient. I've seen you with Holly and Dawn, and even Rachel and Amy's little fellas. They're all so cute."

More wonder filled his chest. A husband was one thing; he was ready for that, no question, but a father? A tiny niggle of alarm traced up his spine. What had happened to *his* father? Had he been killed, leaving Francis an orphan, or had his sire tossed him away unwanted? No way to know. None at all. He'd never want to be like that.

"All this talk of being a father—" He chuckled, but the humor wasn't there. "Let's take one step at a time. We still have a long winter to get through. Only after that, we'll start talking spring flowers, calving season, and weddings."

She quickly pulled back to read his expression. "Are you getting cold feet?"

Seemed she wasn't afraid to talk about anything. She'd said she liked open communication, and she'd proven that fact more times than he could count.

"Not on your life. I just like taking things slow and easy when the talk turns to young'uns. I never had any parents, and I don't really know why. Maybe my father was some horrible person. I just get a little anxious, is all."

She lowered her hands from around his neck and rested them on his biceps, feeling his muscles ever so gently. "And maybe he was a very loving man who was accidentally killed, as well as your mother, leaving you an orphan and no one alive to tell the tale. That explanation is just as plausible as the other. Don't let your fear undermine who you really are, my love. Who I know you to be."

Her understanding smile chased away his anxiety.

She reached up and finger combed his hair behind his ears and then played with the curls around his collar, knowing very well he liked the caress. "You're a natural," she went on softly. "Even the baby animals respond to you. You have the *touch*."

"Well, your mother finally likes me, and that fact must mean something. She sure enjoys her job with Berta May, sewing and darning all day long."

"I think she enjoys the larger town. Having friends, male and female. Starting out new. And I'm enjoying having her in town but living in separate places. I've never done that before. Her at Berta May's and me at Ina's. The move has been good for both of us. And she's the apple expert. Taught me all I know, but there's always more to learn."

Sounds of a jangling harness made them both turn.

"Here come your trees. I hope you're ready." They'd been keeping the saplings inside one of the covered lumber sheds at Klinkner's mill for a few days since the trees had arrived from Priest's Crossing. The ranch hands had come out one day and helped prepare the land to Mrs. Adair's specifications, for the trees from the original orchard in Priest's Crossing and others Ashley and Angelia had ordered. The hundred and fifty holes were dug in one day. Today, the trees would be planted, followed by a picnic with everyone in attendance.

Behind Hayden and Heather's wagon came Roady with Sally and the baby. More townsfolk would arrive any time as well.

When the wagons were close enough, Roady called, "Thought we'd come out early. Hope you don't mind."

Francis smiled and found one of Ashley's hands, a feeling of wonder, peace, and love swirling around inside his heart. His life, one that began on such unstable ground, was now one of deep gratefulness and love. "'Course not. Always glad to see you."

Hayden expertly circled the wagon, parking close to the straight rows of holes, and pulled the team to a halt, the saplings in the back slowly swaying.

Roady followed suit. Gillian howled loudly in her mother's arms.

In all the catching up after they'd come back from Priest's Crossing, he'd only seen Roady's daughter once, and only for a moment. Curious now, he and Ashley walked close as Hayden and Roady helped the ladies down, making sure everyone was safe.

Sally held Gillian to her shoulder, vigorously patting her back. "I think she has a pesky bubble stuck in her craw. Poor baby has been fussing and fretting since we left the mill. I'd hoped the bumpy ride would work out the nuisance, but we've had no luck with that. My little princess is miserable."

Just as Roady went to take Gillian, Francis stepped up with outstretched hands. "Can I give her a go? I've had some experience with Dawn and Holly."

Hayden and Roady exchanged a look and then Roady winked. "As her sleep-deprived father, I give you my blessing."

Francis carefully lifted a squalling Gillian from Sally's hands.

When she looked into his face, she howled so loud an enormous burp sounded, and then she settled down, her face wet with tears.

Francis pushed out his chest and then let his gaze stray over to Ashley, so thankful for the young woman who'd captured his heart. "See, darlin'. One way or the other, I get the job done. You can count on me."

Smiling, Ashley snuggled under his free arm, gazing at the now sleepy-eyed infant. A moment later she looked up at him in adoration.

Their life was just beginning. If he felt this good now, contemplating the rest of his life was exciting. "I love you," he whispered as he fell into her eyes as if the others weren't there, standing nearby. "I promise that will *never* change."

She ran a hand over his chest, staying clear of Gillian who had fallen asleep. "I can see your feelings deep in your eyes, Francis, and it makes me feel like the luckiest girl in the world. I love you more than you could ever know. *I* promise I'll never forget the way I feel this moment in your arms."

Acknowledgments

Thank you to my editors, Linda Carroll-Bradd of Lustre Editing and Anne Victory of Victory Editing & Oops Detection. You make my books shine. To my talented cover artist, Kelli Ann Morgan, for creating a cover so beautiful it makes me want to move to Montana. To Bob Houston eBook Formatting, I think you're great! Working with you is always a joy. My whole team is brilliant and I couldn't do what I do without them.

Tremendous love to my family for making my life meaningful every single day.

Love and gratefulness to my readers! I appreciate every one of you. *Thank you.*

And much gratitude to God for giving me such an incredible life. It's been an adventure I'm so thankful for!

About The Author

Caroline Fyffe was born in Waco, Texas, the first of many towns she would call home during her father's career with the US Air Force. A horse aficionado from an early age, she earned a Bachelor of Arts in communications from California State University-Chico before launching what would become a twenty-year career as an equine photographer. She began writing fiction to pass the time during long days in the show arena, channeling her love of horses and the Old West into a series of Western historicals. Her debut novel, *Where the Wind Blows*, won the Romance Writers of America's prestigious Golden Heart Award as well as the Wisconsin RWA's Write Touch Readers' Award. She and her husband have two grown sons and live in the Pacific Northwest.

Want news on releases, giveaways, and bonus reads? Sign up for Caroline's newsletter at: www.carolinefyffe.com
See her Equine Photography: www.carolinefyffephoto.com
LIKE her FaceBook Author Page:
Facebook.com/CarolineFyffe
Twitter: @carolinefyffe
Write to her at: caroline@carolinefyffe.com

Made in the USA
Monee, IL
05 October 2024

67293008R00194